About the author

A semi-retired solicitor, Philip Harris
is now able to indulge his passion for
writing in his increasing leisure time.

Born to a South American mother and an English
father, Philip has always considered himself to be
a cultural nomad. The Spanish Muse, the fourth of
Philip's books, brings together his lifelong obsession
with Spain and all things Spanish, with his admiration
for the great English poets of the twentieth century.

Philip spends his time between Surrey and Norfolk
with his long-suffering wife, who for fifty years has
stoically tolerated his flamenco guitar playing, from
which their sons escaped many years ago.

THE SPANISH MUSE

PHILIP HARRIS

BookPrintingUK
Peterborough
2019

BookPrintingUK
Remus House
Coltsfoot Drive
Woodston
Peterborough
PE2 9BF

www.bookprintinguk.com

A CIP catalogue record for this book is available from the British Library.

The views expressed in this work are solely those of the author and do not necessarily reflect the views of the publisher, and the publisher hereby disclaims any responsibility for them.

ISBN: 978-1-913284-15-2
eBook ISBN: 978-1-913284-16-9

For Gill.

She tells her love while half asleep,
In the dark hours,
With half words whispered low:
As earth stirs in her winter sleep
And puts out grass and flowers
Despite the snow,
Despite the falling snow.

Robert Graves.

Complete Poems in One Volume
(Carcanet Press Ltd, 2000, Edited by Patrick Quinn)
With permission of the Robert Graves estate.

PART ONE

ONE

It all sounded a bit seedy, really. A little unsavoury. At least when I was first asked. But I went along with it; and then, to my surprise, I began to like it. And it wasn't just because of the money. You see, he treated me like a lady.

All men are a little bit foolish, but some more so than others. It is said that there is no fool like an old fool, and that may have been so in Robert's case. But in fact, of all the men I have known my husband Manuel must have been the most foolish of all. And he was only young – forty-two when his foolishness killed him. He just couldn't keep his mouth shut. Stupidly saying things that he knew would get him into trouble with the authorities. Still angry about things he had seen or heard as a child, long before I was born, and which no longer mattered. Or even things he had never seen or heard, but just imagined.

"Get on with your life," I would tell him. "You have two healthy children. Why create problems for yourself and the rest of us?"

But no. The anger, the rancour, had gone too deep. In Palma, when he saw Italian tourists he would shout at them, call them fascist pigs. Dangerous in a country which was itself fascist, and run by that pig Franco. In the bars of Deià he spoke too raucously, too loudly of the good old days of *la República*, even though he had been too young to know, and was only repeating what his father, and my father, had told him. It seemed he wanted to claim the victimhood, the pain, of our parents' generation – as if we didn't have enough pain of our own.

It was always the Italians who were on the receiving end of

his hate and invective. No one was ever able to explain to me how or why it was that Mallorca joined the Fascists almost as soon as Franco set foot in Spain with his Moroccans, whilst Menorca bravely held out for the Republic until the bitter end. But it is what happened. And then Mussolini's airmen arrived, swaggering and strutting the streets of Palma, leering at the girls. Popinjays, my father said they were: brave men when bombing defenceless cities, but useless in an even fight.

Day after day they used Mallorca's airfields to blitz the city of Barcelona, just a few kilometres across the sea. Our Catalan capital being bombed from our Catalan Mallorca. It makes me sick to think of it, but that's no reason to put your life and the welfare of your family at risk: over something which happened long ago.

I was born in the small Mallorcan village of Deià, the day Barcelona fell: the day General Yague pranced along the *Avinguda de la Gran Vía*, scanning the faces of the crowds cheering him and his victorious army. He wasn't such a fool, though. He knew that the people were afraid and wanted only now to survive. But he had what they called a 'fifth column': those in the city who had lain low and now came out of hiding, or revealed their true colours, to denounce their neighbours as communists, or anarchists, or anti-church. And so the purges followed, cleansing the nation of the poison which had contaminated Christian Spain for so long – as brutal in its own way as the methods used more than four hundred years before to create our Christian Spain in the first place.

I was baptised Maria Jesus in the village church a month after my birth. Franco was now in charge, and the church was back in the ascendant. My mother decided to make a virtue out of necessity. Go the whole hog. She was on her own, and had to make the decision on her own initiative. Maria Jesus. God knows what my father said when she told him my name. He must have thought that he had spawned a little Falangist.

Six months before the fall of Barcelona, my father had

2

escaped in one of the boats that were ferrying men by night to the mainland, to help shore up the tattered remains of the Republican army: one last desperate effort to halt Franco's roll across Spain. It was two years before he was released from a Nationalist prison to return home, emaciated and introverted, a stranger not just to the daughter he had never seen but to his wife as well.

It was another two years before my father could smile or laugh again, my mother told me. And what unlocked the most human of feelings, happiness, was the news that the Allies had taken Sicily from Mussolini and the Germans. They then bombed Rome around the clock – the Americans by day, the British by night – just as the Italians had bombed Barcelona from Mallorca. How the Republican Mallorcans secretly rejoiced: the Italians receiving the same treatment they had meted out to the Catalans. If you live by the sword, you die by the sword. That's in the Bible – something I learnt in the school run by the Catholic Church we all now had to attend.

When Mussolini and Hitler were killed, we thought it would be the end of Franco. The Allies would invade Spain and depose him, or they would arm the seething, silent Republican sympathisers to do the work for them. But they were weary of war, and besides, Franco had been wily, never assisting the Germans or Italians directly with Spanish troops or materials. So the Allies left him alone, for Spain to fester for another thirty years.

As I said, my husband Manuel was the most foolish man I ever knew. Yes, it was hard to let sleeping dogs lie, but we learnt to watch our words. Not him, though. The first time he was arrested was in 1959. We had only been married a year. A certain Fidel Castro had seized power in Cuba, and Manuel and a few friends had celebrated the triumph of communism in Deià's bars, ending the evening carousing drunkenly on the beach at Cala de Deià.

The following day, he was taken to Palma in a police car. I

screamed and begged to go with him, and finally they agreed. I was young and beautiful in those days. That is why, I suppose, they consented to have a communist sympathiser's wife wedged between two Guardia Civil in the back of the car, with Manuel manacled beside the driver.

'*Todos por la Patria*'. The words written above every police station in Spain in those days. *Todos por la Patria*, and don't you forget it.

They put the fear of God into Manuel. When he was released in the evening, they told me to take him home and teach him to behave. He was lucky, they said, but if he could not learn from his wife he would have to learn the hard way. But now he, a barely literate carpenter from the backstreets of Deià, was on the list. The list which was kept in Madrid in the offices of the Interior Ministry close to the Carabanchel.

By the 1970s, we all knew it would be over soon – just a question of time. But Manuel couldn't wait. A little patience was all that was needed. Franco was old and ailing, and Spain now looked hungrily at the rest of Europe, wanting what they had. Change was in the air. Change was inevitable. But maybe, perversely, the authorities were more restrictive in the last few years of the regime, ruthlessly wielding what power they still had before it was taken from them.

There had been a building boom across the island to accommodate the expanding tourist industry. Manuel was never out of work, but he took it upon himself to organise the men on the building sites into some kind of unofficial union, to barrack for higher wages. Syndicalism, the authorities called it, and it was forbidden. Only members of state-recognised and registered unions were allowed to have a voice. They must have put two and two together and realised that the troublemaker, as they called him, was one and the same as the name entered on the records in the Interior Ministry.

"Do I have to go with you?" he asked the two men in civilian clothes who had knocked on our door one evening.

"*Exactamente*," they replied.

I asked them in. They chatted to the children, Alexandro and Josefina, whilst they waited for Manuel and me to pack an overnight bag. He was diabetic, and I wanted to make sure that he had his insulin.

I went next door and asked my neighbour Carmen to look after the children for a few hours, but when I tried to get in the car with Manuel, the police looked at me in astonishment.

"*Señora*," they said politely, "you have done nothing wrong. It is only your husband we need."

"But I want to be with him," I cried. I was becoming frightened for Manuel, who was standing by the car looking solitary and afraid.

"*No posible, Señora.*"

I realised that my looks had faded somewhat in the last fifteen years, and this time Manuel would be on his own. I embraced him, but he remained rigid and unresponsive.

"Where are you taking him?" I asked them.

"To the central police station in Palma."

"When will you let him go?"

"Tomorrow. Or the day after, perhaps."

"I will come down tomorrow to see him, and if possible bring him home."

"*Sí, sí,*" they said, "if that is what you want."

As they drove away, I realised that the children had not said goodbye to their father. Their terrified faces stared through the window, more filled with premonition than I dared to allow.

*   *   *   *

I refused to wear the widow's traditional black for the rest of my life. It was not that I wanted another man, but Manuel's stupidity had left me a widow at thirty-four, and two children of nine and eight without a father. I was angry with him, and it burnt away much of the sorrow which I otherwise would have felt.

'Diabetes complications', the death certificate had said. When they released the body there was no sign that he had been subjected to any brutality, so maybe it was right. Perhaps he forgot to take his insulin, or they took it away from him – I would never know.

People were kind. I took a job as a part-time cleaner in one of the swish hotels in Sóller, down on the coast, and Carmen kept an eye on the children during the school holidays. My parents had moved to a small apartment in Palma and they shared their meagre pension with me. Manuel's parents had, thank God, both died many years before.

TWO

I didn't hear a knock, just the sound of the latch being lifted and a moment later there he was, filling the living room: a large shambles of an old man leaning on a stick, wearing a wide-brimmed Panama hat and holding a bunch of wild flowers in his free hand.

Of course, I knew who he was. Everyone in the village knew who he was. Except for a break during the war, he had been living in Deià for years. We were all so proud of having been chosen as the home of this famous Englishman of letters and his wife that we overlooked their strange choice of friends, with their wayward lifestyles. Even the priest operated a system of 'see no evil'.

It was a Wednesday, my half-day at the hotel. I had just returned home to prepare a quick lunch for myself and attend to the weekly wash before the children came home from school.

"These are for you. I picked them myself," he said slowly, and in perfect Spanish, as he handed me the flowers.

I didn't take them. I was worried that the old man had gone crazy and wanted him out of my cottage as soon as possible.

"Why?" I frowned.

His hand began to shake. "Because I want to be your friend."

"You are old. Why don't you find friends of your own age?" I snapped. It was a little rude, but we Spanish tend to say the first thing that comes into our heads and I suppose that Catalans are Spanish in the final analysis.

"Because it is you I want as a friend."

"You have many friends in your house. They come and go all the time. Why me as well?"

"Because you are beautiful. Your beauty is an inspiration."

"You have a wife, Señor Graves. A wife who, I am sure, loves you. You should not speak to other women in this way, particularly when they are more than forty years younger than you. Please go."

"My wife knows I am here."

"Please go."

I must admit to feeling a pang of remorse as he shuffled towards the door. He turned with his hand on the latch. "And the flowers, do they have to go as well?" I am sure that I saw a twinkle in his eye at that moment.

"Leave them," I ordered, in the loud peremptory way we Spanish have. "And then go."

He tipped his Panama hat to me, as if I were a lady, and then shuffled away.

I felt flustered when he had gone, and then angry with myself for feeling flustered. It was the flowers, I think. No man had brought me flowers for a very long time. Manuel had stopped shortly after we were married, and all I had got from men since his death five years before were salacious leers and mutterings behind my back. But no man had the guts to take on a woman with two teenage children.

No longer feeling like lunch, I found a vase for the flowers, made some coffee, and sat down to consider what had happened.

I had done the right thing. I was sure of that. Firmly sending the old man back to his wife. He must be an embarrassment to her, poor woman. He might be famous, have written great literature in his day, but now he had clearly lost his mind and with it his inhibitions.

But I could not help looking down at my legs – still shapely after carrying two hefty children – and examining my peasant arms, olive and smooth, and downed with light brown hair. What had he said? 'Your beauty is an inspiration.' Well, I suppose when you are over eighty there are many things which appear beautiful through the prism of age, which you wouldn't have looked at twice when you were young. Still, it had been nice to hear.

My train of thought was interrupted by a gentle knocking. I was sure that it was him again and, determined to bring the nonsense to an end, I flung the door open to send him packing. But there, instead of the old man, stood his wife: the elegant, stylish English lady who had borne him four children but still managed to keep her fine figure and looks.

"May I come in, Señora?" she asked graciously, standing well back from my cottage door to make it clear that she at least would not intrude without my consent.

I was sure that I knew the purpose of her visit: to apologise for her husband's behaviour. Maybe she would also want to unburden herself, tell me of the difficulties and strain of living with a man who was losing his mind, and the boundaries of common decency.

"Of course," I said, closing the door behind her and pointing to my best chair beside the fireplace. "Would you like some coffee?"

"That would be very kind."

Whilst I busied myself with the kettle in the kitchen adjoining my living room through an open arch, I could see her gently taking in her surroundings – not in an inquisitive or even curious way, but just noting my furniture, pictures, and bric-a-brac. I was also aware that, very unobtrusively, she was sizing me up. I should have felt uncomfortable about it, but for some reason I didn't.

I pulled a chair up to the other side of the fireplace, arranged a side table between us, and lowered onto it a tray with the coffee cups, milk, and sugar.

"I can see why Robert has chosen you," she said.

I didn't say anything at first, just looked at her sideways. There were many rumours that circulated the village from time to time, about the goings on in the Graves' household. Strange, unconventional English and American poets toing and froing Deià, bringing their Bohemian ways with them but sooner or later leaving Señor and Señora Graves to their respectable family life. I had avoided the gossip as far as I could, but now I had to think hard, and quickly.

"Chosen me for what?" I asked after a long pause.

"His next muse."

"His next muse?"

"Yes. Maybe even his last muse," she added, with sadness in her voice.

She was as mad as her husband.

"What is a muse?"

"A woman who inspires a man, in this case my husband, to release his creativity, in his case poetry. He has written a great deal under the influence of muses, and indeed about muses, in his time." She looked at me enigmatically.

"But he doesn't even know me." I was becoming impatient with her absurdities.

"He has been watching you for some time."

I should have been angry, shouted at her, thrown her out of my cottage. How dare my privacy be invaded, violated even, by that old man. But to my surprise, to my consternation, I found that I liked the idea of being watched. I longed to know what I had that was worth watching.

"How does he watch me?"

"From the upper floor of our house," she said, as if the information was only too obvious.

"From the upper floor of your house?" I said incredulously.

"Yes. Our back bedroom window looks down upon your front door. My husband spends much of his day waiting for you to come home from work. He then watches you weeding and watering your pots of herbs along your front path, talking to your neighbours in the street, and welcoming your children home from school."

"Is that not enough for him?" I asked sarcastically. "What more does a muse have to do?"

These were stupid things to say. I was admitting that his behaviour was acceptable. Perhaps even condoning it. I should have said that he was a peeping Tom and needed help, but somehow those words could not apply to a man who was revered by all and sundry.

"He would like to sit with you – to look at you, to talk to you, to get to know you, just a little. You would not be in any danger."

I took a long swallow of coffee, to give me time to think. "I sent him away this afternoon in no uncertain terms. Are you sure that he still wants all these things of me?" I said, replacing the empty cup on its saucer.

She threw back her head and laughed. "You do not understand the role of the muse, Señora," she cried. "The more the muse rejects the poet in her thrall, the more his passion is incited. Inflamed, even."

She was talking in riddles. I decided to remain silent.

She took several small sips of coffee from her cup, then said in a very practical tone of voice, "And he would probably speak to you in English. A language, I imagine, that you do not understand, which could well be an advantage to you both."

I still said nothing.

"And of course, you would be paid," she said in her matter of fact voice.

"I'm not a prostitute!" I barked.

"No muse could be a muse if she were a prostitute," she said softly. "Please see payment as a gift of gratitude from art. A gift from all those future generations who will thrill to my husband's poetry, inspired by you – poetry which would have remained unwritten and gone with him to his grave."

I dumbfoundedly stared at the floor.

"If it were not for you," she concluded, looking at me pleadingly.

How could I refuse? I, Maria Jesus Gonzalez, widow of

11

a carpenter, cleaner of rooms in a four-star hotel in Sóller, struggling to bring up two teenage children on my own, held a key: a key which would unlock beautiful poetry for all the world to cherish and enjoy.

"*Muy bien*," I said, after a while, to the elegant lady opposite me. "*Muy bien*."

THREE

And so it was that I became the last muse of the great English poet, Robert Graves.

Most Wednesday afternoons in term time he would come to my cottage, but occasionally he and his wife would come down to Sóller and meet me when I came off duty. She would spend time in the shops, while he and I sat on a bench facing the sea.

But it was in the privacy of my cottage, when it was just the two of us, where I learnt to love him.

It seems crazy, I know, to love an old man, particularly one whose faculties were failing. But there always has to be an equality in love: it can never be lopsided. I gave him, he said, something of the Spain he came to in the 1920s, reviving, I suppose, the feelings he had at that time when he was my age, while he showed me a profundity I never thought any human being could hold. Sometimes it seemed like being with God. I know that's blasphemy but I don't care, because I'm not a believer. In his eyes, and in his face, was a wisdom which came from another world. He may have been foolish at times, but you can still be foolish and wise.

Never in my life had I seen or experienced wisdom. At school we learnt that there had been many wise men in our history, but it seemed that when we needed one he was not there, or if he was no one listened to him.

I often wondered if Robert's wisdom came from his great learning, but I'm now sure that was only part of its source. It was how he applied his learning to his experiences that made him truly wise: particularly, fighting for his country, or being jilted in love, and other tragedies which I will not mention. He was able to make sense of them. A sense which he said could only be expressed in poetry, and only then if he had his muse. And that now was me. But, to be honest, I loved him not just for his profundity, but also because he had picked me. That's pride, but we Spanish are a proud people.

I told his wife at that first meeting that I could not see him until the following Wednesday, my next half-day, and he was to leave before the children came home from school.

I was nervous as a kitten as my bus pulled into Deià. He would know exactly when I was home, as he would be watching from that back bedroom window.

Sure enough, five minutes after I arrived home, the latch on my front door lifted and he came into my cottage. Never once did he knock; it was almost as if he saw my cottage as his, part of his life now that he had been given free access to his muse.

At first, I tried not to laugh, but the effort was too great to bear. He was wearing a large blue sunhat garlanded with flowers, trousers of a bright blue – which would not have been suitable for someone half his age – and a loud check shirt. He was holding a box of chocolates in one hand and his stick in the other. From his mouth fluttered a piece of paper, clenched between his teeth.

As I exploded into laughter he began to laugh too, and for the first time since my childhood I felt true joy.

"This," he said, "is for you," putting his stick on the floor and thrusting the piece of paper into my hand. "And these chocolates are for your children." He placed the box carefully on the side table.

I examined the piece of paper. It was a poem, I could see that, but it was in English. All I could understand were the words, 'To my Spanish Muse', written at the top of the page in English and Spanish.

I began to laugh again, and once more he joined in. "Thank you," I said finally, "but I do not understand English."

"Understanding is the first step towards mediocrity," he said.

"And I do not understand that either, Señor Graves."

"Indeed, the less the muse understands, the better for the poetic craft. But call me Robert."

I was for a moment taken aback. How could I call this great man of letters by his Christian name? But it was what he wanted.

"And what shall I call you?" he asked.

"My name is Maria Jesus."

"I don't like the Jesus part. I shall call you Maria, or better still, Madonna."

I put the poem in the drawer of my kitchen dresser and motioned him to sit down.

"No," he said, "but please will you sit down."

It was more in the nature of a command than a request. Obediently, I sat in the best chair by the fire place, the chair in which his wife had sat a week before. Then, to my astonishment, he slowly and painfully knelt before me.

He studied my face at close quarters, seeming to examine and scrutinise each pore of my skin at great length. When he had finished, with trembling hands, he undid the ribbon which held my hair in place, and shook it until it fell about my shoulders.

I remember very clearly what he said next. "I have chosen wisely on this occasion. Very wisely." I dared not ask if this meant that in the past he had made mistakes in his choice of muses. But still, the remark made me feel very smug.

He drew himself to his feet with the assistance of the arm of my chair. I tried to help, but he made an impatient gesture, meaning I should remain seated.

"Until next Wednesday," he said at the door. "Same time."

I was still so full of joy when my children came home from school that I allowed them to eat the chocolates before their tea. I told them that a tourist in the hotel where I was working had given them to me.

I lovingly placed Robert's poem in the empty chocolate box and pushed it right to the back of the dresser drawer.

I looked forward to our Wednesdays. Of course, I saw less of him when the children were at home during the school holidays, but we were not entirely denied each other's company. I would let Robert know when they were not around on a Wednesday afternoon. If, for example, they went to Palma to spend a few hours with my parents, or went on a trip with friends, I would drop a note through his door the night before telling him the hours that it would be safe to come. I always signed 'Madonna.' And if we had not been together for more than a week or so then we enjoyed our company even more. Absence, as they say, makes the heart grow fonder.

Robert would always bring a present, either for me or for the children: an almond cake for our coffee; chocolates; a trinket which he and his wife found in the market at Palma, which they thought might please me, and of course, an occasional poem. These were always in English so I could never make much of them, but I added each to the growing collection in the chocolate box.

The money side of things was treated with great circumspection. The day after each visit, an envelope was pushed through my letter box containing a few hundred pesetas. At first I put the money on one side, meaning to return it to Mrs Graves who I knew was responsible; but bringing up two children is expensive. When I broke my resolve to return the money and used some to buy a pair of running shoes for Alexandro, I never looked back.

And I have to confess that I started to spend a little of the money on myself. I bought new underwear, and one or two outfits that flattered my figure just a little. My daughter Josefina approved, but I didn't think that she suspected. I drew the line at buying perfume, or expensive makeup. After all, I was not a *puta* – a prostitute.

Of course, it soon got about the village that Robert was

visiting me. But as I was a widow, and it was common knowledge that he did nothing without his wife's consent, there wasn't much to be made of it. Carmen told me that over the years he had attached himself to a series of younger women, all with his wife's knowledge and approval, but they had been Americans. Generally there was a feeling of satisfaction in Deià that he was now finding inspiration from a home-grown Mallorcan girl.

Although I was careful to see Robert only when the children were not around, I knew that sooner or later they would find out about us. But I should not have concerned myself.

A few weeks after Robert's first visit, the children came home earlier from school than usual, just as he was leaving. Nervously, I introduced them, but they had seen him around and knew who he was. As far as Alexandro was concerned, if the old buffer wanted to pass an afternoon in the company of his mother, so what? More fool him, and maybe more fool his mother.

But girls are more astute in these matters than boys. As soon as Josefina and I were alone, she broached the subject.

"So it is he who brings the presents for us," she said. "They're not donations from tourists in the hotel in Sóller at all."

"Yes. That is so."

"And it is for him that you have bought those figure-hugging dresses."

Figure-hugging was a bit of an exaggeration, but I saw no point in arguing with her. Besides, I wanted to see where all this would lead. "Yes," I said.

"How old is he?"

"Eighty-seven."

She began to snigger. "So I will not have to march you off to the family planning clinic for advice." Since Franco's death, the grip of the Catholic Church on the country had loosened, and Spain was revelling in its newfound freedoms.

"No, you won't," I said, pan-faced. And then I laughed as well.

"I'm glad, mummy," Josefina said, putting her arms around

me. "I'm glad for you. He is ..." She searched for the right word. "Interesting," she said finally.

It made me very happy.

FOUR

Reluctantly, I had to acknowledge to myself over the following months that Robert was losing his mind. We had never spoken a great deal on his visits, but it came clear to me from his poems. You did not need to understand English to see that the handwriting was becoming less clear, indecipherable sometimes, and the poems shorter and shorter. And then, on a sad winter's day, shortly after my forty-fourth birthday, he presented me with a piece of paper with great panache. But the only word he had written was 'Madonna' at the top of the page.

"What is this?" I asked.

"My latest poem," he said. "Inspired by my Spanish muse. It is one of my best, I think."

"Thank you, Robert," I said slowly, feeling the tears welling up in my eyes. "I shall place it with the others."

I put it in the chocolate box without more ado, to hide it away in case he should realise, in a moment of lucidity, what he had done, or rather not done.

As he knelt before me, I took his head in my arms and pressed it to my breast. His mind was slipping, and perhaps my body might quicken his memory of other women in previous times, and halt the seepage of old age.

*　　　　　*　　　　　*　　　　　*

The summer before he died had come early. Too early. By June the temperature was soaring with no prospect of any reprieve. Normally, a sea breeze relieves our island from the worst of the swelterings of the Spanish summers, but there was not a breath of wind for weeks.

The children spent the whole of July in Palma with my mother. She was now a widow and liked their company, and for them, the disadvantage of being cramped in her flat was outweighed by their being able to bathe in the public beaches around Palma, and in the evening meet other young people in the Plaça Major when it had cooled a little.

I missed my father. He was only seventy when he died; the war, I think, had shortened his life. In a strange way, his death strengthened my feelings for Robert, who, I suppose had now become more of a father figure in my life than ever before.

On the last Wednesday of July, as usual Robert came down to my cottage, but the heat had slowed and tired him. He collapsed into his chair and then began to breathe heavily. I fetched him a glass of water and, kneeling before him, unbuttoned his shirt to the waist. It was then that I saw the livid scars on his chest. Running my fingers over them in amazement, I cried, "What are these?"

"A memorial to my war," he panted.

"What war was that?"

"My war. The Great War. The war to end all wars"

I knew what he meant. He was the right age to have been sucked into the war that destroyed much of a generation of Europe's youth, and which Spain had somehow escaped.

The scars fascinated me. I continued to run my fingers very softly up and down the pale blemishes, feeling the contours of the skin around them grown thick and puckered over the years.

"Tell me about it," I whispered.

He shook his head. I waited. I was usually able to get my own way during the hours he spent with me, and I wanted to know.

"Please tell me about it," I said again after a time. "Your Madonna wants to know."

I stroked his chest, and lay my head on his lap. I knew that he could not resist me when I placed such pressure upon him.

Physical, erotic pressure. "It must have been terrible, Robert. But still, I want to know."

"It was worse for my mother than for me," he said, his eyes fast shut. "You see, they said I was dead."

I raised my head and stared at him in disbelief. "Who said that you were dead? The Germans?"

He laughed mirthlessly. "No, the British. They wrote to my mother and told her I was dead. Lost in action. Dead."

"And then?"

"When they found me in a field hospital, they had to write to her again and tell her I was alive."

"She must have been filled with joy to receive that second letter."

"Maybe, but think how she must have suffered between the two."

Suddenly, he brightened. "But you know, when you've been killed off, and then come to life, you can do what you want. You are no longer frightened of taking risks. Nothing worse can happen to you than dying and, according to the authorities, that had already happened as far as I was concerned."

I did not understand. All I knew was that he was a large, dilapidated piece of history. I very gently nudged my body across his lap to allow him to run his fingers through my hair, which I knew he liked, and to feel my shoulder blades and the bones of my spinal column through my blouse. He always said that he admired my strong peasant back, and I wanted him to touch it and to feel it. Female and alive. Something worth surviving for. Something worth living for.

He suddenly sat up very straight. "Do you have a piece of paper and a pen, please?"

I found an exercise book of Josefina's, and the biro I used for my shopping lists. He wrote very slowly and deliberately across the page, several lines. He read them to himself, made one or two corrections, and then tore the page out of the book.

"For you," he said, handing the page to me.

I was astounded to see that he had written a seemingly

21

continuous and coherent poem. A world away from the scraps of words he had been scribbling for months now.

He knew what was in my mind. "My mother, you see. Talking about her. Together with you. You both have unlocked my genius, which I thought had escaped me for ever."

They were the last sensible words he ever said to me. After he had gone, I carefully wrote the date at the foot of the page, 28th July 1985, and inserted it in the chocolate box.

He hardly spoke another word to me. For a few more weeks he would come down to my cottage, but I could see that it was just force of habit. He would stare at the walls, and occasionally look at me uncomprehendingly. And then the visits stopped. I waited, but not for long. He died on a cold December morning of that year.

*   *   *   *

Carmen expected me to go to the funeral. There was a huge brouhaha of comings and goings of foreigners in the days following his death and somehow, bizarrely, she thought there would be a place for me.

But I had been a muse with a difference. A local girl. Literate, to be sure, but untravelled, and not versed in the airs and graces of the sophisticated world. That, I think, was why he had chosen me; as his life became simpler with age, he needed a simple muse. Besides, I had loved him, and my grief would be out of place in the presence of his wife who, as I have said, had borne him four children.

On the day, I sent my children to school as usual, closed the shutters, and remembered with pride the famous old English poet who had stared wonderingly into my face, run his fingers through my hair, nuzzled my breasts, and rested his head in my lap. Time and again he had told me that I was his muse and called me beautiful. Sorrow and pride, strange bedfellows.

A few days after the funeral his wife came to my cottage. I asked her in, but she refused. "I just wanted to say thank you," she said. We never met or spoke again. She was a lady.

PART TWO

FIVE

No one under the age of sixty could ever understand, of that Maria Jesus was sure. No one could imagine what it was like in that long black night following the disintegration of the Republic. One by one, the last great cities of Spain had fallen to the Fascists: first Barcelona, followed by panic as hundreds of thousands made for the border with France before it was sealed up; then in a matter of weeks Madrid and Valencia, when it was all but over and the executions could begin in earnest right across Spain.

It was not just that they could not understand: people did not want to understand. It was a conspiracy of silence which lasted her lifetime. Not to rock the boat. Put it all behind us. After all, your neighbour's family might have been on the wrong side, and we wouldn't want to open old wounds. Robert's wounds from the Great War had healed. Spain's wounds had supposedly healed, but unlike Robert's there had been no dressing stations to cleanse the flesh before sewing it together again. Cosmetically closed, Spain's wounds remained unswabbed.

When she was a girl, the prisons were still teeming with Republican sympathisers, and for years after the war the necessities of life were in short supply, particularly for those known to have opposed the Fascists, who would always remain at the back of the queue.

Whenever she went to her doctor with her angina or arthritis, he would always say the same: "Señora Gonzalez, you belong to that generation." It was enough. She knew what he meant. She belonged to the generation which did not have the best start in life and now, in old age, was suffering for it.

But it was also the work which had made her old before her time. When the money from the Graveses stopped, she realised how much she had relied on it. To make matters worse, after the death of her mother, Maria Jesus lost the financial support she had provided from her pension. She had no option but to work longer hours in the tourist hotels of Sóller, cleaning out baths and changing the linen on king-sized beds, well into her sixties.

But although little more than a skivvy, she always had the compensation of knowing that, thanks to the generosity of his wife, she had been the inspiration for a great man of letters – a celebrated poet of world renown. It made her important in her own eyes; conferred on her a self-worth which no one could take away.

As the years passed, no one seemed to remember the visits the old man had made to her cottage. Amnesia must be a national pastime, she decided. His own house became a place of great interest, if not pilgrimage, for people from all over the world. But little did they know the full story. Even Carmen seemed to have forgotten Robert's attendances upon Maria Jesus almost as soon as the old man had died.

"I like your necklace," Carmen had said to her one Saturday morning, as Maria Jesus was setting off to the bus stop to visit an old school friend in Palma.

"Robert gave it to me," Maria Jesus said, fingering the loops of aquamarine and pearls supporting a small, gold pendant cross. "He said that it matched my eyes. And that the cross matched my name."

It was the summer after his death, and she wanted to feel close to the memory of that day, almost exactly a year before, when he had spoken of his war and written one last poem just for her.

"Who is Robert?"

"You know. Graves. The Englishman." She nodded her head towards the large house at the top of the village.

Carmen looked bewildered. "Oh yes," she said finally. "Him."

But then, of course, Carmen didn't know about all the poetry Robert had dedicated to Maria Jesus. Why should she? Maria Jesus had told no one. It was all still safely stored in the old chocolate box at the back of the kitchen dresser drawer.

Whether or not anyone else knew or cared, Maria Jesus was proud of the power which had drawn the great man to her side, and proud of what he had written in her honour. But it was the pride which was to be her downfall. A pride which lay dormant, unexpressed, until one January day thirty years after his death.

*　　　　*　　　　*　　　　*

Vanessa, Alexandro's daughter, was putting on too many airs and graces. She was seventeen and attracting the attention of boys. It had gone to her head. She was too big for her boots. At Vanessa's age, Maria Jesus was hardly allowed out of the sight of her parents. Boys had taken an interest in her, for sure, but she was kept on a very short leash. It all seemed so different now.

Success was to blame, Maria Jesus had decided. Not only was Spain now a success story, but her own son had become successful – at least according to the mores of the times. Alexandro and his wife Genoveva lived in one of the more sought-after areas of Palma, close to Alexandro's job at the Mallorcan branch of the Spanish Ministry of Tourism. But it all seemed to have turned their heads. They had got above themselves, forgetting that Alexandro was the son of a carpenter father and a mother compelled to clean rooms in tourist hotels.

Vanessa had been an adorable grandchild, loving to play for hours in the small courtyard at the back of Maria Jesus' cottage and helping her in the kitchen. But now she hardly ever visited, excusing herself when her parents made their twice-a-month duty calls to Deià.

On Maria Jesus' birthday, Vanessa was presented with no option but to visit her grandmother, and on her own. The birthday was in no way special or particular: not a milestone, just a number between seventy and eighty, a number which held no significance. As a result, the family's obligations could, without any compunctions, be deputed to Vanessa. Her parents were hosting a reception at the Town Hall in honour of some high-ranking officials from the Ministry of Tourism in Madrid. Plans were afoot to upgrade the quality of tourism to the Balearic Islands, and Alexandro was to be an important part of the process. There was much at stake for his future career, and he and Genoveva could not absent themselves.

As soon as she walked – or flounced, as Maria Jesus preferred to remember – through the cottage door, a bunch of flowers in her hand, it was all too obvious that she would sooner have been back in Palma: in a café by the Torre de Paraires with her girlfriends, or more likely with one of her admirers.

"Happy birthday, Grandma!" Vanessa said with forced gaiety, placing the flowers on the kitchen dresser and then untying her poncho before swinging it onto the back of a chair. "And many many more."

She was not dressed for the time of year. It may have been mild when she left Palma, but here in Deià there was a wintry edge to the weather and Vanessa's arms were soon goose-pimpled.

The girl's mind was elsewhere. Maria Jesus could see that, but for once did not feel in an indulgent frame of mind as far as her granddaughter was concerned. She was too much a child of the times, seeing her grandmother now as an old lady to be condescended to, to be tolerated for as short a time as possible before she could escape back into the tinsel and pretence that Spain had become.

She surveyed the girl critically. The seventeen-year-old had more the appearance of a tourist from Magaluf than the daughter of a man making his way in an important Ministry of State. Her skirt was so short that it needed constant attention when she sat to ensure that it did not become too revealing, whilst the straps of her brassiere occasionally slipped over her shoulders, requiring her to re-adjust them from time to time.

An Alice band restrained her mass of dark hair, preventing it from falling down over her face. A beautiful face, but arrogant in its beauty, in the knowledge of its power to attract and discard men. Even her father, Alexandro, could be manipulated by his own daughter, falling under the spell of her precocious femininity. The girl, Maria Jesus was sure, had been allowed too much license; her mother, Genoveva, was to blame, reviving her own fading sexuality through her daughter.

But, to her shame, Maria Jesus felt the strangest pang of jealousy mingling with her anger. She had never been allowed to parade her beauty when she had been Vanessa's age. A predictable marriage to the boy next door, after a short clumsy courtship, two children, and then hard work for the rest of her life had been her lot.

But not entirely. There had been a year or two when she had been special, when her beauty had elicited great art. But no one knew, or indeed, would probably even care if they did.

She regretted what she was about to say for the rest of her life.

"You and your friends think that you invented sexual attraction – the art of the seduction of the male – don't you?"

Vanessa sat up and pulled her skirt closer towards her knees. "Whatever do you mean, Grandma?"

"I never needed to strut my wares. No, I never needed to flaunt my body to draw to my side the towering intellect, in fact I would say, the love, of Robert Graves, to be his inspiration – his muse!"

Vanessa knew the name. No one who had any association with Deià could not know the name.

"That Englishman loved you?" The idea was not only incredulous, but risible. Vanessa burst out laughing. In her old age, her grandmother was starting to fantasise.

Maria Jesus hauled herself out of her chair, tore open the dresser drawer, and held the chocolate box aloft.

The picture on the lid was of a boy in a green velveteen suit, white lacy collar and cuffs, staring dreamily at an impossibly large floating bubble wafting above his head of blond curls.

"Is that Robert Graves as a boy?" Vanessa asked, before she could stop herself.

The question only served to further infuriate Maria Jesus, particularly as Robert had in fact been quite capable of garbing himself up in some inappropriate costume for, she always believed, her special benefit.

"Idiot!" she screamed, slamming the box on the dresser. "These are the poems he wrote in my honour, poems which the world, indeed no one, has ever seen."

Vanessa was by her side. "Show me," she said in a hushed voice, her eyes wide.

Maria Jesus carefully removed the lid, to display on top of the sheaves of multi-sized and coloured paper the last poem Robert Graves had dedicated to her: a full page of writing dated 28th July 1985.

Vanessa tried to extract the pages. "No!" Maria Jesus screamed again at her granddaughter, ramming the lid back on the box. She could smell the girl's cheap perfume, and it made her angrier than ever. "No! You have seen enough. Just remember that old people have also had rich and fulfilling lives, seen things of which you can never dream, been things which you can never be worthy to be."

And then she recanted. Vanessa was little more than a child. How could she understand?

"Kiss your grandmother, and go," she said softly. "Catch your bus back to Palma. I'm sorry, and thank you for the flowers."

Vanessa slowly tied the ribbons of her poncho, and then spoke with a perspicacity which took Maria Jesus by surprise.

"I always knew that you had a unique and intriguing life, Grandma, and today I understand that you have had a larger life than I could ever have imagined. But you must allow me to lead my life in my own way, to follow my star, perhaps even to be a muse in the Spain which has changed beyond recognition since you were my age, and which you all too obviously hate. But maybe even you should not hanker for a past which brought such tragedy and unhappiness to so many people. I know that you think I am flighty and shallow, but consider that you might be wrong. Hardship and poverty do not necessarily make you wise. A little cunning perhaps, but not a judge and jury in all matters. But I'm glad that you were special, a chosen one, an inspiration for Mister Robert Graves. Wonderful memories, Grandma, which I am sure will sustain you for many years to come."

There was a note of sarcasm in the way she pronounced 'Robert Graves' with an English accent, prefixed by 'mister,' rather than 'señor.' But Maria Jesus did not notice. She just wanted Vanessa out of her cottage.

After Vanessa had gone, Maria Jesus tried to think over what the girl had said. But she was confused, and her heart was palpitating. Two aspirins were what was needed. When she had calmed, she filled a vase with water and gathered up the flowers from the dresser. They were still in their El Corte Inglés wrapper. He never brought her flowers for her birthday. He always said that he would wait for spring, to pick her the wild flowers with his own hands.

"Ah," she murmured to herself, "they'll never understand."

The chocolate box lay on the dresser. She picked up the last poem he had written for her and read it out loud. There were only one or two words which made any sense, but she knew that it was about her, and especially about her sensuous body which had meant so much to him.

"They'll never understand," she repeated. "Never."

*   *   *   *

"I have been stupid, Robert. So stupid. It was just between the two of us, or three if we count your wife, but now the whole of Spain and beyond will know."

At first light, the morning after her birthday, she had made her way painfully into Deià's small graveyard. The damp was aggravating her arthritis.

She was not a sentimental woman, hardly ever visiting his grave. Most days there were tourists coming and going, even in winter, and that made the graveyard too public a place for a love which had been so private and personal. But this morning she needed to talk to him, and she could only do so before the first bus came up from Palma.

"You see, Robert, they will try and wrest them from me. But I cannot burn them. I can't. At times, I even wonder if it had ever happened. But then I look in the box, and there I have my proof."

She bent down to pick up a discarded crisp packet. "What do they care," she said. "You are just an exhibit. A diversion from their week on the beach, so they can go home and say that they did some culture in Mallorca." She crunched up the cellophane packet. "It wasn't all cheap wine and sun, you know," she said in a strong English accent. "We took a trip to that place where Graves used to live. Up in the mountains. Quite primitive, really."

She traced her finger over the stone bearing his name. "But it's my family now who will be the problem. Alexandro, and his spend-thrift wife. God, I've been stupid."

She made her way out of the cemetery, moving from gravestone to gravestone for support.

"I must leave you," she muttered. "At least where you are no one can sully your memories."

SIX

"How was your grandmother?" Alexandro asked his daughter on his and Genoveva's return from the reception at the Town Hall.

It had not gone as well as he had hoped. He had a feeling that he had been patronised: regarded as the local boy on the block, not quite up to the job. On the way home he had told Genoveva that they might still parachute someone in from the mainland to get to grips with the tourist problems on the island. She only said that, as usual, he was feeling persecuted, and should get over his inferiority complex. He was in no mood to take advice from his wife. She had, in his view, been far too friendly with a large middle-aged owner of a hotel chain in Malaga. They had had a fiery exchange, and by the time they drew up to their apartment they were not on speaking terms. She didn't care. She had never been averse to a little flirting from time to time; it kept Alexandro on his toes.

He was glad to see Vanessa had not yet gone out for the evening. She always managed to calm him down, make him feel that life was good. Without being aware of it, she also helped heal the occasional rifts with Genoveva which, he had to acknowledge, were becoming more numerous as the years went by. His daughter reminded him of the reasons why he had fallen in love with Genoveva twenty years before and married her in the teeth of his mother's opposition.

But now Vanessa was being difficult. She looked at him inscrutably, her expression saying that she knew something he didn't know.

"How was your grandmother?" he repeated, louder, and more slowly.

"I've discovered that she's had an affair," Vanessa said, looking pleased with herself.

Alexandro and Genoveva burst into laughter.

"It's true," Vanessa said.

"And with whom, might I enquire?" Genoveva asked condescendingly.

"The poet Robert Graves."

"Oh, him," Alexandro said, feeling deflated. "I know he used to slip down to see my mother occasionally, but believe me, he was well past it by then."

"Then I suppose that you know all about the poems," Vanessa said truculently. She did not like being laughed at.

"What poems?" Alexandro asked sharply.

"The box of poems. All dedicated to Grandma. Poems no one has ever seen. She showed me. She's kept them all these years in a chocolate box with a ridiculous picture on the lid."

Alexandro and Genoveva stared at each other in disbelief.

"Poems? Dedicated to Grandma? Which no one has seen?" Alexandro asked in quick succession, as Genoveva's heavily mascaraed eyes grew wider and wider.

Vanessa nodded. "Which no one even knows exist," she confirmed emphatically.

"How did you find out about them?" Alexandro breathed.

"I annoyed her. She thought I looked like a tart, and she wanted to prove that she had been tarty once herself. Managed to hook a world famous poet with her wonderful looks."

That, Vanessa said to herself, as she swung her poncho around her shoulders and moved to the door, will teach them not to underestimate their daughter. Discovering a juicy bit of family information: something of which they had been oblivious for years.

"Where are you going?" Genoveva asked.

"To the cinema with Rafael," Vanessa replied, much satisfied with the mayhem she would be leaving behind.

"Don't be late."

"Alexandro," Genoveva said urgently as soon as Vanessa had gone, "you must get up there."

He was used to receiving orders from his wife, orders which often resulted in matrimonial disputes, but on this occasion they were as one.

"I'll get up there tomorrow."

"*No pasarán*, Alexandro. *No pasarán!*"

They were the catchwords, the war cry, of La Pasionaria, the Communist rabble-rouser, who had defied the fascists until the fall of Madrid when she had flown out of Spain to exile in the Soviet Union. When democracy had been restored, she had returned as an old lady to continue to harangue the people for their capitalist ways.

When Genoveva had decided that Alexandro was the man for her, it was necessary to start courting his mother, who was making her opposition to the match only too apparent. As part of her charm offensive, she had invited Maria Jesus and Alexandro to her student nurses' hostel for a meal. The conversation had limped and dragged throughout the carefully prepared main courses, but by the time of the dessert it had come to a standstill. In desperation, Alexandro suggested they should watch a documentary on the television about the disintegration of the Communist states of Eastern Europe. Events were moving fast, country after country defying their governments and demanding freedom.

The Spanish commentary included clips of La Pasionaria in full fiery and bombastic flood. As soon as her image appeared on screen Maria Jesus became animated.

"*No pasarán!*" she had shrieked. "*No pasarán!* But they did pass, and then that bitch buggered off, leaving her followers to be executed and tortured."

As the documentary continued to roll she became more

excited, shouting directly at the flickering image of La Pasionaria. And then, worst of all, the old Communist firebrand was herself being interviewed by a glossy television personality in a plush Madrid studio for a comment.

Maria Jesus became uncontrollable. She knelt before the television screen to shout abuse directly at La Pasionaria's image.

"While you were sucking up to Stalin, eating jelly and trifle in the Kremlin, my parents were starving. Starving, you bitch!"

Alexandro did not know where the jelly and trifle had come from, but thought it best not to ask. He switched off the television and, after an awkward cup of coffee, took his mother home. "*No pasarán!*" she had spat over and over again on the road home. "*No pasarán*, and the devil take the hindmost!"

Ever since, whenever his mother was being difficult, well out of her earshot Genoveva and Alexandro would raise their right fists and shout '*no pasarán!*' to each other, and then grin complicitly.

Except, on this occasion, they were not grinning. There was hard work to be done with an obstinate old lady sitting on a possible gold mine.

She would have to be approached with great tact and delicacy. His mother was stubborn and proud. Proud of the Spain of which she and her parents had been a part, while he, Alexandro, had sold his soul to the devil: cashing in on the waves of cheap tourism which broke on Mallorca's shores from spring until autumn, to occupy the ugly blocks which had mushroomed along the east and south coasts of the island.

She had made her views clear to him on more than one occasion. When he was promoted in the Ministry to chief executive officer, shortly before his marriage to Genoveva, he had expected his mother to be glad. He would be able to support his wife and any children they might have. Instead, they had rowed.

"What are you doing to my island?" she had ranted, when he told her.

"But, Mama," he had pleaded, "times are changing. Do you want to remain poor and bitter for the rest of your life?"

"Yes," she had said, in a quietly menacing voice. "It would be better for all of us. At least Robert Graves preserved Deià for all posterity."

It was well known that Deià's most famous resident had had some influence in limiting tourist development around the village and the nearby coast, persuading the authorities that any building should be suitable to Mallorca's natural beauty. But she was going too far, wanting the island to stay in a time warp to fulfil some romantic notion she had of the past, now fast receding. A past which had brought her and all of Spain such misery.

His wedding had been a few days away. She should be rejoicing that he had found happiness, that one day she might have grandchildren. But she had never shown any enthusiasm for his relationship with Genoveva.

He decided to take the bull by the horns. "It's Genoveva, isn't it?" he had said.

"You are a grown man, Alexandro. You must make your own choices. Just remember, that when you have made your own bed you have to lie on it."

He knew why she had chosen that particular metaphor. She saw her future daughter-in-law as little more than an empty-headed seductress, and Alexandro had stupidly allowed his sexual desires to drive him into an unsuitable marriage.

But now he could see her point of view a little more clearly. If that famous Englishman had been inspired to write poetry just for her, then of course it would turn her head, make her feel superior and contemptuous of people of little intellect or disinterested in the arts, amongst whom, even he had to acknowledge, was numbered Genoveva.

SEVEN

"*No pasarán!*" Alexandro said out loud, as he navigated the bends up to Deià the following evening. "*No pasarán!*"

"*No pasarán!*" he said one more time as he drove into Deià, to give himself a last dose of courage.

She was sitting at her window facing the Graves' old house when he arrived.

"May I come in?" he asked unnecessarily, as he lifted the latch and stepped into the cottage.

"Yes. I have been expecting you." Then, without taking her eyes from the house at the top of the hill, "And the sooner you come the better, I suppose, for my own peace of mind," Maria Jesus said.

"May I switch on the light?"

"If you must. But then, you will need to draw the curtains and shut out the village and the past from me. And right now, I think I need the strength of the past."

"Very well," he said, sitting down in the gloom.

He looked around the cottage, little changed since he was a boy. "The past, Mama, belongs to you; but it cannot, must not, be hoarded," he said quietly and sympathetically.

"How do you mean, 'hoarded'?" She pronounced the word with a snarl.

"Vanessa has told Genoveva and me about the poems. You have kept them for thirty years or more without telling your family, or presumably anyone else, about their existence."

"They are mine."

"Yes. They belong to you – but also to all of humanity. It is only right and just that they see the light of day."

"So there must be no secrets, no magic, no memories which should not be shared?"

"Why should they not be shared?"

"Because they are fragile. They cannot be properly understood, or properly cherished, by anyone but their keeper." She seemed to crumple before continuing in a small voice, "And in the sharing they will be distorted, and eventually contaminated."

He felt a flood of pity for the old woman, mingled with a respect for the fortitude with which she had guarded her secret for what, he had to concede, were good and sound reasons.

He decided upon another tack. "But Vanessa tells me that they are in English, Mama. You don't even understand them," he said gently.

"I understand them better than any professor of English at Madrid University could ever understand them."

"I wasn't thinking of Madrid University."

"What do you mean?"

Alexandro knelt before his mother. For a fleeting moment he brought to her mind the times Robert used to kneel before her in the very same place.

"Allow me to do some research. Discover where Graves' memory is best preserved. Which academic institution, be it in England or America, is promoting, studying, his work. Let me find a place for these poems where, as you say, they will be cherished. Surely you, all of us, owe this much to the great man."

She began to cry silently. It was pitiful to see her shrunken shoulders wracked with sobs.

"Don't cry, Mama," he pleaded. "You will be doing the right thing."

"But you don't understand."

"What don't I understand?"

"He loved me so much. So much. But he was old, and could not express that love as he wanted."

For a moment, Alexandro thought that his mother was referring to a fading sexual prowess. "How do you mean?" he asked guardedly.

It was now or never. He had to be told. "The poems don't add up to much," she wailed. He had elicited the truth, which she had always tried to deny, even to herself. "Although he loved me with all his heart, he found me too late. There is not much there."

"That does not matter, Mama," Alexandro assured her, concealing his disappointment. "Anything from his pen will merit careful academic scrutiny – particularly the work of a great man in the twilight of his years."

He held his mother in his arms and rocked her gently. "Show me," he said softly.

She no longer had the will to resist. But there was one thing that she needed to clear. She extracted a handkerchief from her sleeve, blew her nose, and then looked at him through narrowed eyes.

"Is it just the money, Alexandro?"

"How do you mean?"

"I am not entirely stupid. These poems must be worth money. Good money."

Alexandro stood and returned to his chair. Feeling himself colouring, he was glad the lights had not been switched on for his mother to see.

"You are right. Yes. But the poems are your property, and if they have any monetary value, which is likely to be the case as you suggest, you will benefit," he said briskly, and a little too quickly.

"And then, when I die, one half of what I have will go to you, and one half to Josefina."

It was unnerving. She was reading his mind. But why should she not have a comfortable old age, with anything left on her death split between him and his sister? Not that she needed the money, now headteacher in a private school in Barcelona, only returning to Mallorca for a few days in the school holidays –

leaving him with the responsibility of keeping an eye on their ageing mother for the rest of the year.

"The first priority will be you, Mama, and your needs. You can be sure of that."

"Thank you, Alexandro. It's just that I would not want the matter of the money to remain unspoken. Let us just be clear that I will give up, surrender, the poems in the interests of Robert's memory, his reputation – and you will assist for the money."

He opened his mouth to remonstrate, but she raised a hand to silence him. Painfully, she hobbled into the kitchen and withdrew the chocolate box from the back of the dresser drawer. She had never been sure what she was going to do with the contents now that she was getting old. Perhaps, after all, it was for the best to deal with them while she was still alive; it would be better than their being discovered after her death, when she would have no say over them. At times, she had even thought of burning them but that, she knew, she could never bring herself to do.

She placed the box on her coffee table, and then stood back.

Alexandro ponderously read out the words in flowing gold letters across the top of the lid, above a reproduction of Millais' 'Bubbles'.

"Cadbury's Dairy Milk."

"Yes!" Maria Jesus exclaimed. "Chocolates. You see, he was always generous. Gifts for my children, gifts for me. But the greatest of his gifts lies within this box. And generosity breeds generosity."

"How do you mean?"

"Alexandro, I would have given him anything he asked. For years after your father died, no man came near me. Then he rose up and declared his love. He could have had anything from me that he wanted. Not just my possessions, but my body. All of me. Little did people in the village know. How sweet, they thought, that wild, cranky man is visiting one of our lonely ladies for a little extra female company. All very lovely and above board;

his wife letting him indulge himself in his dotage. But little did they know what went on behind my shutters! How he loved my strong peasant body, my arms, my legs, my back, my hair!"

She was becoming excited, and he had heard more than enough. Whether or not she was fantasising, he had to maintain the momentum of what he had achieved so far.

"May I?" he asked, his hand on the lid.

"You must?"

"Yes, Mama. It is for the best."

Gently, Alexandro opened the box, and rifled through the motley collection of pages of varying sizes and colours: white, cream, blue, even pink.

With a sinking heart, he struggled to contain his dismay. She had been right. There was not very much there: one page of writing, a few half pages of writing, the remainder bearing just a legible word or two. Finally, at the bottom of the box lay one page, inscribed 'Madonna'.

"That is my favourite of all," she said, pointing to the page with the single word. "For me, it speaks more than all the learned works of Shakespeare and Cervantes."

He was tempted to hand them back, to tell her to keep her memories. But she would know why he did so and it might break her heart. He had come this far, and now there was no going back. And, after all, there were one or two pages scrawled with what seemed to be coherent words in English, even running into a few lines. One in particular making it to the end of the page, with a date written in his mother's hand. There might be enough for the academics to analyse and then debate and discuss, as they so loved to do, teasing out something from nothing and then publishing a learned paper on the decline of the mind of a great poet.

And God knows the money, if there was to be any, would come in useful. It was getting more and more difficult to keep up with Genoveva's credit card bills now she had decided that, as the wife of the rising star of the Ministry of Tourism, she needed to dress appropriately. And then, Vanessa was costing him a small fortune wanting to look trendy with the latest fashions, and trend certainly came expensive as far as his daughter was concerned.

Not that the money would be his straight away, and even on his mother's death only half her estate would be his. He couldn't exclude from his mind a venal thought as to how much longer his mother had to live, but then managed to dismiss it at once.

"It will be necessary for me to have the safe-keeping of the box, Mama."

"What do you mean?" she snapped.

"I will need to show your poems to interested parties."

"Not possible, Alexandro. I have guarded the box for nearly forty years. I cannot just hand it over, as if it were a piece of furniture to be sold at auction. At least, not until I know the poems will be with someone who will respect them, even if they cannot love them as I have done."

Again, she narrowed her eyes. "You find the people with the money, and I will decide if they are worthy to have them."

Alexandro felt that he had secured some kind of a deal, but now it was unravelling.

"Very well, Mama," he said, controlling himself. "But I will need to take some photocopies to interested parties, for them to examine."

"Samples!" she cried in outrage. "As if they are curtain material, to take home and decide at leisure if they are what you want, up to scratch, in this case the real thing; whether they really are from the pen of the greatest English poet since Shakespeare!"

"Yes. Exactly so." She was enough of a peasant woman to be business-like and practical when the chips were down. "Yes. Exactly so," he repeated. "After all, you would never buy a pig in a poke."

"And when these samples have been examined – held up to the light, dragged through the dirt – you will negotiate a price

43

for the whole collection, when I will decide if the recipients are worthy."

She was infuriating him. He looked around the small cottage, where he had lived all his childhood and youth right up until the time of his marriage. Nothing had changed. But she didn't want change. The money meant nothing to her. She didn't want a new fitted kitchen to replace the ancient rickety dresser, or a modern boiler, which would relieve her of having to carry wood from the shed in the backyard all winter to feed the range. And now he was sure that it was all because of Graves. She wanted to keep things exactly as they were when the old man had tottered through her door in his final decline. And worse, the few disparate pages in her chocolate box, and her friendship with Graves, had made her feel better and more important than she was. These scraps of paper, these poems – if that was what they could be called – and the memories they induced had served to separate her from the society of others, making her a haughty bitter recluse with no friends, just a passing neighbourliness with a few old village cronies and Carmen next door.

It was always something of a relief when his sister Josefina spent time each school holiday in the cottage with their mother, sharing their meals together and sleeping in her old bedroom. Three times a year his mother had normal human companionship. Josefina never seemed to mind; but then, she always knew that soon she would be off again to her school in Barcelona, and to the status and respect of a headteacher.

"You keep the originals, Mama," he said in exasperation, "and I will take one or two copies to hawk around, as you say, like curtain material."

She nodded. "As long as we understand each other, Alexandro," she said. "As long as we understand each other."

EIGHT

Maria Jesus cut an incongruous figure in Palma's Plaça Major, clutching her chocolate box to her chest.

It was the following Saturday morning. He had picked her up early hoping to miss the tourist crowds, but it seemed that even in February the city hardly slept. The new fad was for week-end breaks. Have a few days away from your north European winter in Mallorca, and if you are lucky, you might even see a shaft or two of wintry sunshine. There were also the stag and hen party week-ends, which held to no season. It was Alexandro's task, somehow, to reduce these to a trickle. How he was going to do that he was not sure, particularly as the local bars welcomed the business, their takings inflated by the revellers' drunken bonhomie, leaving the municipality to clear up the mess afterwards.

Jewellers and souvenir shop keepers were already noisily raising their shutters and shouting loud greetings to their colleagues. The café and restaurant owners were scrubbing their sections of the square and wiping their tables. After all, a few hardier tourists might be tempted to take their lunch al fresco.

Modern Spain had left his mother far behind. She hobbled beside him, an embroidered blanket wrapped tightly around her shoulders to protect her from the early morning mists of Deià which now, as the day wore on, was no longer necessary. He had parked the car in a small side street and they were making for a stationer on the other side of the square.

Their business was soon over. Two sheets were extracted from the box: the poem dated by Maria Jesus together with another which, to Alexandro's eye, seemed to amount to something intelligible. Under Maria Jesus' close scrutiny, they were fed into a photocopier by a disinterested shop assistant struggling to wake up.

"Two euros," she said.

Maria Jesus glared at her while Alexandro paid. "Don't you mean thirty pieces of silver?" she erupted, snatching the originals from her and carefully replacing them in the box.

The girl shrugged. The woman was obviously barmy.

"What is that?" Maria Jesus asked as they drove out of Palma, pointing at a massive cruise ship edging its way into the harbour.

"*The Queen of the Sea*," Alexandro said, without even having to take his eyes off the road. Every other Saturday she docked in Palma at ten in the morning, disgorged her human cargo of wealthy middle-aged tourists, and departed at five in the afternoon. In those few hours, thousands of euros would have been spent without the island having to provide one overnight hotel room. The best possible cost-benefit ratio for the tourist industry and the residents of the city.

"Queen of rubbish, more like," Maria Jesus muttered scathingly.

Outside the cottage Alexandro got out of his car to help her, but she was ahead of him, hirpling between her pots of herbs to her front door and slamming it in his face. It was as if the chocolate box needed to be restored to its rightful place before it was subjected to any further contamination.

He sat in the car for a moment or two checking that the two pages of photocopy paper were safely stowed in the glove box, then glanced down at his mother's cottage, uncompromisingly preserved in its time warp: a challenge to change. Albeit grudgingly, he had to admire her cantankerous implacability in the face of progress.

"Do you have them?" Genoveva asked, as soon as he arrived home.

"Yes. But I feel shabby about it."

For once, she seemed to understand. "It is for the best, Alexandro," she said, putting her arms around him. "Even for your mother."

*   *   *   *

Maria Jesus had dreaded returning home. It was not just that the cottage was empty of its secret, more that it had been robbed of its reason to be, to exist.

Since the children had left it had hosted three personages: Maria Jesus, Robert, and the box. Robert's death had been in the natural order of things, and Maria Jesus had soon come to terms with it. Anyway, everything associated with him was still in its rightful place: his chair, the range where she had made his coffee, the pictures on the walls, which he would have seen many times. Nothing was out of place, to the extent that many a time she felt that he might have left her just a moment or two before; even on occasion she said a word or two over her shoulder to him, but she knew that was a temptation she should not yield to too often.

But now, the third party in the relationship had been violated. She returned the box to its place in the dresser drawer, but there seemed little point in secreting it anymore. The poems would soon become common knowledge, when all that had set her apart, made her special, would ebb away under the examination, maybe even the ridicule, of the common herd. She could not resist a creeping awareness that she had betrayed Robert and had betrayed herself, and she didn't know how she might be forgiven.

She had hardly slept since Vanessa's visit on her birthday. She climbed the stairs and sank onto her bed.

Robert had told her once that his mother had been Irish. She wondered what she had been like. She felt an affinity with her. Between the two, they had inspired that last great poem of his the day he had told her of the letter the army had sent

47

his mother reporting his death, and she had knelt at his feet while he stroked her back and her hair. Irish Mother, Catalan muse. Both nations had been bullied by their neighbours: the Irish by Britain, the Catalans by Spain. Mrs Graves and Señora Gonzalez. They would have had much in common, she decided. Or was it his father who was Irish? She was no longer sure. But it didn't matter anymore, she supposed, as she drifted into a deep dreamless sleep.

NINE

Alexandro felt a surge of parental pride. Without a doubt, Vanessa had much more talent than her school, her mother, or even he, had ever given her credit for.

It was Sunday, and she had woken late after partying with Rafael until midnight. Although Alexandro could have done the job himself, he had been pretty sure that his daughter would be quicker and more competent. Besides, he felt that he had intruded enough into his mother's affairs the day before, at least for the time being, and it was for someone else now to take them to the next stage.

From time to time, he was tormented by the thought that one day Vanessa might end up a clone of her mother, Genoveva. The prospect seemed outlandish, but it might happen. Worse still, might she even end up like his mother? It was all in the genes, after all. But today, looking at his daughter's beautiful, intelligent face, he knew that just could not be possible.

Deftly, she had opened up the sites on her laptop, and after tapping the keyboard with her chocolate brown nail-varnished fingers for a full two minutes, had finally accessed the Spanish language detail of Robert Graves and his oeuvre.

Yes, he had lived in Deià from 1926 until his death in 1985, with a break from 1936, when the Civil War commenced, to 1946, when the second World War was over. Yes, he had drawn inspiration from a succession of women, the first being Laura Riding, who lived with him in their house in Deià, followed by younger and younger women – all tolerated and, it seemed, even encouraged by his wife Beryl. Vanessa read out their names to her parents, ending with a Julie.

"No mention of a certain Maria Jesus Gonzalez then?" Genoveva asked mischievously.

Alexandro frowned. His wife could never entirely forgive his mother for the hard time she had given her when they were courting and, indeed, during their marriage. Now she was having to come to terms with the old woman having a much larger life than she had ever given her credit for.

"None," Vanessa said blithely. "Which, I think you will agree, makes these poems written in Grandma's honour particularly valuable. Obviously they have never seen the light of day until my birthday visit."

It was she who had been responsible for their surfacing, and she was determined to take the credit.

Vanessa tapped away at the keyboard for a little longer, and then stared hard at the screen. "On the death of Beryl Graves in 2003," she read, "all of her husband's notes, manuscripts, and other papers were moved from Deià to St John's College, Oxford. A generous donation by her to her late husband's old alma mater."

"Read that again," Alexandro asked.

When Vanessa had finished the second reading, they looked at each other, leaving unsaid what was in their minds. How would they be able to create interest in two sheets of paper, when there was so much material of the old man's for the experts to pore and pick over?

"Then maybe," Alexandro said, breaking the silence, "we need to make contact with this St John's College, Oxford."

"No!" Vanessa said, without any hesitation. "No, they have too much."

"How do you mean?" Alexandro asked.

"It seems that he was prolific." Vanessa was scrolling down a list of Graves' published works. "Very prolific. I don't think that they will be interested in adding a couple of pages of poems to their collection, with the promise of a few more." She turned to face her parents. "We offer them to their rivals," she said slyly.

"I'm beginning to think that this whole venture is a waste of time." Genoveva started to tidy up the living room, re-folding the Sunday newspapers and re-ordering the ornaments on the mantelpiece. Her obsession with having everything in its proper place was something which had irritated Alexandro's mother, and was now irritating her son. Her damning comment made Alexandro even more determined to pursue the project.

"Please sit down, Genoveva. I think that Vanessa has a point. Academics are always at each other's throats. In fact, they often hate each other."

"So what do we do?"

"We find some learned institution which is in competition with this St John's College, Oxford, and offer them there."

"And how do we find that out?"

"Easy," Vanessa pronounced. "Easy. Everyone knows that the other big university in England is Cambridge."

"So we go to Cambridge?" Alexandro asked.

"Of course."

"But where do we start?"

"Easy." Vanessa looked at her father pityingly. "We Google Cambridge and find out some names of academics in the University specialising in poetry. Modern poetry."

Alexandro turned his head to one side. "Or maybe not such modern poetry."

"Or poetry," Genoveva said crisply, "written for Spanish peasant women by some besotted old men who should have known better."

Another annoying trait of Genoveva's was her inability to see any task through to its conclusion as soon as she met with some obstacle or another.

"But is our English up to scratch for all of this?" Alexandro said, ignoring his wife.

"We can at least try," Vanessa said. "I could have a stab at it. I might even ask Rafael to help."

"No, don't ask. I would prefer to keep all of this in the family."

"Exactly so," Genoveva added. "If we're on a wild goose chase, we wouldn't want the whole world to know."

She stood and left the room, declaring that it was time to prepare lunch. Alexandro waved an admonishing finger at Vanessa pulling a face at her mother's departing back.

"It would seem," Vanessa said, after more tapping on her keyboard and staring at her screen, "that these two English Universities, Oxford and Cambridge, are split into different sections."

"How do you mean?" Alexandro asked.

"They're called colleges. And each college has a department for each subject. So, for example, that St John's College in Oxford will not only teach English, but Mathematics, and everything else as well."

"That's odd."

"I know, but it seems to be the way it is."

"So we can approach any one of these colleges?"

"Yes. So it would seem."

"Read out the names of the Cambridge colleges."

"Christ's, Corpus Christi, Clare, Downing, King's, Newnham for girls only, Peterhouse, Queen's, St John's – like the one in Oxford, I suppose – Katherine the Queen..."

"Which?" Genoveva interrupted. She had reappeared from the kitchen, where she had been eavesdropping.

"Which what?"

"What was the last?"

"Katherine the Queen."

"I wonder if that is Katherine, the Spanish queen. One of ours. Married to that vile king of England, Henry the Eighth."

"A Spanish queen?"

"Katherine of Aragon," Genoveva pronounced authoritatively.

"Enough books have been written about her husband to fill a library."

Genoveva's sole claim to intellectualism lay in her appetite for historical novels of the racier and more salacious kind. The tragic family stories of Ferdinand and Isabella, whose marriage in the fifteenth century united Spain, provided rich material for undemanding novelists. Of all the disastrous marriages contracted for their children, none was more disastrous than the marriage of their youngest daughter, who at fifteen was despatched to England to be betrothed to the king's eldest son, Arthur, sickly and impotent. So important was a union between the two countries, that when Arthur died prematurely she was married off to the next in line, the future Henry the Eighth. And Genoveva was familiar with every detail.

"Never heard of her," Vanessa shrugged. "Anyway, I thought you always said that us Mallorcans were Catalan rather than Spanish, so why should I know?"

"Don't split hairs, Vanessa," Alexandro said. "See if they have a website."

Vanessa clicked onto the name of the college, and started to read slowly in English:

"The College of Katherine the Queen, usually just known as Katherine's, or more familiarly, Kate's, was founded by Queen Mary in 1556 in honour of her mother, Katherine of Aragon."

"There you are!" Genoveva cried triumphantly. "I was right!"

Ignoring her mother, Vanessa continued to read out the information on screen. "The college has followed a high church tradition over the years, and although it offers places for a variety of the arts and science disciplines, its strengths lie in modern languages, particularly English and Spanish and their literatures...."

"That's the one," Alexandro said, interrupting his daughter. "Now, we shall need a contact."

Vanessa nodded enthusiastically. "Now let me see." She clicked her mouse two or three times on the website. "Here it is. Professor Christian Tennenbaum, professor of English literature. Author of *John Keats and the Romantic Movement in English Poetry.*"

"When did this Keats live?"

"How should I know?"

"Do they have this professor's address?"

"Yes," she said, scrolling down the entry. "The English Department, College of Katherine the Queen, Trumpington Street, Cambridge."

"Right. We're going to have to work out what we say."

"But why does he have a German name?" Genoveva asked.

"I was wondering that," Alexandro said.

"Can't see it matters," Vanessa said, closing her laptop, "as long as he's the man for us."

PART THREE

TEN

Christian Tennenbaum wasn't quite sure why he had a German name, either. When his grandparents had arrived in Britain as refugees in 1938, they were determined to rid themselves, and their child Gunther, of all or anything German. But somehow, the name had slipped through the net. 'George' was soon substituted for 'Gunther' in honour of the king of England, but 'Tennenbaum' just seemed to have been overlooked.

At school, George Tennenbaum was subjected to some periodic name calling and bullying during the war. His class mates dubbed him 'Goebbels', not just because of his guttural accent, but also because of his propensity to propound on any topic with great authority. He survived, however, unscathed – or as his headmaster put it, he always bounced back. 'Tennenbaum is nothing if not resilient,' his last school report had said.

Excused National Service on account of his asthma, he moved seamlessly from school to Oxford, to read English. He had sailed his Keeble College entrance interview, explaining to the tutors with dazzling precocity his desire to investigate the influences of Shakespeare upon the great German Romantics, Goethe and Schiller. He left them in no doubt that he was up to the job.

At Oxford he fell in love with Christian's mother, Arabella Pickering, a leggy, intense Somerville College undergraduate and she, a girl with a rebellious streak, fell in love with him.

Her parents were less delighted with the match than were his, but nonetheless, in the summer of 1952 the marriage was celebrated in a small medieval church in a Berkshire village. Not only were the Tennenbaums' German roots now fading and withering, but at a stroke they had lost their Jewish heritage as well, traditionally traced through the female line but now blocked by the very Anglo-Saxon Arabella. The next generation would be as English as apple pie. The naming and baptism of the Tennenbaum refugees' only grandchild as 'Christian,' was the icing on the cake. They had arrived in the safe haven of English respectability.

On graduation, George Tennenbaum had been snapped up by the German Department of GCHQ in Cheltenham. He enjoyed a lack-lustre career, however, hindered by his inability to behave deferentially to those in authority, and to understand the need to ingratiate himself even with those whom he felt to be his inferiors. As a result, he and Arabella focussed their attention on their son Christian and his career which, they decided, would be in academia, where he would be liberated from the requirement of earning a living amongst those of little intellect. They both had the satisfaction of living long enough to see their son become a Cambridge don, and his book, *John Keats and the Romantic Movement in English Poetry*, receive wide acclaim.

But why, Christian often wondered, didn't someone, somewhere along the line, do something about the Tennenbaum bit? And then, as he progressed up the greasy pole of academia, he made an intriguing discovery. Rather than acting as a disadvantage, his name gave him a certain gravitas, a cachet. Here was a foreigner, a German – he must be, with a name like that – looking in at English literature from the outside. He would bring a fresh perspective to bear on the exhausted analyses of the home-grown academics. And what was more, Germans were well-known for their assiduous intellectual rigour.

But at the time that Alexandro and Vanessa's carefully constructed letter landed on his desk in the small room where he conducted his tutorials, with its fine view of King's College Chapel, he was not feeling very fresh at all, and certainly devoid of any intellectual rigour. Time seemed to have passed him by. The years were leaking away, and he didn't have much to show for them. He was now pushing sixty, as he liked to put it, still a bachelor, and still waiting for some life changing event to occur. The long-held desire that he might yet find love was fading, but he still held out hope that he would discover some earth-shaking fresh insight into the Romantic Movement, which would at least secure his name and reputation, if not in perpetuity, then for a long time to come.

The first edition of his book was now nearly thirty years old. He revised it from time to time, more to adapt it to changing tastes than to introduce fresh perspectives. Twice in the last ten years the college had released him for teaching sabbaticals in the United States, but on each occasion he had returned to the security of Cambridge with relief. And that, he knew, was his main problem. As he grew older, he was becoming more timid, more fearful of risks and above all, terrified of making a fool of himself.

It was in such a frame of mind that he read and re-read the letter from Mallorca. He, Christian Tennenbaum, was being invited to a meeting with a family from Deià who held unpublished, indeed, unseen works of the great English poet Robert Graves. The manuscripts were in the hands, and were the property of, the Spanish family of Maria Jesus Gonzalez. It was not commonly known that this lady, Maria Jesus, had been an inspiration for Señor Graves in the very last years of his life. The relationship had been very pure, very beautiful, and needless to say it had produced some magnificent final poetry. They were approaching him in confidence, as the senior lecturer in English literature in the English college with particular Spanish connections, but if he was not interested then they would happily go elsewhere.

The halting, fractured English, put together by Vanessa with the aid of a Google translation and a Spanish/English phrase book, had stretched her abilities to the very limit.

On each reading of the letter, Christian Tennenbaum felt less inclined to feel dismissive about it. Over the space of a week he re-read it several times, removing it from below the glass paper weight on his desk and then staring through the window at the spires of King's College Chapel, as if they might provide illumination.

A small hope started to flicker in his breast. Was this the big break he had been waiting for? Would his name be associated with a literary coup, the magnitude of which was unforeseeable? Of course, it might amount to nothing. It might be a con, even a scam to prise money out of the college, but it would be reckless to ignore the letter, or to send a discouraging reply.

First, he needed to mug up on Graves. He knew a bit about his long, extraordinary life, and remembered the general feeling of loss when he died: the last of the great poets who had spanned the inter-war years and beyond. He had not been a great fan of his poetry, finding it too abstruse and obscure compared to the early nineteenth century Romantics. But at school he had read *Good-bye to All That*, a vivid first-hand account of life in the trenches in the First World War, and as an undergraduate had dipped into *The White Goddess*, a required work of reference for aspiring literary academics of the nineteen-sixties and seventies.

Ten days after the letter had arrived, he made his way over to the college library between two first-year tutorials and borrowed a copy of *The White Goddess*. Flicking through the pages that evening, he remembered how densely written and tangled were the threads of Graves' arguments. But nonetheless, the book must have some enduring appeal, running through numerous editions since its first publication sixty-five years before.

A short refresher course on Graves was all that Christian Tennenbaum needed to be convinced that the letter demanded a positive reply. Graves had led a whacky, unconventional life, and there was no reason to assume that what these people were saying on behalf of Maria Jesus Gonzalez was anything but the truth.

There was little time to lose. He had taken ten days to make his decision, and as the letter so plainly pointed out, there were other institutions which would be very interested in seeing this Maria Jesus Gonzalez and what she might have to offer.

But he needed help. It was quite clear from the letter's broken English that he could only deal with these people with the assistance of a fluent Spanish speaker.

The College of Katherine the Queen had no shortage of Spanish lecturers, from the head of the Spanish Department, Professor Gilbert Pym – full of bombast and self-importance – down to a newly appointed junior lecturer, Tristram Jones. And he, Tristram Jones, would be the ideal choice. He would do what he was told, and if he was foolish enough to try to overshadow or upstage Christian Tennenbaum at any time he, Christian Tennenbaum, would not hesitate to pull rank on him.

The only drawback with Tristram Jones was that he was too jolly by half: always happy and smiling, as if the world was an infinitely good and beautiful place. It could sometimes get on Christian Tennenbaum's nerves.

ELEVEN

The College of Katherine the Queen was well endowed. Not as wealthy as some of the more senior Cambridge colleges, but certainly not devoid of the income required to provide half a dozen scholarships each year for students from deprived backgrounds, and to keep the wine cellar well stocked for fellows' dinners and other celebratory occasions.

The Bursar, Major Anthony Grace, who had served the college for almost as long as Christian Tennenbaum, had been a wily investor of college funds, at the same time sedulously extracting donations and promises of legacies from alumni. He and Christian Tennenbaum had become good friends over the years. Roughly the same age, they enjoyed sharing their misgivings as to the stupidities and failings of dons, heads of departments, and proctors, who seemed to get younger with each passing year.

As soon as he had made his decision to respond to the Gonzalez' letter, it became obvious to Christian Tennenbaum that at some stage, if there was to be a successful outcome, money would have to change hands. It would be prudent, therefore, to involve the Bursar in his plans right from the start. Otherwise he might find himself embarking upon a fool's errand.

The following morning he marshalled his forces. As soon as he was sure that the Bursar would be at his desk, he picked up his telephone and dialled the internal number.

It was lifted at once. "The Bursar." Anthony Grace's voice boomed down the line. His short-term commission in the army had been put to good use over the years. His voice, his military demeanour, everything about him made it clear that he would not be a soft touch.

"Anthony, it's Christian. There's something I need to speak to you about urgently. Would you be able to join me in my study after dinner, say nine o'clock, for a drink and a chat?"

"Of course, Christian. Nine it is."

Christian Tennenbaum often speculated as to the relationship between the Bursar and his wife. Anthony Grace was always available for late night emergency meetings, financial advice, and support at any time. Apart from the occasional sighting of a slight, mousey, timid creature at a reception or occasional drinks party, one would be forgiven for thinking that the Bursar was wedded to the college.

Christian Tennenbaum now needed to get hold of Tristram Jones before he made off to the university Spanish Department. He caught him leaning on his bicycle in the quad, surrounded by a small gaggle of female undergraduates looking at his thick blond hair and fine features in admiration and hanging on his every word.

As he approached, he could hear him speaking to them in Spanish and gesticulating theatrically.

"*Adios*, Franco. *Adios!*" he was saying. After a few more words, the gaggle exploded into laughter.

"What was all that about, Tristram?" he asked, when the girls had dispersed.

"Ah, Christian, I was just telling them that deathbed story about that old fox, Franco. You must know it."

"No, I don't. What deathbed story?"

"Well, apparently when Franco was dying a crowd of his supporters gathered under his hospital window and chanted, 'Farewell, Franco. Farewell, Franco.' The old boy then raised himself onto one elbow and said to his nurse, 'Where are they going?'"

Tristram Jones could hardly contain himself until the end of his story, and then laughed like a hyena.

"That's a very good story," Christian Tennenbaum said, just wondering at the same time if he and Tristram Jones would be compatible partners on the Spanish enterprise after all. But it was too late for second thoughts.

"Tristram, something's come up on which I will need your help. Can you join the Bursar and myself for a drink in my study at nine this evening?"

"Yes, of course, Christian, of course," Tristram Jones said, feeling flattered to be asked.

*　　　　*　　　　*　　　　*

"White or red?" Christian Tennenbaum asked his guests as soon as they had taken their seats in his superficially tidied study and settled.

"White for me, old boy, as you well know," the Bursar said dryly.

"Is the red Rioja?" Tristram Jones asked.

"No, it's not bloody Rioja, Tristram. I can't stand that stuff. It's Merlot."

"Persevere with the Rioja, Christian. Persevere." Tristram Jones grinned as he took a glass of Merlot from Christian Tennenbaum's hand. "Queen of the Spanish wines. But Merlot's a close second."

"Rioja gives me a headache," the Bursar said in a manner that made it clear that the debate over the wine was closed.

There was no point in wasting time. "I want your advice on this," Christian Tennenbaum said, handing the Bursar the Gonzalez' letter for him to read and then pass on to Tristram Jones.

The Bursar passed it on in silence. Tristram Jones read the letter carefully. "Wow!" he said, when he had finished. "Wow, and wow!"

"Do you know anything about Graves?" Christian Tennenbaum asked, not without some misgivings.

"I certainly do. We have so much in common."

"What do you and Robert Graves have in common?" It was downright absurd that this whipper-snapper should presume to link his name with that of Robert Graves.

"Our love of Spain, of course."

"Well I know nothing of Robert Graves," the Bursar said. "I know his name, but nothing more. Please enlighten me."

Christian Tennenbaum leant back in his tutorial chair, placed the fingers of his hands together and addressed the dark shape of King's College Chapel through the window.

"One. Robert Graves, born 1895, died 1985, was one of the greatest poets of the twentieth century. At least of those writing in the English language.

"Two. He declared that his poetic genius was inspired by muses. Females, usually much younger than him. First there was Laura Riding..."

"She wasn't much younger than him, actually." Christian Tennenbaum was taken by surprise. Tristram Jones knew more than he had given him credit for.

"That's as maybe." Christian Tennenbaum did his best to conceal his annoyance at the interruption, and then took a sip of wine before continuing. "But after her departure, freed of her baleful influence, he started to write his best, attaching himself to a succession of girl muses usually in their early twenties."

"And that's where *The White Goddess* comes in," Tristram Jones said brightly.

"Please, allow me to make my points uninterrupted. Three. *The White Goddess.*" He smiled patronisingly at Tristram Jones. How he was going to be able to work with him on the project, he just wasn't sure. "The extraordinary mish-mash of convoluted thinking," Christian Tennenbaum continued, "tracing poetic inspiration from almost prehistoric times to the present day, concluding that true poetry springs only from the influence, patronage, face, body, demeanour or whatnot, of a woman or women. They themselves, the muse, or muses, may or may not be seen as worthy of such a role, may be educated or uneducated. What is essential in every case is that they are young, beautiful, and even aloof. When those qualities are no longer apparent, or available, a fresh muse needs to be found. It's all in the book."

"Some would say," Tristram Jones said earnestly, "the longest incoherent rambling in literary criticism. Full of anachronisms and non-sequiturs. Intellectually dishonest." He flapped his hands in the air, to wave away *The White Goddess* before leaning forward in his chair. "But, if that is the case," he continued dramatically, "if that is the case and these pundits are right, why has the book never been out of print since it was published in 1946? And why then has it become a totem, a mantra, a touchstone for generations of aspiring poets, hippies, and drop-outs? Particularly in America, and particularly in California." He drained his glass in one conclusive gulp.

"And that," the Bursar said, more to himself than to anyone else, "is where the money is."

"Which brings me to my fourth and final point." Christian Tennenbaum drummed his fingers on his desk. "If, as has been suggested, a last muse has surfaced – who in addition is found to be in possession of some as yet unknown and unpublished poems of Robert Graves – not only would that be the literary event of the decade, but it would provide the person, persons, or institution with the right to such poetical works with an economical potential beyond imagining."

"Exactly!" Tristram Jones exclaimed. He could hardly believe his luck in being included in the unfolding narrative.

"Now, to bring a little reality to bear," Christian Tennenbaum continued after a short silence, "during the last years of his life, Graves was beginning to lose his mind. As far as anyone knows, nothing of worth was written from about 1975, until his death in 1985."

"When were these poems purported to have been written?" the Bursar asked, picking up the letter.

"Late seventies, early eighties, I would have thought," Christian Tennenbaum said.

"Then I think that you're wasting your time, and would be wasting our money," the Bursar pronounced.

"Perhaps, but perhaps not." Tristram Jones was not going to let the project go. "Suppose, just suppose, that a Spanish peasant woman, a *duende* if you like, re-ignited his creativity. Maybe just a little. Maybe spasmodically. But still, she brought a shaft of light into his life sufficient to burn away his senility and release his mind to write as a youth again – and let's face it, he never really grew up – she would be holding a treasure trove which the literary world would be agog to see. And for us to bring it to light, would be a *golpe militar* beyond imagining."

"Please Tristram, stick to English," Christian Tennenbaum said irascibly. He had been irked as much by Tristram Jones' youthful enthusiasm as by his knowledge of Graves' muses, but at least they were both singing from the same song-sheet.

"You're the boss," Tristram Jones responded brightly. It was going to be fun, and he saw no reason not to make himself amenable.

Christian Tennenbaum turned to the Bursar. "Tristram's right you know, Anthony. We just can't afford to let this pass us by."

"It might be worth a punt, I suppose, Christian," the Bursar conceded. "If, with Tristram's assistance, you can beat her down to a reasonable figure, it might, just might, be worth considering. Obviously though you'll need to inspect the goods first."

"I'll do my best." Christian Tennenbaum nodded, barely managing to conceal his delight at the Bursar's decision.

"Maybe there's a film in all of this," Tristram Jones cried chirpily. "Penelope Cruz could be the muse, and Ian McKellan, Robert Graves."

"Don't get carried away, Tristram," Christian Tennenbaum said, smiling indulgently. "One step at a time."

The Bursar decided to draw the proceedings towards practicalities. "How much, do you reckon might be needed, top whack?"

"I've no idea, Anthony," Christian Tennenbaum said.

The Bursar looked around Christian Tennenbaum's book-lined study, and then at the two eager academic faces before him. They're very clever, he thought, but they'll screw up the financial side of things between them. They're not money savvy, and they're dealing with foreigners. These Gonzalez people will take money off them like candy from a child. He needed to assert himself.

"Get them over. Offer to pay their expenses. We can put them up in the college. See what they want, then we'll start negotiating. If it all comes within the college slush fund, all well and good, but we can't work in the dark."

"How much is in the college slush fund?" Tristram Jones asked, replacing his glass on the desk and standing to go.

"That, my boy, is confidential. A secret known only to me and certain members of the Senior Common Room," the Bursar said, pointing to Christian Tennenbaum.

At last! Christian Tennenbaum thought to himself. Tristram Jones has been put in his place.

"I would like us to keep all of this to ourselves, at least for the time being," Christian Tennenbaum said, as he collected up the empty glasses.

"Suits me," the Bursar said.

"No problem," Tristram Jones agreed. And then, "I think I'll get on with that letter now. Strike while the iron's hot."

"No, you don't," Christian Tennenbaum countered. "I'll write the letter, and when it's ready, you will make the translation."

"Okey-dokey, Christian. Anything you say. You're the boss."

TWELVE

Although it was never going to be plain sailing, Alexandro had not fully appreciated the number of obstacles that needed to be overcome to bring the project to a satisfactory financial conclusion.

The Cambridge College of Katherine the Queen had taken the bait. Their response to his letter, written in faultless Spanish, was as much as he could have hoped for. Yes, the fresh information he had supplied as to the last years of Robert Graves had been duly noted. Yes, they would be interested in investigating the material held by the Gonzalez family, and yes, all being well, matters might be settled to each party's mutual advantage. In Alexandro's book, that meant money in return for the poems.

But it was the particularities which were giving him a headache. The letter went on to invite him and his family to Cambridge to discuss the matter further and, needless to say, to produce the documents in question.

By 'family', they must mean, or at least be including in their thinking, his mother. It was, of course, quite out of the question. Never in her life had she left Mallorca, and even supposing that she could be persuaded to go, God knows what she would come up with. He smiled at the picture in his mind of her hurling abuse in Catalan at the clever professors of Cambridge the moment they stepped out of line – the line she had drawn for the proper behaviour of those approaching the sacrosanct relationship between herself and Graves. And those academics were so clever that one of their number would probably understand every word that she said.

But he did not want to go alone. Tactically, it would be a mistake, appearing as if he was serving no purposes but his own selfish interests, and anyway, he would need someone with whom to discuss the progress of any negotiations and assist in the formulation of any deal. Genoveva would be worse than useless. She spoke no English, would want to go on spending sprees in London, and generally would be uncontrollable.

That left Vanessa. She had a rudimentary command of English, was sensible – at least as sensible as a seventeen-year-old might be expected to be – and above all, was cunning.

But she had lost interest. She had done her bit: brought the poetry to light, been instrumental in finding a market for it, and to her mind it was all now done and dusted. She was the only possible candidate for a travelling companion, but would need some persuading.

These difficulties paled into insignificance beside having to produce to these university academics two photocopied sheets of paper, lightly written with a few lines of poetry in a language he did not understand. He took heart from his recollection of snatches of old Mozart or Schubert scores being discovered in Vienna flea markets from time to time, and then being auctioned for a small fortune. He wasn't sure though, if Graves would fall into the same category. And then, somehow, he would have to convince them about the box: tell them there was plenty more where those two pages came from, and if possible extract the cash up front before they discovered the scantiness of the remaining material and made some kind of objection.

Time and again in the small hours, listening to Genoveva breathing and turning in bed beside him, he would decide that the whole procedure should be aborted. He was leading himself and his family into a disaster, and no money was worth the shame and infamy. But then in the morning his feelings changed. Those pieces of paper were all of significance, each handled by the great man himself. If a Picasso drawing of a couple of pencil strokes could be sold for hundreds of thousands of euros, then for the doyens of English literature there was much of value in that chocolate box.

Genoveva told him time and again that he lacked self-confidence, even courage. He would have to prove that on this occasion she would be disabused. It might also do his marriage a world of good.

*   *   *   *

Vanessa drove a hard bargain.

"England? England? I don't want to go to England!"

He knew that wasn't strictly true. She would love to have gone to England with Rafael, or with some of her school friends, but a night or two in a Cambridge college with her father and some university lecturers held no appeal.

"Will you not do it for your grandmother?"

"My grandmother?" she shouted. "Get real, Papa. You're interested in the money, not Grandma!"

Her eighteenth birthday was approaching. She had been holding out for a grand party at the Hotel Can Cera, the prestigious venue in central Palma for local and national events. When Genoveva and Alexandro had tried to persuade her that the occasion would best be celebrated with a family dinner to include a few of her close friends, her godmother Josefina – who would doubtless come over from Barcelona for the day – and her grandparents, she had flown into a tantrum, citing the generosity of the parents of her friends who had gone to great lengths to provide their daughters with fit and proper celebrations.

There was currently a stand-off, but following urgent discussions with his wife Alexandro re-opened the topic late on a Friday afternoon. He had come home early to catch her on her own, Genoveva not returning from her cookery class until seven.

Vanessa was preparing to go out for the evening with Rafael, slamming the bathroom door and then noisily moving around the flat, picking up her bag and poncho and putting on her shoes.

"Vanessa!"

"What?"

"I've been speaking to your mother. Come with me to England after your birthday party."

"What birthday party? A meal with my charming family in a rubbishy downtown restaurant?" She glared at him from the front door, her hand on the knob.

"Well, let's talk about that, Vanessa. Your mother and I have been having a re-think. We want you to be happy, feel that you are provided with a celebration which will make you..." He moved his head from side to side. "Well, happy," he concluded.

Vanessa suddenly twigged. "Then after my party, you want me to go to England?"

She re-traced her steps into the sitting room and sat down.

"Yes."

"How long for?"

"Two nights, three the most."

"I want all my friends at the party. At the Can Cera."

"How many would that be?"

"Say thirty."

Thirty. Add ten for family – forty. At sixty euros a head, two thousand four hundred euros. God, he thought, those poems had better be worth it.

"And I'll need a band."

Three thousand, Alexandro thought, with a sinking heart.

"And then afterwards, we go to England. OK?"

"All right, but I must have a new dress for my party."

Genoveva was pleased with the arrangements. The party would give her an opportunity to excel as the beautiful young mother of the belle of the ball, and she'd make sure that she would add in one or two of her own friends as well. Then she would have the apartment to herself for a few days, whilst

Alexandro and Vanessa were in England. It was all a win-win situation for her.

*   *   *   *

His mother would have to be invited. There was the risk that her lowering presence would put a dampener on the festivities, but there was nothing that could be done about that.

Genoveva had driven up to Deià two weeks before the party and delivered Maria Jesus' invitation.

The old woman had read and re-read the multi-coloured piece of paper, plastered with script which looked as if it had been cut out of a variety of newspapers. Vanessa wanted to study at the College of Design in Palma when she left school later that year and had exercised her talents to the full on her birthday invitations.

Genoveva broke the silence. "We are sure that you will want to be there, Mama. Alexandro is arranging for a taxi to pick you up at seven, and of course you can go home whenever you want, or when you get tired."

"Hotel Can Cera," Maria Jesus said finally.

"Yes. Alexandro wanted the best for his only child."

"*Muy bien*. I shall be ready at seven on the day."

"By the way, next week Alexandro and Vanessa are going to England for a day or two to see some people at Cambridge University about those poems," Genoveva said as she was leaving, and as casually as she could. Alexandro had not been sure when to break the news to his mother, and after some discussion Genoveva had agreed to drop it into the conversation on her errand to deliver the invitation.

Maria Jesus remained silent, her face impassive.

"See you at the party, then," Genoveva said, as she left. "Taxi at seven."

Once the money had been paid over to the hotel, Alexandro began to look forward to the party. Then, to his surprise, he found that he enjoyed the evening more than he had dared to expect. He made a rambling toast to Vanessa, his beautiful, unpredictable, fiery daughter, and she had replied to thank her parents for being there for her in the bad times as well as the good. Josefina's onerous duties as a headmistress prevented her from getting over from Barcelona, but she sent Vanessa a cheque. Not so much as to spoil her, but enough to be worth banking.

During dinner Maria Jesus sat between Genoveva and Alexandro, and opposite Genoveva's parents with whom she made polite conversation.

Alexandro had hoped that when the dancing began, his mother would ask him to summon her taxi. But she didn't. She just stared at the young people throwing themselves around the dance floor, singing the words of the pop songs in loud disjointed English phrases. Vanessa had chosen a scarlet, low-cut dress for her big day, with Spanish frills and flounces below the knee. It didn't look quite right for the style of dance as she spun Rafael around the floor to the sounds of Queen and U2, but she was a dazzling sight nonetheless.

Maria Jesus' face became severe and forbidding. "Shall I call your taxi, Mama?" Alexandro bellowed in her ear, above the din of the band and the revellers.

"Not yet, thank you," she said, staring wide-eyed at her granddaughter.

And then, he had an idea. He sidled up to the band leader, a corpulent middle-aged lead guitarist, and whispered into his ear.

"OK. When?"

"As soon as you like."

At the conclusion of *Glad All Over*, and as the dancers, temporarily exhausted, fell into each other's arms, the band leader walked over to the microphone.

"Our host, Señor Gonzalez, will dance the next number with his daughter, the birthday girl, Vanessa."

With a broad smile, Vanessa moved to her father and stood before him, glowing with her exertions. All now had been forgiven, the misunderstandings over her party were now well

73

and truly in the past. Vibrating with excitement and happiness, not knowing what was to come, she placed her hands on his shoulders and waited for the music.

The keyboard player imitated the sound of the trumpets at the start of the corrida, and then the band crashed into the fandango. In an instant, Vanessa transformed herself from a modern party and club goer into an arrogant temptress of Andalucía. The music began slowly, Vanessa stamping out the rhythm clearly and deliberately. Then, as it accelerated, she flailed her bare arms and spun her dress, occasionally holding a hem to preserve her modesty. Alexandro kept up with her as best he could, flinging himself about the dance floor until it was no longer possible to do so, Vanessa becoming a whirlwind of spinning stamping scarlet.

As he stood aside, Alexandro saw out of the corner of his eye that his mother had raised herself from her chair, moved to the front of her table and was clapping the rhythms and shouting encouragement with the other guests. She looked happy for a moment, even ecstatic. For the first time in a long time, he had done the right thing by her.

The dance came to a sudden halt, exactly anticipated by Vanessa, who threw both arms up in a triumphant final gesture. As the guests clapped and whistled wildly, Alexandro took Vanessa's hand, solemnly walked her over to Rafael, and with a bow joined his mother.

"I would like to go home now, Alexandro," Maria Jesus said into his ear.

"Come, I'll take you outside and we'll find a taxi."

She leant heavily on his arm as they walked into the chandeliered entrance hall.

"Can we sit for a moment?" she asked.

He lowered her into a billowing velvet settee and sank beside her.

"So, all is not lost," she said when she had found her breath.

"How do you mean, Mama?"

"All is not lost of the old Spain. Vanessa's dance. It has made me very happy."

"I did not think that you liked the people of Andalucía."

"They are Spanish, just as we, I suppose, are Spanish. And we all of us have those rhythms in our blood."

The music had reverted to the pop idiom. Alexandro could hear the lead guitarist asking for the road to Amarillo in the party room.

"So you are taking Vanessa to England. Genoveva told me," Maria Jesus continued.

"Yes. We leave on Thursday."

"I have something for her."

Maria Jesus fished into her bag and withdrew the aquamarine and pearl necklace with the small pendant cross which Robert Graves had given her thirty years before.

"It is for her birthday. I know now that she is worthy of it. Robert gave it to me, but I no longer have any use for it, I suppose."

Alexandro took it in both hands and, after holding it up to the light, carefully placed it into his inside pocket.

"It is very beautiful. She will be pleased."

She sat on in silence, staring distractedly at the opposite wall hung with full-sized reproductions of the Goya tapestries at Santiago de Compostela.

And then, very quietly, she began to speak. "One day, Robert told me that once, when he was about fifteen, a little younger than Vanessa is now, he discovered that he understood everything. It was a mystical revelation; all things had become clear to him. He decided to write down his new-found knowledge, but as soon as he began to write it all began to slip away. The more he wrote, the less he knew, until he was right back to square one."

She laughed at what she had just said, as if it were a private joke. "And that, you see, is what my box is all about."

"How do you mean?"

75

"Those pages. Some have little to say, but maybe they are the most interesting. Interesting in what they leave unsaid."

A mischievous expression passed her face. "But how are you going to explain that to those clever men of Cambridge? Those clever men, who think they know everything but know nothing. How can you explain to them that a long time ago, the man who chose me as his inspiration knew everything, but in the expressing, the writing, it all escaped him? Perhaps if they wrote and said less, and looked more at the world around them, even at people like me, they might become wise themselves."

She struggled to stand. Alexandro took her arm and helped her to her feet.

"I wish you luck, Alexandro," she said, as they moved to the front door. "Don't let them insult or damage Robert's memory. I don't care for myself. And don't let them tie you into knots. For that is what they are: knot tiers. Robert taught me that life should be simple, and in the simplicity we find the truth and beauty and, if we are lucky, even love."

"*No pasarán!* Mama."

Maria Jesus smiled thinly. "Just make sure that you do better than that bitch Pasionaria."

THIRTEEN

The spring term was ending. A few students had been collected by their parents, driving away from Trumpington Street in the family car, crammed with washing files and books. Others would be leaving over the next few days. The remnants would remain in Cambridge to work in the libraries and common rooms, preparing themselves for the exams to be held immediately after Easter.

Early blossoms were already showing themselves in college gardens. The sheltered quadrangle of the College of Katherine the Queen had been planted with four magnolia trees in 1953 to mark the four hundred years between the coronation of Mary I and that of Elizabeth II. Their tulip-shaped pink and white buds were now swelling by the day, encouraged by the rays of sunshine appearing a little earlier each morning above the surrounding buildings designed by Christopher Wren. The Tudor originals had been destroyed by an arson attack during the Protectorate, as a punishment, it was believed, for the college continuing to indulge in Popish practices despite numerous warnings.

Tristram Jones had been granted one of the few college parking lots off Trumpington Street. It was a privilege to be treasured, given the fierce competition in Cambridge for parking space, even resulting in the occasional outbreak of parking rage.

His car was in regular use, not just for visits to his parents in Marlborough but also to take girlfriends to Ely or St Ives for dinner on a Saturday night, well away from the Cambridge scene. The girlfriends, though, had become fewer and further between since his arrival in Cambridge as a newly graduated lecturer four years ago. He was, he realised, getting a little more choosey the older he became. After one or two mistakes he now made it a rule, for professional reasons, to resist the advances of female undergraduates, who he no longer found particularly attractive, anyway. But on the other hand, the women of his own age, postgraduate students or junior lecturers, were rather too intense for his tastes. And there didn't seem to be very much in between.

Christian Tennenbaum had just assumed that Tristram Jones' car would be available to pick up the Gonzalez, as soon as he had decided that both he and Tristram Jones should constitute the Stansted Airport welcoming party. In his letter accepting the offer of an all-expenses paid meeting, Alexandro Gonzalez had said that he would be accompanied by his daughter who spoke a little English. Christian Tennenbaum decided that it would create a good atmosphere right from the start for this daughter and Tristram Jones, presumably much of an age, to rub along together in advance of the hard bargaining which lay ahead.

What he had not expected was such a young daughter. Tristram Jones had prepared a handwritten sign, saying '*Señor Gonzalez y Hija*,' which he held up at the Arrivals at Stansted, opposite the door which slid open with monotonous regularity to allow holidaymakers in shorts and T-shirts readmission to their country.

Before they knew it, beside them were standing a stocky middle-aged Spaniard in a brown double-breasted suit and sober tie, and a girl tightly wrapped in a poncho, her eyes smiling up at Tristram Jones. "We are the Gonzalez," she said in English.

"*Bienvenido a Inglaterra,*" Tristram Jones said to the pair in turn, dumping his notice in a waste bin, and then taking Vanessa's case from her hand. Christian Tennenbaum shook each of Alexandro and Vanessa's hands, and the four made their way to the car.

"Have you been to England before?" Tristram Jones shouted

in Spanish over the din of the airport traffic, as they rolled the cases across the road to the car park.

"Me, yes," Alexandro shouted. "To the Holiday Designers exhibition at Earl's Court. Five, maybe six years ago. But my daughter, never."

"I went on a school trip once to France," Vanessa mouthed. "To Perpignan."

"It is a little cooler here than in Mallorca, I imagine," Christian Tennenbaum said, wanting to be included in a conversation which he did not understand, as they stowed the cases in the boot of Tristram Jones' Skoda. What a fatuously obvious statement to make, he then thought. Whether or not they understood, Alexandro and Vanessa nodded and smiled in agreement.

There was a polite exchange as to who should sit where in the car, but finally everyone seemed happy with Vanessa sitting next to Tristram Jones, and Alexandro sitting in the back with Christian Tennenbaum.

"What made you choose the College of Katherine the Queen?" Tristram Jones asked Vanessa, as they swung onto the M11.

"I Googled the Cambridge colleges, and yours came up as the college with strong Spanish links."

"Yes indeed, our college has a great historical affinity with Spain," Tristram Jones said. "A great affinity. Are you at university yourself?"

"No, but I hope to go to the Mallorca College of Design in October, providing I pass my school leaving exams. This trip, I hope, will improve my English."

"Then we must make a point of speaking a little English while you are here."

"That would be very helpful."

It was pleasant with Vanessa sitting beside him. Her Spanish was attractively accentuated but lighter than his Castilian, which he thought must sound a little heavy on her ears. But best of all, he thought how stylish she looked. She must be about the same age as the university's first year intake, but she was not wearing slashed jeans or a floppy jumper, which seemed to be the Cambridge female undergraduates' hallmark.

From time to time she stared wide-eyed out of the window, absorbing the changing scenery. Tristram Jones noticed that her eyes were neither brown nor blue, but a luminous metallic green. He had seen the eye colour before on the Continent, particularly in Spain, but it looked unusually arresting in England.

"Welcome to our college," Christian Tennenbaum announced as they drew up outside the Porters' Lodge. "Katherine the Queen, commonly known as Kate's." He and Alexandro had remained totally silent during the drive from the airport, the language barrier preventing any meaningful exchange.

It was time for Tristram Jones to launch into the programme, carefully organised with Christian Tennenbaum over the previous few days.

"I am off now to park the car. Professor Tennenbaum and I suggest that after you have settled into your rooms and rested, we have our first session over afternoon tea in his study. An exploratory discussion. And if you feel able to bring the poems with you, that would be most welcome."

The Gonzalez agreed that would be a very good plan.

"Very well," Tristram Jones said, before climbing back into his car. "The professor will take you up to your rooms now. Then why don't I meet you here at four, when I will take you to his study for our chat?"

Christian Tennenbaum conducted Alexandro and Vanessa around the quadrangle, and into the East Wren Building. They refused all assistance with their cases, carrying them up three flights of stone stairs to the Jacobite landing.

"It is rumoured that King James the Second spent the night in these rooms on his way to King's Lynn in 1688."

The Gonzalez had no idea what he was saying.

He unlocked two adjacent doors and threw them open in turn. "Take your pick," he said hospitably.

The rooms had been vacated by their student occupants the day before. Fresh towels and soap had been laid on the wash hand basins and flowers placed in hurriedly procured vases.

"And the lavatory and shower," Christian Tennenbaum pronounced, "are here, at the other end of the landing."

He threw open a third door to reveal the facilities.

The Gonzalez' smiled and nodded.

"Four o'clock," Christian Tennenbaum said, raising four fingers. "Down at the Porters' Lodge," he concluded, pointing down the stairs.

"*Sí, sí,* Professor. *Gracias,*" Alexandro smiled and nodded again.

"Mother of God!" Vanessa said to her father, even before Christian Tennenbaum was out of earshot. "They may want to live in medieval times, but do we have to as well?"

"It's only a couple of nights, Vanessa. Which room would you like?"

"What difference does it make? They're both like prison cells."

Vanessa walked into one of the rooms, felt the bed, smelt the soap, and examined the view from the window.

"Do they have any money?" she asked her father. "They seem to live here like paupers, and that young professor, Tristram or whatever is his name, his car must be at least seven years old."

"They've got money, alright. The big question is will they spend it."

"We'll see."

"You have this room, Vanessa. I'll go next door. I'll see you at four."

Alexandro closed the door to his room, carefully removed the two photocopied sheets of poetry from his hold-all and placed them on an old ink-stained rickety desk pushed beneath the window.

"God knows if they will be enough," he said, before lying on the bed and closing his eyes.

Christian Tennenbaum had not been idle. During the past few days, he had returned to his research on Graves with fresh urgency, delving ever more deeply into his poetry and prose. The exception was *The White Goddess*. He had persevered as far as he could through the tales of Celtic myths and legends before deciding on some selective skipping, moving on to those passages specifically referring to the inspiration of a muse and attaching yellow Post-it notes to the pages for further inspection.

The life of Robert Graves was as absorbing as his poetry. He read Seymour Smith's biography from cover to cover, and for good measure threw in *Good-bye to All That*, which he had not read since he was a teenager.

As his research programme progressed he became increasingly certain that what Alexandro Gonzalez had written about his mother was true. It entirely tallied with the character and previous life of the great man, and could hardly be fabricated by an ordinary Spanish family with little or no command of English.

Whatever might transpire as a result of the Gonzalez' visit to college, he decided that the English Department should introduce a new module next year: 'Graves – the Link between Romanticism and Modernism.' It would follow on very well from his own specialisation, Keats and the Romantic Movement. Of course, if the college could get its hands on some previously unseen prime source material that would make the module all the more relevant.

But above all he harboured the hope that the Gonzalez papers, as he now thought of them, would yield up sufficient material to produce a detailed study of the final years of a creative genius. It would provide him at last with the academic renown he deserved after so many years of waiting for something, anything, to turn up.

Anthony Grace, the Bursar, had also been a little proactive.

Christian Tennenbaum had been summoned to his office on the Monday before the Gonzalez' arrival and quizzed about their visit.

"When exactly do they touch down?"

"Thursday. On the midday plane from Mallorca. Going into Stansted."

"And the old lady?"

"Not coming. Gonzalez told me at the last minute that it would not be possible. Presumably she's too old. He's bringing his daughter instead."

"I've made some enquiries in the Law Department. The property in letters, papers, et cetera, which are the subject of a gift lies with the recipient. As does the copyright, apparently. Now, does the old lady's son have authority to deal with us?"

"I don't know. It's too late now to clear the point before they arrive. I'll have to raise it at the first meeting."

"No. I'll raise it. I shall be mister nasty, and you can be the bumbling academic."

"So you're going to be in on all of this?" Christian Tennenbaum felt his hackles rising. The Bursar was quite capable of sinking the whole operation, and all because of money. A paltry few thousand pounds was probably all that was needed to secure something of inestimable worth, but if he drove too hard a bargain it would all be at risk.

"Don't even think of discussing business with these people without me being present. You and Tristram can talk to them about didactic pentameters and Spanish irregular verbs until the cows come home, but the moment you move onto business, shut up until I'm there."

Christian Tennenbaum felt his plans for his new module and his book receding. "Tristram and I have decided on a preliminary meeting on Thursday afternoon."

"I'll be there. Just tell me when you've agreed a time."

"What's in the slush fund?"

"Thirty thousand pounds. But if there's going to be a deal, I want to go well below that. Well below."

FOURTEEN

Vanessa was not the best of time keepers. She had developed the art of arriving for a date just at the moment the boy in question had given up hope and was ready to go home. If there was a row and he marched off, so what? He was the loser. More often though, the boy would be relieved to see her, and the evening would proceed with her having the upper hand.

At last, after her father's persistent banging on her door, it finally swung open at four fifteen.

"We shall be late," he said, restraining the impulse to give her a piece of his mind.

"It will be good to keep them waiting."

"And what are you wearing?"

"My smart casual suit."

"No, on your nose."

"Oh, these," Vanessa said, taking off a large pair of owlish glasses and posing with them against the bannister. "Just a fashion accessory. They are plain glass, but it is important that they do not see us as a couple of simple Spanish peasants."

Tristram Jones was full of bonhomie at the Porters' Lodge. "I do hope that you are rested after your journey."

"Yes, thank you. In fact, we overslept a little," Alexandro lied. "I am so sorry."

"We will be joined by a Major Grace at our meeting," Tristram Jones said as casually as he could, as they crossed to the far side of college and mounted the fellows' staircase.

"He is a man from the army?" Vanessa asked.

"No." Tristram Jones laughed. "He left the army years ago, and now is our money man, running the college finances."

In silence, Vanessa and Alexandro thought through the implications of the Bursar's presence.

They shook hands with the Bursar, waiting for them in front of the window. Vanessa took an instant dislike to him, sensing that he looked down on her as a naïve, inexperienced girl who had no place in the deliberations about to take place. If he thinks I'm just a pretty face he'll soon discover otherwise, she said to herself.

Christian Tennenbaum's study was a little cramped after they had all taken their places.

"That," he said, to break the ice, and pointing to the view from his window, "is the famous King's College Chapel. Tell them, Tristram, that it is where the annual Christmas service is relayed around the world."

"That?" Vanessa said, when Tristram Jones had done as Christian Tennenbaum had asked. "Famous? But it is so puny. You could fit twenty of those in the cathedral of Palma, La Seu."

Tristram Jones smiled and nodded, as if Vanessa had paid the chapel a compliment.

"Let's get down to business," the Bursar said.

They all turned to look at Alexandro. "Ah," he exclaimed, as if suddenly aware that the initiative lay with him. He reached inside his jacket, removed from his inside pocket the two photocopied sheets, and handed them across to Christian Tennenbaum.

Picking up his glasses from his desk, Christian Tennenbaum read each page very slowly to himself. He then turned the pages over, to see what might be written on their reverse. When he was satisfied that there was no more to be seen, he made to hand the pages to the Bursar.

"*No Señor!*" Alexandro said, holding out his hand. "*Por favor.*"

Christian Tennenbaum folded the sheets and handed them back to him.

"Well?" Tristram Jones asked.

"They're Graves. Almost certainly. At least as far as I can tell. Not at his most brilliant, but still Graves. A little mildewed, but still Graves. The best of them is dated the year he died. When we thought the springs of his inspiration had long since dried." He was speaking rapidly to exclude the Spanish from any understanding of what he was saying.

Tristram Jones raised an eyebrow and nodded knowingly, while the Bursar looked at him blankly.

"Don't you see, Anthony?" Christian Tennenbaum continued, struggling to contain his excitement. "If Graves was writing good coherent work in 1985, we can only conclude that this muse of his holds some very interesting pieces for the few years before his death."

"OK then, ask him what else he has to show us," the Bursar demanded of Tristram Jones.

"Nothing," Alexandro said, after the translation. "Nothing. This is as much as my mother would allow me to bring."

"But there is more, I imagine," Tristram Jones asked anxiously.

"Yes. A whole box full. But I have not examined it in detail."

Vanessa glanced across at her father. He looked small and vulnerable. He was out of his depth, overawed by the place and the people. If he was not careful, they would swallow him up.

"There is much for you to understand," she said in a voice which could not be ignored, removing her glasses, and examining them. "I even wonder if you are capable of understanding."

"Please explain," Tristram Jones asked.

Vanessa replaced her glasses and leant back in her chair. "My grandmother is a fine lady of the old Spain. Born into a country with a history and an ethos, even now, very different from what I see here in England. She is possessive of her history, as are all Spanish people. It was no easy matter for my father to convince her that she was under an obligation to reveal the papers in her possession and ownership to the world at large, for its benefit, and not to cling to them for her own selfish recollections of her past. But my father has done so, even at the risk of endangering the sacred relationship between a mother and her child. But this was all she would allow." Vanessa paused to wave a hand at Alexandro's jacket, where the two sheets had been replaced before continuing. "At least until she could be sure that your interest was serious, your intentions genuine, and the poems would be duly honoured."

Tristram did his best to keep his translation going as Vanessa said her piece, his English sounding insipid against Vanessa's long Spanish vowels and rolled 'r's.

As she took breath, he smiled at her. "I understand," he said, "as I am sure that we all do."

The Bursar glared at him. "Ask her if her father has her grandmother's authority to sell the papers, along with their copyright."

"Yes, absolutely," Vanessa said, as soon as she had listened to Tristram Jones' translation.

"We will need written confirmation, countersigned by your grandmother."

"Of course."

Alexandro saw no reason to intervene in the exchanges between Vanessa and the Bursar. She was doing a very good job.

"How can we see the other papers?" The Bursar asked.

"You can't."

"Why not?"

"You must trust."

"Trust?"

"Yes, trust. My grandmother will not have her property picked over as if it were merchandise in a Saturday market. These papers are unique. You cannot measure the worth of the sunrise, the grandeur of the sea in a storm, or of a lover's poem to his mistress. You have seen enough to know that she, my grandmother, is in possession of what is both priceless, but also, what has great price. Whatever my grandmother holds is hers, to do with what she wants: to release to you, if you are willing to recompense her for them in a full and proper manner, to offer them elsewhere to other people in other places that may be interested, or even to burn them."

The Bursar found Vanessa's passion and eloquence irritating in the extreme, made more so by his feeling that both Christian Tennenbaum and Tristram Jones were being taken in by it.

"How much more is there? Please try and be a little specific," the Bursar said impatiently.

"Difficult to say," Alexandro replied. He needed to take control of this very difficult area. Vanessa's flight of oratory had taken him by surprise. She had proved that they were not a pushover, but the detail was best left to him.

The door edged open, to admit two college porters in their worn-out suits and bowler hats carrying trays laden with tea pots, jugs, sandwiches, and cake.

"Tea!" Christian Tennenbaum announced. "In England, everything stops for tea."

There was a re-shuffling of chairs to enable the trays to be placed on the desk. The porters asked each in turn how they liked their tea, poured, and handed round the cups with an empty plate.

"Help yourself to sandwiches and cake," Christian Tennenbaum said, as the porters departed. Then, turning to Vanessa, he cried, "Ladies first."

Alexandro had been granted a brief respite in which to plan his response to the Bursar's awkward question, but he was going to be confounded by his daughter.

Vanessa placed her cup on the floor. She had asked for tea, no milk, no sugar, but the thick slab liquid in her cup would be impossible to drink. She examined the contents of her sandwich. She thought that she had chosen a salami sausage filling, but on close inspection it proved to be stale pressed ham.

They had no money, of that she was sure. If she was wrong, as her father had assured her, they were miserly – mean with themselves and consequentially mean with others. Either way, it was now time to call their bluff.

"Take it or leave it!" she cried.

"What do you mean?" Tristram Jones asked her.

"Take what we have to give, at a proper price, or forget all about it."

Tristram Jones effected a hasty translation. "And what is a proper price?" he then asked Vanessa.

"The poems you have seen," Vanessa said, slowly and clearly, "a box with, say twenty or so others, which you will not see until you buy, for fifty thousand euros."

The Bursar belonged to the old school of wheeler dealers, who made it a rule never to be the first to walk away from the negotiating table however outrageous might be the demands of the other side – or in this case, however annoying the girl before him.

"That is a very high price for unseen goods," he said calmly to Alexandro on hearing the translation.

"Partly seen," Tristram Jones corrected, to be met with a withering glance from the Bursar.

"Forty thousand, last price," Alexandro said.

On the flight to England Alexandro had unburdened himself to Vanessa, telling her that apart from the copied poems they were taking with them there seemed to be little else of any worth in the chocolate box. Preoccupied with the preparations for the trip to England, for a short time he had blocked the unwelcome reality from his mind. But with the meeting in Cambridge imminent, it had returned with a vengeance. Vanessa had listened to him carefully, and then simply said they would cross that bridge when and if they had to. And now the whole affair was assuming a momentum of its own, a momentum which Alexandro could not stop, and indeed was helping to accelerate.

"No, fifty!" Vanessa screamed.

Now that's a good development, the Bursar thought, they're bidding against themselves.

"I think that we all need to reflect a little on what we have discussed so far," Christian Tennenbaum said genially, placing his plate with a half-eaten sandwich on his desk. "Why don't the Bursar and I withdraw for a few minutes for a short discussion, whilst the rest of you finish your tea?"

As soon as they had gone Vanessa and Alexandro burst into Mallorquín, their local dialect, speaking rapidly and simultaneously. Tristram Jones understood nothing of what was said.

When they had finished, Vanessa jumped to her feet and stared out of the window, her arms folded.

"My daughter and I were just discussing how much this money will mean to my mother. She is now infirm, and every euro will count."

Vanessa snorted loudly.

An awkward silence ensued, finally broken by Alexandro. "You speak very good Spanish, Señor Tristram."

"Thank you. I was lucky enough to have spent a year as an undergraduate at the University of Salamanca."

"Salamanca!" Vanessa exclaimed. "I have always wanted to go there. I have heard that it is very beautiful."

It was as if her tirade of a few minutes before had never occurred.

It was more than an hour before Christian Tennenbaum and the Bursar re-appeared. Conversation between the Gonzalez and Tristram Jones had all but dried up. They had explored the differences in tertiary education between Spain and England to the full, moved onto graduate job opportunities, and even touched on the chances of each of their countries in the approaching European Football Cup – a topic on which Tristram Jones had very little to offer – when at last the door was flung open by Christian Tennenbaum.

"We have a proposal," he announced grandly, making for his chair. "A sound proposal which I think you, Mr Gonzalez, will be pleased to accept on behalf of your mother."

The Bursar, leaning against the back of the door, maintained a heavy silence.

Christian Tennenbaum consulted his notes, and then began.

"Your mother, or you, Mr Gonzalez, on her full authority, will make over to the College of Katherine the Queen – the college – all poems paper writings and notes – the material – written or made by the late Robert Graves – Graves – which are in her possession as of today, together with all copyright.

"You warrant on behalf of your mother, that title to the material is vested in your mother, and that no previous pledges or dealings with the material have occurred.

"Your mother will grant an interview of one hour to the college's representative describing how the material came into her possession and outlining her recollections of her meetings and friendship with Graves. And allow her photograph to be taken.

"On fulfilment of the above terms and conditions, the college will pay to your mother, or her duly authorised representative, the sum of twenty thousand euros."

Christian Tennenbaum looked up from his notes. "I suggest that when we have agreement in principle, we pass this before our Law Department people tomorrow and then arrange a certified translation so that you will have something on which you can rely to take back with you to Mallorca."

Tristram Jones completed his translation with foreboding.

Vanessa fixed Christian Tennenbaum with a cold stare. "You are a thief, Professor, a thief, that you could even think of robbing an old woman in this way for a paltry twenty thousand euros."

It gave Tristram Jones a strange existential pleasure to turn to Christian Tennenbaum, and tell him directly to his face, that he was a thief.

"Vanessa," Alexandro said in Mallorquín. "It is their opening shot."

"Exactly. Leave it to me." And then, "Forty thousand euros," she cried, reverting to Spanish.

Christian Tennenbaum looked across at the Bursar pleadingly. He so desperately wanted to get his hands on the papers that he had even suggested in his separate session with him that he should chip in some of his own money. The Bursar had told him not to be a fool, and that patience and perseverance would win the day.

"Twenty-five thousand pounds," the Bursar said quietly. "Our last figure."

"Thirty thousand pounds," Vanessa spat.

"What about thirty thousand euros," Christian Tennenbaum said. "Full and final."

"Pounds!" Vanessa cried. "Or we go."

"Twenty-seven thousand, five hundred pounds," the Bursar said. "Believe me, I will not go a penny more."

"With ten thousand pounds paid up front now," Vanessa said.

"No. If you fail to deliver I don't want the inconvenience, to put it mildly, of chasing you through the Spanish courts to get our money back."

"I need to take something back to my mother," Alexandro pleaded. "To encourage her to sign."

The Bursar and Christian Tennenbaum looked at each other.

"All right," the Bursar said at last. "Five thousand pounds now, twenty-two thousand, five hundred pounds when the heads of agreement are fulfilled."

"What is the pound-euro rate today, Tristram?" Vanessa asked. She had grown a little fond of Tristram Jones during the time they had spent in Christian Tennenbaum's study with her father. Also, throughout the negotiations, he had played fair.

"It's about one-eighteen to the pound, I think," he said, a little flattered by Vanessa's special attention. "I'll check."

Vanessa took off her glasses, threw them in her bag, and extracted her iPhone. She pattered her fingers on the keyboard at great speed and then studied the result.

"Let's say one-twenty euros to the pound." After a little more pattering, "That's six thousand euros now, and twenty-seven thousand euros when the deal's done."

She looked across at her father. It was less than either of them had hoped, but they had done their best and she doubted they could extract a euro more. And in reality, given that there was little left in the box worth having, at least as far as her father could tell, it was a good deal.

"We will do our best to procure an interview with my mother, but nothing can be cast in stone in that regard. She is old. The agreement needs to take that into account," Alexandro said.

"We cannot twist her arm," Vanessa added.

"Well, maybe just a photo shot in her house might do," Tristram Jones contributed helpfully, after his translation.

"Why don't you keep quiet?" The Bursar's patience had snapped. "Mr Gonzalez will, as he says, use his best endeavours to procure an interview between the representatives of the college and his mother, to include a photograph. God knows, it's all costing us enough."

"Now," Christian Tennenbaum said, "we will need to congregate some time tomorrow after I have spoken to my contact in the Law Department. I can't, though, envisage any problems: I'm convinced of that. But we must be sure, and then I will provide typed up copies of our agreement. Tristram, are you around tomorrow to translate the final version for the Gonzalez? And then certify it as true and faithful?"

"Yes, of course."

Christian Tennenbaum was relieved to be back in some control. He had been battling the Bursar as much as the Gonzalez. His separate session with Anthony Grace had strained their friendship to the limit, but at last it was a done deal and he could reassert his authority. "Suppose we all re-assemble here at two-thirty tomorrow afternoon," he said expansively. "I do think that our guests have earned some leisure time, and a free morning will give them an opportunity to see our beautiful city."

Except for the Bursar, they all nodded in agreement.

"Splendid!" Christian Tennenbaum consulted his watch. "The Senior Refectory is now open for supper. Why don't we all go for a bite, and then perhaps the Gonzalez will appreciate an early night."

"What about the money?" Vanessa asked, keeping her seat.

"We'll deal with that tomorrow," the Bursar said. "Mr Gonzalez can give me his bank details, and of course a list of travelling expenses to be added to the six thousand euros."

"*De acuerdo!*" Tristram Jones exclaimed, jumping to his feet. "Everyone is happy."

It was getting dark as they made their way through arches and courtyards, and around the college chapel to the Senior Refectory reserved for graduates and lecturers. When Vanessa stumbled over an uneven flag stone, Tristram Jones took her arm for a few steps.

"Thank you," she said when he released her, treating his hand to a squeeze. "They need to install more lights."

As they arrived at the refectory, Christian Tennenbaum noticed to his relief that they had lost the Bursar along the way. He was now in total command, summoning waiters to run through the day's specials and taking his time to order the wine.

"You know, one of the best ways of getting to know Cambridge is to take one of those open top tourist buses," he said when they had given their orders.

Alexandro nodded distractedly. He was tired now, and wanted to get back to his room, have a few words with Genoveva on his mobile phone, and go to bed. As far as the nagging matter of the quality of the remaining items in the box was concerned, it was best to try and put it out of his mind, at least for the time being. As Vanessa said, cross that bridge when you get to it.

Tristram Jones was suddenly struck with an idea. "Vanessa, would you like to come with me to Peterborough tomorrow morning for a quick visit?" he asked on impulse.

"What did you say about Peterborough?" Christian Tennenbaum said uneasily.

"I asked Vanessa if she would like to come with me to Peterborough tomorrow."

Christian Tennenbaum looked at him aghast.

"Well it would only take you half an hour or so to speak to someone in the Law Department, get their imprimatur, and it wouldn't take me five minutes to run out a translation when we meet in the afternoon," Tristram Jones said. "You could take Señor Gonzalez out on the bus, and I could take Vanessa on a trip to Peterborough."

The open top bus tour had suddenly become less appealing to Christian Tennenbaum. "And who would translate for me, while we drove around Cambridge?"

"Not a problem, Christian. All Señor Gonzalez has to do is put on the ear phones in front of his seat, and press the button marked 'Español.'"

Christian Tennenbaum felt a sharp pang of jealousy at the thought of Tristram Jones careering off on a jaunt with the feisty Spanish girl. It was ridiculous. She was no older than the average fresher, but so different, so self-assured and fearless. He was ashamed of thinking about her in that way, but he couldn't help himself.

"What is this Peterborough?" Vanessa asked.

"It's not the most exciting of cities," Tristram Jones said, leaning across the table, his eyes sparkling. "But its cathedral holds the tomb of Katherine of Aragon, the daughter of Ferdinand and Isabella who married our Henry the Eighth. She is the queen after whom our college is named. Each year on our Founder's Day we have a special service in the cathedral, close to her tomb."

It didn't sound much of a fun trip, but it would be a relief to get out of Cambridge. And Tristram was handsome in an English way, and young. Certainly less than thirty. Not young enough for her, but at least younger than the Methuselahs, Christian Tennenbaum and the Bursar. It would also give her an opportunity to test her powers of attraction on a foreigner.

"I would like to go to this Peterborough," she said to Tristram Jones, looking up at him under her dark eyelashes.

FIFTEEN

Tristram Jones was only too pleased at the prospect of driving out of Cambridge with a pretty girl in his passenger seat. The spring term had dragged. He had not had a proper girlfriend for nearly a year now, which had made the time pass even more slowly. He would be going back to his parents' Old Vicarage near Marlborough for Easter, but there would be no opportunities for meeting anyone of his own age in their picture-book village, let alone any attractive members of the opposite sex.

He had arranged to pick Vanessa up at the Porters' Lodge at nine-thirty. She didn't appear until nine forty-five, leaving Tristram Jones parked on a double yellow line for fifteen minutes checking over his shoulder for the ubiquitous parking attendants. At last she glided through the Lodge, wrapped in her poncho, and after looking in the wrong directions spotted him waiting by his car in Trumpington Street.

As he opened the passenger door for her she pecked him on each cheek, for a moment overwhelming his senses with her exotic continental perfume. She reminded him of the girls he had taken out in Salamanca, erotically arousing but at the same time frustratingly, tantalisingly inaccessible.

"You slept well?" he asked, as they nosed into the Friday morning traffic.

"No. The bed was like a board, and too narrow."

"I'm sorry."

"Tell me about this tomb we are about to see," she said, briefly touching his knee.

"Well, it is the last resting place of Katherine of Aragon, the mother of our college's founder, Queen Mary. She established the college in honour of her mother's memory. Katherine of Aragon came to England to marry our king's son, Arthur, but when he died she married his younger brother, who became Henry the Eighth. Unfortunately, she only had a daughter, Mary, her sons dying at an early age. Henry wanted a son, so when she was too old to have any more children he divorced her."

"For a younger model, I suppose."

"Yes. Ann Boleyn."

"Nothing changes," Vanessa said indignantly. "What became of Katherine's daughter?"

"Like I said, she did become queen but only after her brother Edward had died. And then only for a short time."

"Did she have children?"

"No. She married her cousin Phillip the Second of Spain, but sadly they had no children."

"Thank God for that," Vanessa cried, "they would be imbeciles. You shouldn't go around marrying your cousin, that's for sure. It's sick."

Vanessa looked out of the window to make it clear that the topic of conversation had come to an end, as far as she was concerned.

Tristram Jones thought hard for a mile or two. He had got Vanessa into the car and was now well out of Cambridge – two plusses – but he didn't want to spoil the outing by dragging her around a dingy cathedral to see something that did not interest her in the slightest.

"Vanessa," he said, as they approached the A14 interchange, "shall we go to Ely instead? I know of a nice pub overlooking the river where we could have an early lunch."

"That sounds like a very good plan, Tristram. I don't like to hear of kings and queens making fools of themselves, and what's more I'm not very fond of their tombs either."

"The Ship of the Fens," Tristram Jones said, as Ely Cathedral appeared on the horizon.

"The ship of what?"

"The Fens. These flat lands. The tower of Ely Cathedral can be seen for miles and miles around, like a great galleon on the ocean. So they call it the Ship of the Fens.

"But we're not going inside, are we?"

"Don't worry."

Tristram Jones knew most of the pubs in Ely, a forty-five-minute excursion from the noisy Cambridge watering holes patronised by the city's undergraduates. The George and Dragon was the most picturesque, but it would be filling up well before lunchtime. They were early enough to be seated on the balcony overlooking the Cam.

"I like this," she said, looking down on two eights rowing up the river in slow rhythm. "It is very English."

Tristram Jones brought across two menus. Vanessa chose a salad niçoise and a lemonade, and Tristram Jones bangers and mash with a pint of Wherry.

Soon, the pub was descended upon by a groom and his wedding party, including six ushers in grey tails sporting white carnations in their buttonholes.

"I think the groom is being provided with some Dutch courage by his friends," Tristram Jones said. "I reckon the wedding will be in the cathedral, probably at two."

Vanessa looked around her and became more animated, staring and smiling across at the other customers, and nudging closer to Tristram Jones. When the sun rose above the cathedral tower, she draped her poncho over the back of the chair. She was wearing a half-sleeved cream dress which showed off her olive complexion and figure to advantage. She had pinned up her hair and secured it with a tortoiseshell comb to reveal the nape of her neck.

"It is fun here," she said.

"I'm glad that you like it."

"I like people to have fun, and I like to have fun myself. You see, I have much to make up for."

"How do you mean?"

"I need to have fun for the whole of my family."

"Explain."

"My grandmother, she never had fun when she was my age. In fact, I wonder if she ever knew the meaning of the word, except maybe for the short time that she was with Graves. My father, he married too young – maybe my mother as well – so I need to have fun for both of them. And as for my aunt, the dutiful headmistress of a school in Barcelona..." She shrugged her shoulders dismissively.

Vanessa poked her straw up and down in her lemonade, making the ice cubes clink, before continuing. "They all missed out on fun, either because of circumstances or character. I'm not going to make the same mistake. I want real fun, not like the tourists in Mallorca who manufacture their fun with alcohol or sex, but good, light hearted fun. Life has to be serious sometimes, like yesterday, but most of the time it should be fun. Don't you agree?"

"Yes, I do." Tristram Jones needed little convincing.

She placed a hand on his arm. "You do now, Tristram, but don't let Cambridge and all those stuffy old people like the Bursar and Tennenbaum knock the fun out of you. Promise me."

He looked down at her slender hand and chocolate painted fingernails. It was weird, being given advice by a girl who was only just leaving school.

"I promise," he said, just before she withdrew her hand.

"And that's why I admire Graves."

"Why do you admire Graves?"

"He had fun right up until his dying day. And he didn't mind making a fool of himself, as long as he had fun. My grandmother is a serious and staid person, but he had fun with her and gave her, I think, the only fun she had in all her life. Just for a few months. But think what it means to her, even now."

She took a sip of her lemonade. "I wish I could make life more fun for her, but families are difficult beasts. Your relations have preconceptions. My grandmother thinks I'm a flibbertigibbet, just after the boys, but she's wrong, so wrong. And as for my parents, it's almost impossible for a teenage girl, particularly a Spanish teenage girl, to be seen as anything more than a family asset to be protected at all costs."

Tristram Jones noticed that as Vanessa's Spanish became more passionate, the more attention she was attracting from the men in the wedding party.

She looked at Tristram Jones with a mischievous smile on her face. "It is fun, those men in tails admiring me. I like it, and they like it, so we are all happy. The world is a happier place."

Tristram Jones finished his meal and drained his pint of Wherry.

"Thank you for bringing me here and not to the tomb of a great Spanish queen, important as she may have been. And do you know, if that queen was alive now and my age, I would hope that she would sooner be here than poking around some old cathedral."

Vanessa had picked at her food whilst she spoke, separating out the lettuce leaves and eating them slowly. She pushed her plate away.

"The pub is now full," she said, reaching for her poncho, "and we have the best seats. It is time to give them up, and let other people have the fun of looking over the balcony at the river with its boats and swans."

He paid the bill at the bar and, slipping his arm in hers, they walked towards the stairs.

The wedding party opened to let them pass. "*Mucha suerte*," she said to the young man they had both presumed to be the groom.

"Thank you," he said in reply.

"One day you will get married, Tristram. Make sure the girl is lighthearted," she said, as they made their way to the car.

"And what about you?"

"That is so far away it is not even worth thinking about.

Maybe I won't even get married. Thank you again," she said when they arrived at the car, brushing each of his cheeks with hers as he opened the passenger door for her. "I will remember this place, and will always remember you, Tristram."

Her mobile rang as they drove out of Ely. She looked at the number and let it ring on until it fell silent.

"Who was that?" Tristram Jones asked.

"Rafael, my boyfriend. He is getting too serious. I will have to speak to him when I get home."

They took the direct route to Cambridge, down through Waterbeach. As they entered the outskirts of the city, Tristram broke the silence. "After we've parked the car, I think we had better go straight to Christian's study. We don't want to be late for him."

"Or late for that money man."

"The Bursar."

"I can't stand meanness, and he's mean," she said. "God has been extravagant to us, and we should be extravagant to others."

"So you believe in God?"

"I am a Catholic, Tristram. We are allowed to believe so many things without having to believe in God. It is the great advantage which our faith holds over the others."

They were seated and waiting when Tristram Jones and Vanessa tentatively opened the door of Christian Tennenbaum's study.

"Not a moment too soon," the Bursar said.

"We are only five minutes late," Vanessa said to her father, sensing the Bursar's impatience.

"I know, Vanessa," Alexandro said in Mallorquín, "but the morning has dragged. That tourist bus with the professor. I would not want to wish that upon anyone."

"How was Peterborough Cathedral?" Christian Tennenbaum asked distractedly, studying his notes.

"We didn't go," Tristram Jones replied. "We went to Ely instead."

"Ely!" Christian Tennenbaum exclaimed, looking up. "How wonderful! The Ship of the Fens! My favourite cathedral."

"We didn't go to the cathedral. We had lunch at the George and Dragon, overlooking the river."

Christian Tennenbaum glared at Tristram Jones. "I hope the little excursion did you both a power of good. And now, down to business. Yesterday we did the heavy lifting, but you will remember that I wanted to pass the agreement before our lawyers this morning before it is signed. The lawyers saw no reason to criticise the agreement, but they want a time frame included. What, Señor Gonzalez, do you think would be reasonable?"

After Tristram Jones had translated the question, there followed a lengthy exchange between Vanessa and her father in Mallorquín.

"It will not be an easy task to pin down my mother," Alexandro said, when he and Vanessa had finished their discussion. "But we will get there in the end, I'm sure of that," he added quickly. "And maybe she will need a little bribing with the six thousand euros we are taking home."

"Three months," Vanessa said. Her father was taking his eye off the ball, talking too loosely. "The deal to be completed by first July, say."

"Very well," Christian Tennenbaum said. "And I am also advised to include a provision to the effect that if the agreement is not fulfilled within the stipulated time frame it is null and void, and all funds which may have been made over to your mother, or on her behalf, are to be returned."

"Except for our expenses," Alexandro said.

"Yes, of course."

Christian Tennenbaum laboriously wrote out the two additional paragraphs at the foot of the agreement. He then read them out for the Bursar's approval.

"Fine," the Bursar said when he had finished. And then, "Señor Gonzalez, may I have details of your expenses, and the particulars of your bank account?"

Alexandro produced a previously prepared sheet of paper and handed it to the Bursar.

"Thank you. The funds will be in your account next week. Now, if I am no longer required, I will excuse myself." The Bursar shook Alexandro and Vanessa's hands cursorily and left the room.

"Tristram, as I mentioned yesterday, the Gonzalez will need a certified copy of the agreement in Spanish to take with them when they go home tomorrow."

"Not a problem," Tristram Jones said, taking the sheet from Christian Tennenbaum. "I can do that this afternoon."

"And now," Christian Tennenbaum said. "And now." His voice grew in volume. "And now! Something very special. Something very special for you this evening!"

Christian Tennenbaum looked at his audience as if he were a children's party entertainer about to produce his pièce de résistance from a top hat. "The college is inducting a new fellow into the Chair of Chemistry. The ceremony will take place later this afternoon in the chapel, with a celebratory dinner in Great Hall at seven this evening." He dropped his voice to a hush. "And for the dinner I have procured not just two additional places for our guests from Mallorca, but also, Tristram, a place for you!"

After they had listened closely to Tristram Jones' translation, Vanessa and Alexandro looked at each other in bewilderment.

"We do not understand this thing," Vanessa said.

Tristram Jones gave them a lengthy resume of what they were likely to expect.

"It sounds a wonderful occasion for English tradition," Alexandro said, when Tristram Jones had finished. "My daughter and I will be very pleased to accept your kind invitation."

SIXTEEN

Vanessa had been in two minds about taking the dress to England, but it had made quite an impression at her birthday party and maybe it would be necessary to make an impression at Cambridge. Anyway, once folded into tissue paper it took up only a small space in her case.

Genoveva had come into her room while she was packing. "You think you are going to England for a party?" she had said, when she saw the flash of scarlet in Vanessa's case.

"You never know," Vanessa had said with a shrug.

Genoveva had seen the men's eyes on Vanessa as she had danced the fandango on her evening at the Can Cera. It had given her a vicarious kick. She had produced something beautiful, and she relished the male admiration at one remove, reliving a piece of her own teenage allure and attraction, before her father had taken her down the aisle of the Church of the Immaculate Conception on the outskirts of Palma at the age of twenty to give her away to Alexandro, to whom she had solemnly vowed to be faithful for the rest of her life. There had been a need to escape the cloistering of her parents and the only way was through marriage. But nonetheless, the marriage had been successful in its own way and Vanessa, for all her imperfections, was its crowning achievement.

She had looked from the case to Vanessa, and back to the case. "Take it to England," she had then said. "I don't think that you'll be able to use it, but at least you will be prepared."

Vanessa examined her reflection in the Spartan bathroom on

the Jacobite landing of the East Wren Building. The dress looked wildly out of place. She had removed a rose from the vase in her room and attached it to the side of her hair, which was still pinned up for the morning excursion to Ely but was now held in place with two silver combs.

"I look like an Andaluza going to her first fiesta," she said to the mirror. To prove her point she stamped her feet and performed a short flamenco pass. She couldn't help sniggering: it was all so comic. She slipped across the landing to her room to put the finishing touches to her makeup.

To Alexandro's surprise, it only took about five minutes of intermittent knocking on Vanessa's door for it to open, just after seven.

His pleasure at her punctuality evaporated as soon as he saw what she was wearing. He opened his mouth to say that she was inappropriately dressed for a serious function in a venerable seat of learning, that she should change into something more sombrely suitable, but stopped himself just in time. If he had not, if he had spoken his mind, he was sure that in all likelihood she would have flown into the mother and father of a tantrum, slammed the door on him, and not reappeared until it was time for breakfast.

As directed by Christian Tennenbaum, they made their way towards the entrance of Great Hall, where a cluster of dons and lecturers were congregating in their gowns and academic hoods. Whereas Alexandro, in the dark suit he had worn on the flight from Mallorca, blended into the crowd, as he feared Vanessa stood out like a sore thumb. But she seemed to be unaware of the mistake she had made.

Tristram Jones materialised, it seemed, from nowhere. "Vanessa," he said, "how splendid! A splash of welcome colour for what can be a rather dull occasion."

They filed into Great Hall and paused to study a table plan behind the door before taking their seats.

"Don't bother with that," Tristram Jones said, as Vanessa

searched for her name. "We've made sure that the Spaniards are together. You are besides your father at the very end of top table, me on his right, next Christian Tennenbaum. On your left is Justine Goodenough, a lecturer in Spanish classics, and opposite you Gilbert Pym, our head of department. So! You will be in a comfort zone."

Grace was a long rambling Latin affair. Vanessa found that hers was the only head unbowed, everyone else piously staring down at their side plates and cutlery.

As soon as they sat down Christian Tennenbaum said something to Tristram Jones, pointing at Vanessa and Alexandro.

"The professor wants me to tell you that, believe it or not, after the accession of Queen Elizabeth the First men could go to prison for saying that grace."

"Why?" Vanessa asked.

"It invokes the name of the Pope."

"I hadn't noticed."

Examining her surroundings whilst the waiters served the first course of smoked salmon with a half lemon wrapped in muslin, Vanessa had the first inkling that her appearance might attract more attention than she would have liked, or as her mother would have put it, the wrong sort of attention. It was very much a male evening. Despite a sprinkling of middle-aged women, it brought to mind those English men's clubs she had seen on television, in dubbed re-runs of *Poirot* or *Morse*. Some of the men were glancing at her surreptitiously, and in one or two cases, quite openly and salaciously. She was just beginning to feel uncomfortable when the lady beside her offered her hand.

"Justine Goodenough," she said. "Lecturer in Spanish literature. An odd name, Goodenough. In Spanish it means *bastante buena*. Thank you for bringing a little youth and glamour to our proceedings."

Her bright blue eyes shone kindly upon Vanessa, putting her at her ease. "Thank you," Vanessa said, shaking her hand. "My father and I are guests of Professor Tennenbaum." She felt that she needed to explain her presence.

"I know," Justine Goodenough said. "He notified us all by email that you would both be here this evening as his guests. He was very secretive, though, as to why you are staying in the college."

Vanessa smiled enigmatically. "You speak very good Spanish," she said, by way of a change of subject.

"I have to," Justine Goodenough laughed. "I am working on a new translation of the poems of Lorca. Do you know his poetry?"

Vanessa racked her brains as she squeezed her lemon onto her plate of smoked salmon. "No," she said, finally. "I have never heard of him."

"Probably just as well. They are very gloomy, and there will be time for gloom when you get a little older."

Vanessa warmed to Justine Goodenough. She hadn't been tarnished by the trappings of learning. She looked sideways at Tristram Jones, suddenly seeing him in a different light. He was talking earnestly across the table to Gilbert Pym, his gown enveloping his smart suit and tie, with his academic hood falling neatly over the back of his chair. He was proud of what he had achieved, she could see, and maybe he was right. He spoke faultless Spanish, and no doubt knew all about the poetry of Lorca. If he was not careful though, in a few years, he would be like all the other men: pompous, and self-opinionated.

As the plates for the first course were removed, a voice from the centre of the table boomed, "We shall take wine with our Lady of Aragon, Katherine, Queen of England."

A corpulent man with a florid complexion raised his glass towards a faded portrait of an austere-looking woman in Tudor costume. Everyone stood, as they tossed back the remnants of the Sancerre, served with the salmon.

"He is the head of our Chemistry Department," Justine

Goodenough said to Vanessa, as they sat down. "Our host for the evening."

One of the many glasses before Vanessa was filled with Burgundy in preparation for the main course of Welsh lamb. It was then that she noticed that as fast as glasses were emptied, they were refilled by over-attentive waiters. In fact, a considerable quantity of Burgundy was drunk before the lamb was served.

As soon as the lamb, potatoes and peas were arranged on the plates, the same voice as before boomed out, "We shall take wine with our foundress, Lady Mary Tudor, Queen of England."

They raised their glasses towards a second portrait of a woman in Tudor costume, on the opposite wall. Again, the wine was downed with great alacrity. The evening seemed to be rapidly deteriorating. The drinking matched anything Vanessa had seen amongst the British tourists at Magaluf.

At one point Gilbert Pym raised his glass in Vanessa's direction, and shouted, "*Arriba España!*"

She looked down in embarrassment. It had intended to be a compliment to her beauty, she supposed, but his expression was one of bare faced lechery. Justine Goodenough winked at her sympathetically. "They can't resist a pretty woman," she said, "particularly when they're drunk and feeling brave. One of the advantages for a woman growing old in the academic world is that they stop looking at you and start listening instead."

After a dessert of jam roly-poly, served with a sweet Marsala, silence was called for a lengthy resume by the head of the Chemistry Department of the career and achievements of the professor about to be appointed a fellow of the college. At the conclusion of the eulogy there was wild applause as the new fellow – a bony, angular man, ascetic to the point of emaciation – stood and took a bow.

"That is the end of the formal proceedings," Justine Goodenough said to Vanessa, "and maybe, you'll think, not a moment too soon."

"Vanessa!" Alexandro said to her out of the blue. "Professor Tennenbaum has asked Mr Tristram Jones to enquire of us how Graves first courted your grandmother."

"With flowers," Vanessa said. "Certainly, it would have been with flowers. She loves flowers."

She had almost forgotten their reason to be in Cambridge, so far removed from that small cottage in Deià was the junketing of the wise men around her.

"I couldn't help overhearing you talking to your father about flowers," Justine Goodenough said to Vanessa. "I think the Spanish word '*flores*' is so less pretty than our English 'flowers.' One of the few words which gives my language the upper hand over yours. But there speaks the poetic translator. And now, I think it is time for my departure. Will you be alright?"

She wanted to say 'No, could we leave together,' but it would be an insult to Professor Tennenbaum's hospitality for him to see that she was not happy to remain for what was left of the evening. She would have to wait until her father was ready to go.

Scarcely had Justine Goodenough walked through the door of Great Hall, signalling goodbye to one or two of the dons and lecturers, than Gilbert Pym moved into the vacant seat beside Vanessa.

He was a large, overbearing man, labouring under the delusion that all and sundry were grateful for his words of wisdom.

"You are from Mallorca, I hear." His Spanish was quaintly old fashioned and stilted, sounding as if he had learnt it from a text book rather than from mixing with real people.

"Yes." Vanessa forced a smile.

"In the eighteenth century, the British colonised Menorca. You can still see their Georgian architecture all over the island."

It was immediately apparent that Gilbert Pym's attentions were not limited to imparting historical facts and figures. Blatantly, he fixed his eyes on her cleavage, where lay the cross hanging from the necklace her grandmother had given her for her birthday. At the last minute, she had decided to wear it, just as her father was banging on her door. Not that he had noticed.

"Exquisite!" Gilbert Pym said. Vanessa was sure that he was hinting that she was free to decide whether the remark referred to her or the cross. She felt sick, being sized up for her physical attributes. She had to get back to her room, change into her night dress, and go to bed.

"Excuse me, please," she said to Gilbert Pym, turning to her father. "I want to go back now," she said to him in Mallorquín. "I don't feel well."

"Not yet, Vanessa," he replied in Spanish. "I am talking to Professor Tennenbaum about the effect of the banking crisis upon our tourist industry."

He was flattered to find himself amongst intellectuals who were interested in what he had to say. Tristram Jones was translating for him and Christian Tennenbaum, but had suspected what had passed between Alexandro and his daughter.

"Did you say you want to go back to your room, Vanessa?"

"Yes, I did."

"I'll take you. Professor Pym can do the translating for your father and Christian."

"Thank you, Tristram. What time should we leave for the airport?"

"Nine o'clock, to be safe. Shall we say breakfast at eight in the Senior Refectory?"

"Did you hear, Father?"

"Yes, yes," Alexandro said. "Goodnight, Vanessa."

It was a relief to walk into the fresh April air. She realised that Tristram was guiding her gently away from the East Wren Building but decided not to object, curious to see what his intentions might be.

Before she knew it they were walking arm in arm along the tow path behind the college. They stopped by the King's Bridge. He turned to face her and kissed her exploratorily on her lips. When she did not resist, he kissed her again.

111

"Grow old gracefully, Tristram," she said, breaking free. "Remember what we said about having fun in that pub at lunchtime. Always have fun, but not like those men tonight. They were making fools of themselves. And as for all that history stuff – talking of the past, toasting long dead people – those men are no better than my grandmother, who also loves tradition. But there is no excuse for them. They are educated people, while my grandmother left school at fourteen."

"Don't judge them harshly, Vanessa. For some of them it is all that they have."

"Well, you make sure that some day you have more." And then, "Can you take me to my room now please," she said. "I am so tired."

They climbed the stairs of the East Wren Building with their arms around each other. On the Jacobite landing, Vanessa removed a key from her bag and unlocked her bedroom door.

She kissed Tristram long and passionately, then placed a restraining hand on his chest as he made to cross the threshold of her room.

"No, Tristram. You are a gentleman, I know, but those men made me feel cheap. I do not want to behave cheap and prove them right."

She wriggled free, slid through her bedroom door, and locked it.

SEVENTEEN

At first, Christian Tennenbaum had struggled not to feel ashamed of himself for the feelings which had come out of the blue. Jealousy is a humiliating emotion, particularly when you have no right to be jealous. Of course young people will be drawn to each other, hold a shared, youthful world view in which he at his age could not, should not, participate. Years of teaching had brought that much home to him, but yet he could not help himself.

It began as a small impulse of anger towards Tristram Jones when he had asked Vanessa to accompany him to Peterborough and she, without much hesitation, had agreed, leaving him to take her father on the open-top bus around Cambridge. Alexandro had clapped the earphones over his ears, tuned into the Spanish commentary, and stared at building after building with an expression of profound boredom. Later, crashing into the meeting that afternoon, Tristram Jones and Vanessa's faces said it all – they had had a good time in their pub in Ely.

And then, once more, Tristram Jones had abandoned him at the end of the fellows' dinner, deputing that crushing bore Gilbert Pym to translate a lot of garbage about the prospects of the tourist industry in Spain, and Mallorca in particular. As if he cared.

But somehow, he could have coped with all of that. What was so unbearable was the sight of Vanessa, stunningly, breathtakingly beautiful, being shepherded out of Great Hall by another man. Again, Tristram Jones would be having her all to himself. Maybe only for a few minutes. Or perhaps, and this hardly could bear thinking about, for much longer.

The moment he first saw her at the airport, when she had fixed her green luminous eyes upon himself and Tristram Jones and said, "We are the Gonzalez", he had felt an immediate attraction. The attraction had grown during the negotiations for the Gonzalez papers when she had fought the Bursar for the last euro. She had proved herself strong and unflinching, an equal match for his old friend Anthony Grace who prided himself on his financial acuity.

But his feelings had come to a head when she had appeared outside Great Hall in her Spanish finery, for all the world as if she had walked out of a portrait by Murillo. Feelings which became all but unmanageable when she was ushered away by Tristram Jones, looking up at him with gratitude. It was the moment when he no longer felt ashamed of himself: just angry and searingly jealous.

Christian Tennenbaum and Alexandro were just about the last to vacate Great Hall, a good hour after Tristram Jones and Vanessa had departed. Tired-looking waitresses were loading vast numbers and assortments of glasses onto trays, each with a small residue of wine colouring their base, when at long last Alexandro had looked around and declared that it must be time to go. Gilbert Pym, whose translating abilities, Christian Tennenbaum suspected, were not as quick or accurate as Tristram Jones, wasted no time in beating a hasty retreat.

"Let me show you your way to the East Wren Building," Christian Tennenbaum had offered, speaking in English but gesticulating to make himself understood as they walked into the night, lit only by a few converted gas lamps placed on the corners of buildings.

It was not an offer made entirely in the interests of Alexandro. Christian Tennenbaum wanted to see if there were lights or voices coming from Vanessa's room, or any evidence of her and

Tristram Jones' comings and goings. Maybe they would bump into the pair, and they would say where they had been.

"*No necesario*," Alexandro had said, waving his hand. "*Hasta mañana*."

Over the years Christian Tennenbaum had ensured that his small flat in the college, consisting of a bedroom, drawing room, kitchen and bathroom, was just to his liking. He had exacting standards and impeccable taste, and these were reflected in his rooms' decor and furnishings. The flat was situated on the floor above his study, offering from his drawing room a spectacular view towards King's College Chapel and beyond. But as he let himself into his rooms at nearly midnight, he could take no pleasure in them.

His mind was alive with Vanessa. Images of her hair decorated with a solitary rose, her long vulnerable neck, her bare arms, her cleavage adorned with a chaste gold cross, crowded his brain. When he could bear it no longer he raced down to his study, taking the stairs two by two, pulled out a volume of Graves' poetry from his bookcase and returned to his flat. Feverishly, he turned the pages until he found what he wanted. It was the poem of a man who maybe should have known better, acknowledging his attraction for a much younger woman; not only acknowledging his attraction, but letting it run its course. It was the last stanza which he read over and over again. "Why not me?" he asked, each time he read the stanza. "Why not me?" He looked at the date of the poem. Graves would have been about ten years older than him when he wrote the poem, and the girl in question probably a year or two older than Vanessa, five at the most.

The relationship between a creative genius and a muse is first and foremost one of respect. It inspires something unique, of inestimable value. How had she put it yesterday? Something not just priceless, but of great price. Of course, if within the relationship there followed an intimacy, intellectual, or even physical, that would be dealt with in a decent, proper manner.

115

And God knew he needed some inspiration. Years of teaching had drained him of that. Sucked him dry. The Gonzalez papers, he had hoped, would be a catalyst for some new learned project, reviving his creativity. But suppose, just suppose, that the real inspiration was the girl who had brought to him her grandmother's secret hoard of poems; what an enchanting narrative that would be. History would be repeating itself through the Gonzalez line. First Graves and his muse, and now he, Christian Tennenbaum, with the granddaughter as his inspiration.

He was going to have to be bold, even thick-skinned: make himself impervious to what people might think or say. But what he had resolved would be in the interests of art, and that would justify any ridicule he might suffer.

Having made his decision he calmed a little, and for the following hour or two was able to snatch some fitful sleep. At six o'clock he bathed, put on his summer suit, and at first light made his way to the Saturday market which soon would be setting up at Parson's Piece.

*   *   *   *

Tristram Jones had to admit to himself some relief when Vanessa had refused to allow him into her room. He couldn't stop himself from trying, but he would have breached not only college rules, but also the respect owed to a guest. Furthermore, her father would soon have been returning to the room next door. The added frisson which that kind of caper gave to his love making was no longer as attractive as it used to be. He must be getting a bit older, he thought.

She had, though, been a marvellous diversion during the last forty-eight hours. Not afraid of speaking her mind and standing her ground, with an intelligence years beyond her age. It must be the peasant blood, he decided. And how refreshingly out of place she had looked at the fellows' dinner. Not cheap, just herself.

Putting on his pyjamas, he smiled to himself as he visualised the expression on his parents' faces if he had taken her home and shown her off as his girlfriend. It would serve them right, with their upper middle-class tastes and ambitions for their son.

He woke later than he had intended. The plan was to have breakfast with the Gonzalez in the refectory at eight and leave for Stansted at nine, before the build-up of the Saturday traffic. He was going to have to put his skates on.

As a junior lecturer, his rooms were on the top floor of the Queen Mary block overlooking Trumpington Street, noisy and unmodernised. Standing at his bathroom window cleaning his teeth, he was looking out distractedly at the first stirrings of the city, when his attention was caught by the figure of a man bearing a semblance to Christian Tennenbaum. He was emerging from a side street onto the main road with a garish bunch of flowers in his hands, wearing a powder blue suit and a wide cravat. Freezing in the motion of cleaning his teeth, Tristram Jones couldn't take his eyes away from the figure. And then, as he drew closer, he was certain: it was Christian Tennenbaum, walking determinedly over the zebra crossing in front of the college and disappearing through the Porters' Lodge. Tristram Jones ran out of his rooms to the window across the landing to track his progress. Christian Tennenbaum marched around the side of the chapel and made for the East Wren Building. At the foot of the stairs he paused to adjust his cravat.

"Fucking hell!" Tristram Jones said out loud. "He can't be serious!"

Grabbing his dressing gown, Tristram Jones fell down the stairs of the Queen Mary Block and raced across the quadrangle. He intercepted Christian Tennenbaum on the first landing.

"What the hell do you think you're doing?" he cried, tearing at his elbow.

"Nothing."

"What do you mean 'nothing'? You're going to the Jacobite

landing with a bunch of flowers. Do you know what you look like?"

He forced Christian Tennenbaum down the stairs and onto a seat fronting the college's manicured gardens. Pulling the flowers out of Christian Tennenbaum's hands, he rammed them under the seat. "We'll get rid of that lot, for a start."

"It was no different to what Graves did," Christian Tennenbaum said in a small, defensive voice.

"No different? I'll tell you the difference. You are Christian Tennenbaum, and he was Robert bloody Graves – that's the difference."

"Why should there be a difference?"

"God alive, Christian, do I have to spell it out? Robert Graves had great courage. Read his war exploits in *Good-bye to All That*. He also was a genius. Courage and genius – a potent combination. People like him are few and far between. Very few and far between. But even for him, Christian, it must have been risky. But for you it would be catastrophic. You see, you are not a genius; people would not try and understand, excuse, forgive, or say, 'Well if he keeps writing great poetry, so what. It's a small price to pay.' You would be deemed unfit to hold a fiduciary appointment. It would finish your career."

He felt a touch hypocritical, given that last night he had tried to enter Vanessa's room, but it would have only been with her consent which, in the event, had not been forthcoming. If she had agreed and they had found themselves in difficulties with the authorities then somehow, between the two, they would have managed the situation. A far cry from what had now presented itself: the college's senior English professor making a very public fool of himself.

Christian Tennenbaum sank his head into his hands. "Thank you, Tristram," he said at last.

"No problem."

A porter appeared before them. "Are you two gentlemen alright?" he asked attentively.

"Yes, thank you, Forbes," Tristram Jones said, and then, reaching beneath the seat, he pulled out the bunch of flowers. "Could you dispose of these, please?"

"Certainly, sir."

The porter walked back to the lodge, holding the flowers behind his back and whistling quietly to himself.

"Why?" Christian Tennenbaum asked.

"Why what?"

"Why did I do it? What got into me?"

"You've just got a bit carried away with all this Graves stuff." Tristram Jones touched Christian Tennenbaum on his arm comfortingly.

"No, it's more than that. Did you know that my father's parents came from Germany?"

"Well I always assumed that there was a German connection somewhere in your family tree with a name like Tennenbaum, but I never gave it much thought."

"My parents always used to say to me, 'Put education first. The Nazis took everything from your grandparents – their house, their money, their furniture, their jewellery – but no one can take education away.'"

Christian Tennenbaum leant back and stared at the sky before continuing. "And so, I studied and studied and studied. Whenever a girl came along, my parents would say 'There's plenty of time for that later.' They weren't exactly discouraging, but they weren't encouraging either. Get your A levels, get your degree, get your PhD, get your lectureship. And then one day there are fewer girls around, and you become more particular, more fastidious, while the important things in life are beginning to leave you behind."

Tristram Jones was becoming a little anxious that time was ticking by. He had to meet the Gonzalez in the refectory in a few minutes. But above all, he didn't want them to stumble upon Christian Tennenbaum pouring out his heart to him, Tristram

Jones, in his dressing gown on a seat in the college gardens, when they emerged from the East Wren Building.

"It's getting on a bit," Tristram Jones said. "I think I should be getting dressed."

Unperturbed, Christian Tennenbaum pressed on. "And then you're stuck in a Cambridge college at the age of fifty-five with not much going for you. And that's when you begin to think a little irrationally. You become a little peculiar."

"It's never too late, Christian," Tristram Jones said, looking at his watch.

"In some ways that's true, but in other ways it's not."

"How do you mean?"

"It's too late for the simplicities of life. Straight forward people and simple things." He stood to go. "Thank God you stopped me just in time. I don't think that I can face the Gonzalez today. Will you make my excuses for me?"

"Yes, of course."

"And Tristram, this won't get any further will it?"

"Of course it won't, Christian."

"By the way, I was going to show her this." Christian Tennenbaum produced a folded sheet of paper from his top pocket.

"What's that?"

"A poem by Graves."

Tristram Jones scan read the sheet. "Well, I can only just make head or tail of what he's saying, and she can't even speak fucking English."

"Let me explain."

"No, Christian, it's too early in the day for that sort of stuff. Throw it away," he said, handing back the poem.

A few minutes later Christian Tennenbaum stood in his book lined study, staring blankly at the shelves. Row upon row of intellectualism: his refuge and substitute for the reality which had escaped him, or from which he had fled. He was not sure.

But Tristram Jones was right. It was important at least to believe that it was never too late, whether or not that was in fact so.

*   *   *   *

Alexandro and Vanessa were sitting alone in the refectory when Tristram Jones joined them at eight-fifteen. Their cases were leaning neatly against a wall, with Vanessa's folded poncho placed on top.

"It is very quiet here," Alexandro said, as they helped themselves to the buffet.

"The college always takes time to wake up and get going on a Saturday morning. Students sleeping off Friday-night drinking," Tristram Jones said with an indulgent smile. Just as well, he thought, or it could have been more than just me and the porter seeing Christian making an exhibition of himself.

"And some lecturers sleeping off the drinking as well, I think," Alexandro said impishly.

"Where is Professor Tennenbaum?" Alexandro asked as they got into Tristram Jones' car.

"He sends his apologies," Tristram Jones said breezily. "He had forgotten that he had promised to do some coaching at the other side of town. He's looking forward to seeing you in Spain. In fact, we're both looking forward to going across, just as soon as you let us know that your mother is ready to seal the deal."

"I think that Professor Tennenbaum is a very wise man," Alexandro said as they got under way. "He has many good ideas for tourism in Spain: upmarket, intellectual tourism, to our great cultural heritage."

"*Amare et sapere vix deo conceditor*," Tristram Jones said under his breath.

"What was that?" Alexandro asked.

"Even a god finds it hard to love and be wise at the same time. A Latin saying."

"I will have to think about that," Alexandro said. "Although I can't see how it applies to the professor."

Vanessa remained almost totally silent on the journey to Stansted, looking out of the window from the back seat.

"We haven't been speaking much English," Tristram Jones said over his shoulder as they turned off the M11.

"How do you mean?" Vanessa asked.

"We decided when you arrived that we might speak a little English. Improve your language skills."

"Never mind."

Alexandro would not hear of Tristram Jones parking in the short-term car park and helping them with their cases. He insisted that they be dropped outside the Departures Hall.

When the car came to a standstill Tristram Jones opened the glove box and handed an envelope to Vanessa.

"What is this?" she said, aghast. Surely he had not written some soppy love letter for her to take back to Spain?

"The contract of course," Tristram Jones said with a grin, half-suspecting what she had feared.

"Thank you, Tristram," Vanessa said, much relieved, as she took the envelope and put it in her bag. "I nearly forgot."

As soon as the boot had been emptied, Vanessa put out her hand to forestall an embrace. "Thank you so much for your hospitality, Tristram," she said. It was important to put the frolics of the day before behind them. They were now in a business relationship, and nothing should stand in its way.

In the Departure lounge Vanessa busied herself with her text messages, notifying her friends that she was on the way home.

"Did you like England?" her father asked her.

"Do you know," she said, without looking up, "I can now see why Graves spent most of his life in Spain."

EIGHTEEN

Spring was the best of times, but now was also the worst of times. As the yellow broom erupted on the hillsides and the eaves of the buildings were re-inhabited by the swallows, Maria Jesus became acutely aware of her waning physical powers. When just a few years before she would have walked along the road that led to Sóller to pick the spring flowers and watch the swallows swooping and diving amongst the hills, now her wracked joints and swollen ankles kept her for much of her life tied to her house and garden.

She rarely took the bus to Palma now: not just because she felt a stranger in her own capital, bewildered by the changes that affluence had inflicted, but also because of the pain of negotiating the steps and squares of her old haunts.

Alexandro visited her every two weeks or so – sometimes with Genoveva, sometimes without – and on Friday evenings she might play cards with Carmen and one or two elderly neighbours. On her seventieth birthday Alexandro had bought her a television and she occasionally watched old 1950s Hollywood films, dubbed unconvincingly into Spanish. But the highlights of her year were the three annual visits her daughter Josefina made to Mallorca to see her mother. A few days at Christmas and Kings' Day, Easter, and a week or two in the summer.

Josefina was smart and clever – a breath of the great Catalan capital Maria Jesus had never seen. But she felt she belonged, if only at one remove, when her daughter spoke of the school

123

of which she was the headmistress, and to which so many politicians and businessmen sent their children.

There was a mutual respect between the two. Josefina did not try to change her mother's life for the better, just taking her as she found her. In return, Josefina did not expect her mother to enquire or pry into her affairs. In particular, and instinctively, Maria Jesus knew that there was no purpose to be served in delving into Josefina's emotional life. It had occasionally crossed her mind that she might be a lesbian, but it was not worth dwelling upon. Maria Jesus valued the short spells of her daughter's company too much to spoil them with enquiries, demands, or requests for declarations which in all likelihood could not, or would not, be made.

Three days after Alexandro and Vanessa's return from Cambridge, Maria Jesus awaited her daughter's Easter visit with more impatience than usual. The night before, Alexandro had made a special trip to Deià to make his report, as he put it. And what a damning, self-incriminating report it was.

"And?" she had demanded, when they had sat down over a pot of coffee and a plate of almond cakes.

"Very good news, Mama," he had declared, shifting uneasily in his chair. "For all of the poems, the men of Cambridge will pay thirty-three thousand euros." Just for the moment he had thought it best to hold back on the other terms: the one hour interview and a possible photo shot.

"And that is good news?" she had asked sarcastically.

It was time to be realistic. "There is not much there, Mama. This money, what is it for? A few sheets of paper, most with little or nothing to show. They may yet say that we have double-crossed them when they see what we have."

"What I have," she had corrected. "Give me back those copies."

Alexandro had felt in his pocket and placed the two sheets of paper on her dresser. There was to be no opportunity for realism, for straight talking, for enlightening his mother as to the monetary value of what she professed to hold so dear.

"You would have been proud of Vanessa, Mama," he had said, to keep the conversation going. "Without her, I would have been at sea."

"I can believe that," Maria Jesus had agreed contemptuously. Alexandro was never the cleverest child: outshone by his sister at school, and now admitting that even his daughter could do better than him.

"I will have to think it over." It was tempting. Just. But she was not going to let herself be rushed. At least it sounded as if Vanessa had done the bargaining, and she would have given them a run for their money, that was for sure. Maybe it was all that the box of poems was worth, but she was not going to say as much to Alexandro.

"To show their good intentions, they have deposited six thousand euros in my account. For you."

"Send it back."

"Mama, that money could be used now. For you."

"What would I do with it?"

"Genoveva thought that you might like an electric wheelchair. To take you around the village."

"And show to all the world that I'm old and decrepit?"

"You have never cared much what people think."

She had stood, laboured across the room, and returned with a newspaper in her hand. It was a monthly distribution delivered by the local municipality to keep the residents up to date with its achievements.

Opening it at the centre page, she had read, "Permission granted for new hotel complex in Sóller, to be financed by consortium of Spanish government and German businessmen. Cost eighteen million euros."

Lowering the paper, she had looked at him scathingly over her glasses. "Eighteen million euros for breeze blocks to be stuck together with cement, and a hole dug in the ground and filled with water. All to attract the scum of northern Europe, never mind the blighting of our island. And you tell me that for Robert's life blood you have secured thirty-three thousand euros!"

It was time to leave. She was working herself into a state. It had not gone well, but at least she had the facts. She now needed time for it all to sink in. Josefina would be arriving soon for Easter. Her visits always put his mother in a good frame of mind, and perhaps she would win her round.

"When is Josefina arriving?" he had asked, as he stood to go.

"Tomorrow."

"Maybe you could talk to her about the offer."

"Maybe, maybe not. I shall make my own decision."

He knew she would. She admired her daughter. It had always made him jealous.

As soon as he had gone, she had climbed the stairs to Josefina's room to ensure that everything was in order for her visit: the ornaments properly arranged on the mantelpiece above the old iron basket fire grate, the freshly laundered counterpane turned back on her bed, with her favourite old teddy bear resting its head on the pillow.

She closed the window. The room had been well aired, and the nights were still chilly.

* * * *

Josefina often speculated as to where she would periodically escape, where she would find refreshment from the fraying pressures and conformity of the big city when her mother was no longer alive. It was true that she was a dutiful daughter, but that was by no means the whole story. Her regular visits to her childhood home and ageing mother in Deià were a counterpoise to her busy life in Barcelona, a release from friends and colleagues whose lifestyles were so different from hers. All of them were now married with families of their own, many of them deftly juggling work and children. But in Deià she felt liberated. No comparisons. No tedious talk of the progress of children, their schools, universities, and careers, or the waywardness of husbands. Just a few days of tranquillity with a mother who asked few questions, said little, and just seemed content to have her presence under her roof.

Alexandro and Genoveva would invite her round to their apartment for an evening meal, but she always left with the impression that marriage was a burdensome institution – at least as far as her brother and sister-in-law were concerned. Try as she might, she could find little her brother, who was somewhat dull, had in common with Genoveva, who was somewhat flighty. Josefina would leave their apartment with relief amidst exclamations of what an enjoyable evening it had been.

The compensation was Vanessa: bright and loving but, like so many of the only children Josefina had seen at her school, grown up before her time, missing out on part of her childhood. When she had been told that Vanessa had applied for a place at the College of Design in Palma, she had been tempted to suggest that she might consider going to university in Barcelona where she could keep an eye on her, and where perhaps she might read a more weighty subject. But then Josefina decided that she did not want her niece too close to her and her private affairs.

There had been romance in Josefina's life. Short, discreet liaisons with other women, but nothing permanent. It was still too risky in a country emerging from decades of conservatism for a high-profile headmistress to disclose too blatantly her particular sexual orientation. Instead she had to pose as a dedicated pedagogue, wedded to her calling, with no time for the activities and inclinations of ordinary mortals.

She always picked up the same make of car at the airport. A Seat 600, if possible in white. As soon as Maria Jesus saw the little car winding down the main street of the village her heart beat a little faster. Her daughter had arrived, was safe home. And on this trip there would be much to talk about, for Josefina to think about, to comment on, and advise.

*   *   *   *

Maria Jesus had prepared an evening meal of lobster stew with mussels to celebrate her daughter's return home. When the plates were cleared and the pair were standing by the sink, Maria Jesus washing up, Josefina drying, she launched into the subject which was dominating her thoughts.

"Do you remember Robert Graves, Josefina? That Englishman?"

"The one who fancied you? Of course I do."

"He was a famous poet, you know. At least judging by the number of people who still come to the village to look over his house and visit his grave."

"Yes. I know. And he did you good. Made you feel a little special."

"He thought I was so special that he wrote poetry for me."

"That's what poets do," Josefina said with an admiring smile. "Write odes to pretty women."

She looked at her mother. There were still traces of what she had been. Strong and defiant: attractions for a certain type of man, who would have had to be strong and defiant himself to court her which, she remembered, Robert Graves was in his elderly way.

"Yes, but you see, he gave me the poems he wrote. Showed them to no one else, just gave them to me. And I've kept them."

"They must be a lovely memory of him."

"But they're in English."

"I understand English," Josefina said brightly. "I'd like to see them."

"Everyone has now seen them, it seems. At least the ones that count."

"How do you mean?" Josefina paused in the motion of wiping a dinner plate.

"Alexandro has taken them to England. There is great interest in them. I have been offered money for them. Good money. He's organised everything. In Cambridge University."

"Alexandro!" Josefina cried. "But he's useless! *Inutile!*"

128

She exclaimed both the English and Spanish words by way of emphasis.

"He took Vanessa with him. She did the bargaining."

"Thank God for that."

Josefina felt a great anger welling inside her. Of course the poetry was valuable. Not that Alexandro would see any value in them apart from the money. They were family property, a memory of their childhood. When their mother was struggling to keep her children clothed and fed, out of the blue something very special occurred. She began to be gently courted by a celebrated poet who saw in her something beautiful. She had responded by blossoming in her own way, becoming beautiful herself. How dare her brother hawk something magical around for the best price available, the going rate.

"Where are the poems now?" Josefina asked

"I'm not stupid, Josefina. I've kept them here."

Maria Jesus was beginning to feel a little frightened. Her daughter was formidable; she couldn't be otherwise, holding down her job as headmistress of a leading school in Barcelona.

"So Alexandro took the poems to England, and brought them back?"

"No. He just took photocopies of two – the best. To show them. Samples, if you like."

"Where are the photocopies now?"

"I insisted that he gave them back to me."

"Please show me what Graves has written in your honour."

Maria Jesus leant across to the dresser drawer and extracted the chocolate box. "Here, look. Here are the poems Alexandro took to England, and here, beneath them, are all the others."

Josefina rifled through the sheaves of paper. "But apart from these two, there's hardly anything here. How much have you been offered for all of this?" She waved disdainfully at the contents of the chocolate box.

"Thirty-three thousand euros."

"Jesus!" Josefina said, before she could stop herself.

"Alexandro isn't so stupid after all. Or, as you say, it was more likely the work of that cunning little madam Vanessa."

"Everything in there is valuable, Josefina," Maria Jesus said reproachfully. "They are the best of my memories."

"When does this transaction take place?" As she said 'transaction,' Josefina raised her hands and wiggled her fingers to qualify the word with imaginary inverted commas.

"Soon, I suppose. They have paid Alexandro six thousand euros to show they mean business, and I'll get the rest when I hand them over."

"I think that I had better see Alexandro about all of this."

"Yes. Please do." It was a relief that Josefina was going to participate in the whole affair. If she ran true to type she would soon take command, and somehow, matters would be resolved for the best.

"What will you do with the money?" Josefina asked, softening. After all, it was not fair to vent her frustration on her mother. It was Alexandro who would need to answer some questions.

"I don't know. Give some to you, give some to Alexandro. Genoveva wants me to buy an electric wheelchair out of the money Alexandro's now holding for me, but I told him I wasn't interested."

"It's not such a bad idea, Mama. Your arthritis isn't improving."

If only all of this had come earlier, Josefina thought, when she could have enjoyed it. Maybe travelled a little. Stayed with her in Barcelona. She might also have spent some money on the cottage. It was too late for that now. She liked the cottage as it was: a memory of the past which gave her so little but somehow, in her mind, was still worth preserving.

"How did all this come about?"

"It was Vanessa. She was putting on airs and graces and stupidly I wanted to show her that I was young and pretty once as well." She paused before continuing. "Maybe not that pretty, but at least one man thought me attractive, even in middle age."

"And a great man at that, Mama."

In bed that night, sleep eluded Josefina. Her brain teemed with memories of the past, and the fear, verging on certainty, that the whole business of the Graves poems would not go well with her brother at the helm. He had never been the brightest banana in the bunch. She was going to have to take some control before it was too late. It had been a difficult term and she had been looking forward to a quiet Easter, but there was not much hope of that now.

NINETEEN

Elder sister syndrome. Headmistress mode. Or just Josefina being Josefina. Alexandro and Genoveva used a variety of derogatory terms to describe his sister when she took over, or waded in, as they sometimes put it. It had been a relief when she had taken up her appointment as headmistress and moved to Barcelona. Alexandro could at last move out of her shadow and be himself.

He had been proud to do something off his own initiative for the family – go to England without Josefina's knowledge, and with his daughter's help cut a brilliant deal on behalf of his mother. But now, even that had fallen under his sister's scrutiny. Sitting in his and Genoveva's apartment on the settee beneath the long window which opened onto one of Palma's moderately fashionable squares, she was ponderously studying the agreement which he and Vanessa had so painstakingly hammered out with Professor Tennenbaum and the Bursar in Cambridge. What was particularly galling was that she was holding the paper almost at arm's length, as if it were an offence to her.

"Now, let's unpack this, paragraph by paragraph. First, our mother is to surrender to this college in Cambridge all the poems et cetera in her possession written by Graves." She lowered the paper. "I understand that they've seen two of them."

"Correct."

"Those two, Alexandro, are the only ones that count. The rest are..." She shook her head from side to side with a vacuous expression on her face, "Nothing. Just nothing."

"What are you saying?" Genoveva asked in bewilderment. "Alexandro, is this true?"

Alexandro had been completely honest about the sparseness of the box's contents with Vanessa, but had seen no reason to share that particular piece of information with his wife. She had held him in some esteem since his return from England, a new-found status he had found enjoyable. There had even been a positive impact on their sex life.

"Of course not, Genoveva. There are some bits and pieces of writing. Something for the academics to get their teeth into. You know academics."

Josefina looked at her brother and sister-in-law with undisguised contempt mingled with pity. "No, Alexandro," she continued, "don't fool yourself. There's nothing else worth having. Not even for your academics." Josefina returned her attention to the paper. "You warrant that title to the so-called material is vested in our mother."

"Any problem with that?" Genoveva asked curtly.

"No. Absolutely not. Those two pages, and the rest of the box are hers alright. Never mind, I suppose, that they're mainly waste paper."

Genoveva struggled to contain herself. It was her, and only her prerogative, to criticise her husband. The debatable merits of the Graves poems were not as important as protecting her husband's honour from his harridan of a sister.

"Next," Josefina said, getting into her stride, "our mother is to grant an interview, presumably with this Professor Tennenbaum, to explain how the material came into her possession, outline her recollections of her meetings and friendship with Graves, and allow her photograph to be taken."

"That, Josefina," Alexandro said earnestly, "is where we can deliver. In some ways that could be for them as important as the papers themselves."

"I agree," Genoveva said. "And even if there is a little

fabrication, a little elaboration on Maria Jesus' part, who's to know?"

"Primary sources," Vanessa added. She had been half listening to the conversation, wafting between her bedroom and the living room, but now had decided to make a full contribution to the discussion, planting herself on the edge of the settee beside Josefina. She was not going to have her father ridiculed and belittled by her aunt if she could help it, and anyway, the agreement had been as much her work as his. "Primary sources," she repeated decisively. "That's what's important."

"Well let's look into that," Josefina said. "I agree with Vanessa. We are talking about a primary source, but our mother is not highly educated; she will not say what they want to hear, and I doubt she is capable of the elaborations Genoveva mentions. She is getting old. And she will not want her photograph to be taken."

Josefina looked back at the page. "If this agreement is not fulfilled, et cetera et cetera, it is null and void, and all monies already disbursed are to be repaid."

She looked up. "Send the money back, Alexandro. Send it back."

"No, I won't," Alexandro said petulantly. He had achieved something good for his mother which now, true to type, his sister was determined to demolish. "I think that you are envious that it is me, and not you, who has had these dealings. You feel that you are the heavyweight academic, and can't stand the fact that I, the dunce of the family, have done something so worthwhile. And what's more, in Cambridge. In Cambridge!"

"Send the money back, Alexandro," Josefina repeated calmly and deliberately.

"You have no right to speak to my father like that," Vanessa said.

"You should be helping your brother in all of this," Genoveva added, "not, as usual, rubbishing everything he does."

So there it was. It had become clear to Josefina that the whole escapade had now devolved into a battle between brother and sister, and they were not going to buckle.

She read again from the paper. "This agreement is to be completed by the first of July."

"Help us," Vanessa pleaded.

Josefina couldn't let them stew in their own juice. Besides, there might be as yet unknown repercussions for her mother, who would need some protection from someone a little more level-headed than the trio sitting before her.

"Very well. As Vanessa said, our strongest suit is the interview."

"Actually, Alexandro said that," Genoveva corrected. "He is not as stupid as you are trying to make out."

"Maybe that is where I can help," Josefina said, ignoring the interruption. She looked at the foot of the page. "Who is this Professor Tennenbaum?"

"He is head of the English Department at this college." Alexandro could feel control of the enterprise slipping away from him.

"Would he be sympathetic?"

"How do you mean?" Genoveva asked.

"Would he be sympathetic, patient, painstaking, caring, understanding, unhurrying, when he interviews Maria Jesus? Because, otherwise, he'll get nowhere."

"*Bastante buena*," Vanessa announced.

"What are you saying?" Genoveva asked her daughter.

"*Bastante buena*. Good enough. That is the name of the lady professor I sat next to at that dinner. She helped me when all those old men were gawking at me. She should interview Grandma."

"What old men?" Genoveva looked askance at Vanessa.

"The old men at the dinner in the college papa and I were invited to. They were gawking at me in my party dress."

"I was always in two minds about you taking that dress to England."

"Tell me about this Goodenough," Josefina asked.

"She was a professor of Spanish. Was translating the poetry of someone called Lorca. I had to admit that I did not know who he was."

"Federico Lorca," Josefina said. "Shot by the Fascists in Granada in 1936."

"I think, Auntie," Vanessa said after a short silence, "that you should maybe act as a go between. Deal with these Cambridge people on our behalf."

Reluctantly, painfully, Alexandro had to acknowledge that his sister was best placed to deal with the people of Cambridge and their requirement for an interview with their mother. She could relate to them in a way he could not. With all her learning she would command their respect, which he had been all too aware was a little lacking when he and Vanessa had taken up the cudgels on the family's behalf. They had looked down on him, soon realising that he was not one of their number. The young lecturer Tristram Jones had fallen a bit for Vanessa, whisking her off for some jaunt – but that had just been a sex-driven diversion. At least, though, it had shown that the Gonzalez had something going for them. But they now needed some gravitas in fulfilling these terms and conditions, and only Josefina could supply that. She might even prove her worth in assisting with any recriminations that might arise over the all-but-useless remains in the chocolate box.

"Alright," he said, as if making an important concession. "You, Josefina, make contact with the men of Cambridge for this interview. But you must keep me fully informed."

"No!" Vanessa interjected. "The interview must be conducted by Goodenough. Auntie Josefina and Goodenough will deal with the interview, and you, Papa, can deal with the rest."

"Very well," Josefina said. "But it will have to be when school ends."

"When will that be?"

"About the end of June."

"They will want to hear before then," Alexandro said.

"I suggest that I write direct to this Tennenbaum, and say that we have agreed that I will assist in this interviewing process..."

"And the college's representative must be Justine Goodenough," Vanessa insisted, interrupting her aunt. "Justine. I've just remembered. Her Christian name is Justine."

"Very well. I shall let you know how I get on."

The atmosphere relaxed. They had reached a compromise: as good a solution as could be expected in the difficult circumstances.

"I have suggested that some of the money sent to Alexandro by the college, might be used to buy an electric wheelchair for Maria Jesus." Genoveva had cast herself into the role of the practical member of the family.

"I know," Josefina said. "She mentioned it to me. But if we have to send the money back?"

"Then we will have to make good the cost," Alexandro said. "But at least it will show our mother that there are benefits to be gained from these Cambridge dealings. Give her some encouragement to fulfil the other terms of the contract."

"I think I could persuade Mama the electric wheelchair is a good idea. I'll work on it."

"Her arthritis is bad," Genoveva said. "It's what she needs. Freeing her up to get about the village."

The wheelchair had become a unifying factor. Something on which they could agree without dissent or argument.

Alexandro produced a bottle of local herb liqueur, and four glasses. "Let us drink to our mother's health." It was a little too early for Josefina, but she took a glass from Alexandro containing a few drops of the livid liqueur. She knew that he needed to feel that the confrontation was over; he had always disliked dissention or conflict of any kind. A likeable trait, but it could not have assisted him much in his career. Certainly, she would not have got anywhere in education, if she had been similarly inclined.

"To the family," she said. "*Salud*!"

She looked out of the window. The small church at the top of the square was disgorging a long line of the faithful in their best clothes, silently following an oversized wooden cross carried by a dozen or so young men struggling under its punishing weight. It was the annual Good Friday pilgrimage from all the city's churches to the cathedral, where they would converge at midday for the three-hour service of solemn reflection. It gave her the creeps. At least in the vastness of Barcelona, you could escape such things.

She watched as the column disappeared down an alley leading to the monolithic sandstone Cathedral of La Seu.

"Thank God Mama kept me free of all that," she said, to no one in particular.

"They're good people," Genoveva said, joining her at the window.

"And it's harmless," Alexandro added. "They're not running the country with Franco anymore. That ended years ago."

Maybe, Josefina thought. But try telling them that you are gay or a lesbian, and then see just how good and harmless they are.

TWENTY

It had not been Lorca who had drawn Justine Goodenough to Granada, but Granada which had drawn her to Lorca.

At the age of eighteen, she had backpacked on trains and buses down to Andalucía with her cousin Jane. That summer she had been awarded a place at Newnham College Cambridge to read Spanish literature, and had persuaded her parents that an indispensable preliminary to her taking up her much-celebrated achievement was a trip to Spain. Jane, three years older than Justine, was reading sociology and architecture at Bristol University. She was writing her last year's dissertation entitled: 'The conversion of mosques into churches and cathedrals following the reconquest of Andalucía by Christian Spain in 1492: adaptation or assimilation?' Jane took the responsibility of finding an answer to the question posed by her dissertation very seriously indeed.

Justine Goodenough's parents had consented to the trip on the premise that Jane was solid, safe, and cautious, and could be relied on to look after their sometimes wild and wayward daughter.

On a dusty afternoon, they had stepped out of the Córdoba express onto the platform at Granada. A tour around the Alhambra and the cathedral merited at least two full days, according to Jane, before they could feel free to move on to Seville. But something unexpected was happening; the streets were alive with music and dance. The last of the three-day Granada fiesta was in full swing. The youth hostel was full, but they were able to find a room in a pension in a side street off a half-hidden square, heavily decorated with streamers and bunting. For two blond English girls, availability in cheap hotels and hostels could usually be found, however high the season.

That evening, the two watched the parade of the young caballeros from the countryside into the town: boys wearing black circular hats strapped tightly beneath their chins, riding trotting mules and ponies, whilst pillioned behind them, side saddle, sat teenage girls in frilled polka dot dresses holding their heads high, their ornamental combs and mantillas bobbing to the motion of their mounts.

Justine Goodenough couldn't tear her eyes from the girls. Their long features and black eyes, wild and untamed, stirred in her something she could neither resist nor deny.

Much later, in the melee of the music and dancing and the reek of horse and pony which hung over the city, she lost her cousin, parted in the clapping, stamping, and elbowing of the flamenco rhythms. It was something of a relief to be shot of Jane, who had bored her to tears with her corbels, buttresses, and arabesques during the past few days.

She wandered amongst the sinuous streets, drawn towards caressing and fondling boys and girls; a succession of half-drunk youths pressed unwanted kisses on her, but then she was swept into the bare arms of a girl of about twenty. As they embraced and then kissed, she made the discovery which had always been there to be made, but which she had never dared to find. Then the girl was gone, leaving just a memory and an aroma of sweat and garlic.

She returned to her pension in a daze. Jane was lying awake on her bed, naked in the heat. "Thank God, you're back. I was getting worried," she said, before turning on her side and falling asleep.

Justine Goodenough crept to the window and looked up at the stars. In the immensity of the universe, at last she, Justine Goodenough, had her own significance, her own place. Too excited to sleep, she lay awake until dawn when at last the city became still.

Mid-morning after a makeshift breakfast, she and Jane picked their way over the detritus of the festivities and made their way up the Calderería Nueva to the Moorish Palace. But now she was a different person, and the world a different place. The Alhambra was more magnificent than she could ever have imagined, the town below more splendid in the blazing heat than she could ever have envisaged. And she was light-hearted, laughing generously at the guide's puerile jokes, even tolerating Jane's intensity which previously had become so tiresome. She was free at last, free of everything which hitherto had tarnished her existence.

Granada was the place of her liberation, and she would never forget it. During her third year at Oxford she returned to the city to research her thesis on the life of Lorca. Later, when she undertook the challenge of translating Lorca's plays and poetry into English she spent a few weeks each summer at Granada University as a visiting academic, studying, reading, delving into the university's archives.

Even though it was lunacy, she could not stop herself from searching the city's crowd for the girl who had kissed her that night. She would scan the faces of the women haggling in the market or waiting at a pedestrian crossing for the light to turn green. She knew she would never recognise her, had she seen her; but it was something she could not help doing, pointless as it was. Forever youthful, the girl had become her epiphany, sparing her from confusion and prevarication.

Lorca became Justine Goodenough's life work, and Granada her second home. And it was there that she forged bonds with academics of her own sexual orientation: women who to all the world had sacrificed husbands and children in the pursuit of matters of the intellect, but clandestinely were living and expressing their emotions as they wanted and needed.

Obligingly, Lorca had been prolific in his short life. There was always more to discover, and Granada was the place to discover it. Even the revisions of her English translations were best conducted in Granada, close to the bars and cafes Lorca would have known, and in the unobtrusive hotel rooms where she could pursue her passions away from the hypocritical sagacity of Cambridge.

*　　　　　*　　　　　*　　　　　*

Christian Tennenbaum had summoned her to his rooms on the first Wednesday of the summer term, by way of an enigmatic note deposited in her pigeon hole.

'We are both in thrall to 'La Belle Dame sans Merci'', it said. 'Please, can we, as common supplicants, have a few words together in private? Would this afternoon be convenient in my little pad, at, say, 3.P.M? Just let me know if not convenient. Otherwise, I shall be expecting you.'

The reference to Keats' Belle Dame had amused, if not intrigued her. There were similarities between Keats and Lorca, and not only in their early untimely deaths. But then she was outraged to discover that she had been invited to his rooms under false pretences. He expected her to join him in Mallorca, of all places, to do a bit of free interpreting.

"You can't be serious!"

"Justine, that's the third time you've said that." He wagged a finger at her. "I'm going to have to call you Justine McEnroe."

"I don't care what you call me, Christian, you just can't be serious!"

"Fourth time."

"Do you seriously expect me to sacrifice a week of research in Granada to go to a tourist trap in the Mediterranean, heaving with half-naked package trippers throwing up on the beach, to help you elicit some old lady's reminiscences of Robert Graves?"

"Three days should do, Justine. Otherwise, put very succinctly. But the operative words are 'Robert' and 'Graves'. Admittedly, the island has now become a focus for package tourism, but that is incidental to discovering the workings of the mind of a giant of English literature."

"I would have thought that everything that could possibly have been written about Robert Graves has been written."

"I could say the same about Lorca."

"Bear in mind, Christian, that I am engaged in translating Lorca's work into English. There is always latitude for improvement, re-thinking, revision, where that discipline is concerned."

Christian Tennenbaum knew that it would only be a matter of time before winning her round. She was kind, and always wanting to help and to please. The Spanish had been very astute in identifying her as the candidate for the interview with Maria Jesus; certainly more astute than he would ever have given them credit for.

"You met two of the old lady's family at the Chemistry Department fellows' dinner last term. Lovely people." He had decided upon a fresh approach.

"Well I was beginning to put two and two together. So it's all to do with that cloak and dagger stuff about special guests from Spain, and could I please treat them nicely, make sure that they felt at home. As if you could feel at home at one of the college's drunken debaucheries."

"Tradition, Justine. Admired and valued around the world."

"Rubbish. And where does that poor girl fit in?"

"What poor girl?"

"The girl sitting next to me, being ogled by all the men. I'm surprised she didn't walk out."

"That is Vanessa Gonzalez, the old lady's granddaughter. And it is her aunt who has now written to me, praying in aid your special skills and services. You made quite an impression that evening, Justine, despite what you say about drunken debauchery."

Christian Tennenbaum consulted Josefina's letter. "'Justine Goodenough's compassion, her sensitivity, are the qualities required for a productive interview with my mother,'" he read.

"I was probably the only person there that night who was sober enough to see what that girl was having to contend with."

"Please do it. If not for me, for the college. And at some time I too will be there with you in Mallorca, to ensure that we get just what we need, and that everything is in order."

Justine Goodenough sighed heavily. "I'll think about it, Christian."

"Thank you, Justine. Thank you so much." He knew that he was home and dry. "And by the way, Justine," he said to her retreating figure, "this must remain confidential between the two of us, please. Not even a word to anyone else in the department."

On that, he said to himself when she had gone, I can rely. She's not a blabbermouth.

The letter had been a godsend. Written in passable English by Maria Jesus' daughter, about whom Christian Tennenbaum had previously known nothing, it gave him carte blanche to eliminate Tristram Jones from the whole project and substitute Justine Goodenough.

He had carefully rationalised his thinking almost as soon as Josefina's letter had arrived.

First, Tristram Jones knew too much. He had been in on all the negotiations. He wasn't at all convinced that it was necessary to mention to Justine Goodenough anything more than that an old friend of Robert Graves had been discovered, and he needed help to download her memories of the old man. It was best that he dealt with the hand-over of the poems on his own. The fewer of his colleagues who were involved in the first glorious examination of them the better. He was feeling possessive. They were almost his, and he alone wanted to savour the moment of examination – the moment when they would be seen for the first time by a compatriot of Graves, who could speak his language and appreciate his genius.

Second, he was envious of Tristram Jones. Not just envious of his success with women – whisking Vanessa off to Ely, or marching her into the night during the fellows' dinner – but envious of all that there was about him. His youth, his ability to be at ease with himself, to see the funny side of things.

And finally, of course, there was the debt he owed him for preventing him from making an utter fool of himself. He was grateful for what he did, but the whole embarrassing saga came to mind every time he saw Tristram Jones; he was sure that every look Tristram Jones gave him, every smile, every expression, was laden with meaning.

Moving around the college, waiting to come across Tristram Jones, he kept Josefina's letter in his inside pocket. He needed to make it look casual.

At last, two days after speaking to Justine Goodenough, he saw Tristram Jones wheeling his bicycle up Trumpington Street. With a firm step, he walked out of the college grounds and made towards him, as if on a visit to another part of the town.

"Christian!" Tristram Jones exclaimed, as they drew level. "Any news from Mallorca?"

"Yes, indeed. A letter's just arrived, Tristram." Christian Tennenbaum fished in his pocket. "From the headmistress of a school in Barcelona, in fact."

"Barcelona?"

"Yes. A daughter has come out of the woodwork, believe it or not."

"What daughter?"

"Apparently Mrs Gonzalez has two children. A Josefina as well as Alexandro. Josefina is the headmistress of a school in Barcelona. She was told all about the Cambridge trip when she went home to Mallorca for Easter. Still there by all accounts."

"So?"

"I think that she wants to play a part in all of this. But the interesting thing, which I'm afraid affects you, is that the family now want Justine to handle the meeting with Mrs Gonzalez."

"Justine? What's it to do with her?"

"Apparently Alexandro and Vanessa were much taken with her."

"How do they even know about her?"

145

"She was at the fellows' dinner, Tristram. Don't you remember? They say that she has all the right qualities to deal with Mrs Gonzalez. Sensitivity, and so on. And of course, she's a woman."

"Let me see that letter." Tristram Jones scan-read the flimsy sheets of typing.

"Her English isn't bad," Christian Tennenbaum said, when Tristram Jones handed the letter back to him, "but of course we'll still need Justine to do a proper job. You know, approach the old lady from our perspective."

"But what about me?"

"I fear, Tristram, that you are surplus to requirements." It sounded a bit brutal, but it was best not to beat about the bush.

"Well, that's just about the giddy bloody limit, after all I've done. I'm going anyway."

"Tristram, three of us would appear a trifle overbearing, don't you think? And I don't believe that I can persuade Anthony Grace to stump up for three people's expenses."

"Sod the Bursar. I'll pay my own expenses. I'm coming, Christian, and that's that."

There was no point in remonstrating. He should never have involved Tristram Jones in the first place. Why he didn't approach Justine Goodenough right from the start he just didn't know, but now he was stuck with both of them accompanying him to Mallorca. Keeping Justine Goodenough in order would be difficult enough, but now Tristram Jones was going to be a millstone around his neck.

"Damn and blast!" he said out loud, as he continued his way up Trumpington Street to nowhere in particular. "Damn and blast!"

"There's gratitude!" Tristram Jones muttered to himself, as he climbed the stairs to his tutorial on the influence of South American writers on the Spanish idiom. "Did he honestly think I'd let him get away with it? What a bastard."

TWENTY-ONE

Josefina's advice always came at a premium as far as Maria Jesus was concerned. She couldn't entirely trust Alexandro. He was, she knew, influenced by his wife – what husband is not, to a greater or lesser extent – and of course, married to that particular woman, there would always be financial issues. She lived and dressed extravagantly, and now it was only too clear that the contagion of extravagance had been caught by Vanessa. Josefina, on the other hand, held down a good job, which combined with her modest lifestyle, enabled her to live easily within her means. And she was single, free of a husband's influence. There could be no ulterior motive, no axe to grind, when she took it upon herself to advise her mother. Furthermore, she was a woman of the world, living in the great Catalan capital.

"I have been thinking over Genoveva's idea that you might use some of the money from England to buy an electric wheelchair to get you around."

They were eating boiled eggs for breakfast, in recognition of it being Easter day. The bells of the village church had been banging on and off since dawn.

"What does Genoveva know about it? I can get around fine without, Josefina."

They continued to eat in silence.

"Robert would have approved," Josefina said, when there was a break in the cacophony of the bells.

"How do you mean?"

"He loved life." Josefina leant across the table, patted her mother's hand, and winked at her. "He loved life, right until the end, as you of all people well know. And being a little more mobile would give you a bigger life."

Maria Jesus took time to think over what her daughter had said. As usual, she had to acknowledge she was right. Robert had been lucky; he was active into old age. But if he had become infirm, like her, he would have done something about it.

"And if it doesn't suit you, we can return it and get our money back." That, Josefina knew, would appeal to her mother's parsimonious peasant instincts.

"Maybe."

"It's worth a try, Mama. I'll get Alexandro on my mobile after breakfast and ask him to make some enquiries."

Three days later, Josefina drove into Deià with a top of the range electric wheelchair folded into the back of Alexandro's car. Her hired Seat 600 was too small for the delivery, so she had swapped cars with her brother outside the suppliers. It had taken some persuading to stop Alexandro from accompanying her back to Deià, but in the end he accepted that Josefina, and on her own, was best placed to overcome the last hurdle: introducing their mother to the wheelchair and finally convincing her of its benefits.

Josefina cleared the short path down to her mother's front door of her pots of herbs, and with her firmly sitting on the chair, explained the controls. Maria Jesus was won over the moment the chair lurched forward. She had never driven, and the power of controlling the small electric motor went straight to her head.

When she had been up and reversed down the path several times, Carmen appeared at her front door. "*Brava!*" she shouted, clapping her hands. "*Brava!*"

Later that evening, when the tourists had returned to their hotels, Josefina opened the front gate so that Maria Jesus could propel herself up the road towards the Graves' house. People came out of their cottages, smiling and waving. Some, Maria

Jesus realised, she had not seen from one year's end to the next. Her eyes were sparkling when Josefina helped her out of the chair at her front door.

"If the English want their money back, I'm afraid we're going to have to pay up for the chair," Josefina said to Alexandro when she returned his car that night.

"Perfect." Alexandro said. "Maybe now she'll be a little cooperative over that interview."

"And the photograph," Genoveva added, joining them on the pavement outside their apartment.

"Dates," Josefina said to her brother, as she unlocked her car. "We now need to sort out the dates."

*   *   *   *

"What time did you say you are leaving for the airport tomorrow?"

Josefina had delayed her return to Barcelona by a week, telephoning her deputy, and citing family affairs as the reason. Still, her mother seemed more reluctant than ever to see her go.

It was the third time that morning Maria Jesus had asked the question. It was as if she might be provided with a different response if she asked often enough. Hanging on to the hope of a later departure, so that she might have her daughter for a few hours longer.

"Three o'clock, Mama, as I've said."

"Three o'clock. And when are you back?"

"The twenty-sixth of June."

"The twenty-sixth of June. I'll put that on my calendar."

"It's there already, Mama. As well as the meeting with the English lady, Miss Goodenough." During the past few days, Josefina had skilfully woven the other contractual arrangements into her conversations with Maria Jesus.

"When's that again?"

"The twenty-eighth of June."

"Oh yes."

149

Fixing the meeting with Justine Goodenough had been a straightforward matter. Josefina had decided that it all needed to be dealt with before her return to Barcelona, to ensure that everything was in place when she left. Efficiency. That, she knew, was one of her strengths. The letter to the Cambridge college extolling the virtues of Justine Goodenough had been written on Good Friday and posted the following day. It was time for the follow up.

The contract written on the college's English Department notepaper gave several telephone numbers, including its professor's direct dial. A telephone call from Alexandro and Genoveva's apartment two days before Josefina's departure immediately made contact with an effusive Christian Tennenbaum.

"Miss Gonzalez, what a pleasure, what a pleasure! And how I am looking forward to meeting you in Mallorca! Looking forward so much!" he repeated, before arranging a return call from Justine Goodenough later that evening.

"You made an impression on my niece," Josefina said at the start of the conversation.

"I am sure that is an exaggeration." Justine Goodenough spoke with the clipped Spanish pronunciation of the far south. Odd, Josefina thought, for an English academic.

"I don't think so. Vanessa said that you rescued her from some embarrassment at a dinner in Cambridge."

"Poor girl, she was having a hard time. I just hope that I made her feel a little more at ease. Now I understand that I am to meet your mother."

Justine Goodenough could not stop herself from being a little brisk. The whole prospect of the excursion to Mallorca was depressing her. She looked forward to when it would be out of the way so that she would be able to get back to Granada, her researches, and her long-standing Andaluz friends.

"Yes, I believe that is the plan."

A schedule was soon worked out. Justine Goodenough was

leaving Cambridge in mid-June to complete some research in Granada. Josefina would arrive in Mallorca on the twenty-sixth of June, and Justine Goodenough would join her from Granada on the twenty-seventh. Professor Tennenbaum would be arriving on the twenty-ninth to ensure, as he put it, that everything was in order. By the beginning of July, Justine Goodenough would be back in her Granada apartment and it would all be behind her.

"All done," Genoveva exclaimed when the receiver was replaced. "Us women get things done quickly and without a fuss, don't we Josefina? Are you happy, Alexandro?"

Genoveva's admiration for her husband, to his astonishment and relief, had increased since the admission that the chocolate box might not contain the priceless pieces of work she had been led to believe. She had never liked clever-clever people who looked down on her, and if they were going to be cheated all well and good. She was glad that her daughter would not be going to one of their fancy universities, but instead would be studying a useful subject at the College of Design which one day would land her a proper job.

"We need to talk money," Alexandro suddenly exclaimed with a start. "While you, Josefina, are here. Now."

"Wait until we have eaten," Genoveva pleaded.

"No. Now. It is getting late."

Alexandro dialled Christian Tennenbaum's number and then conducted a long, tortuous conversation, Josefina standing beside him translating as best she could. Alexandro was pressing for the English to bring the agreed sum with them in cash. Christian Tennenbaum on the other end of the line explained that their finance man would not allow him to travel with such a large sum. Josefina knew what was in Alexandro's mind. He was worried that when they discovered the poverty of the material in the box, the English might not want to pay up.

The best Alexandro was able to do was to persuade Christian

Tennenbaum to authorise a transfer to his account the day the transaction was complete.

"So if they didn't like what they saw, you were going to mug them of their cash?" Josefina asked her brother sarcastically, when the call was over. "Or they wouldn't notice that the box was all but empty until they got back to England? Or maybe you thought..."

"Enough!" Genoveva shouted at her sister-in-law. "Please, give Alexandro some credit. He is the business man, not you. Remember that he runs half the tourist industry of this island."

"Just accept, Alexandro, that this whole affair might come to nothing," was Josefina's parting shot as she left the apartment for the last time before returning to Deià, and two days later, to Barcelona.

The morning of her departure, Josefina went to great pains to ensure that everything was settled in her mother's mind. Bags packed, over coffee and almond cakes she took down her mother's calendar from the wall and once again ran over the course of events with her.

"When I arrive on the twenty-sixth of June I will make sure that you are well prepared, ready to talk to this lady of your memories of Robert. I can help, if you like. Remember I saw something of him as well."

"What lady?"

"Justine Goodenough, Mama. The lady I have spoken about. The lady Vanessa says is kind and gentle. I have spoken to her on the telephone and Vanessa is right."

"You will be there?"

"I will not leave your side for a moment."

"And when she is done?"

"A day later a Professor Christian Tennenbaum will arrive from England for the formal hand over of Robert's poems, and the payment of the money."

"What was that name?"

"Professor Christian Tennenbaum."

"He sounds German, not English."

"Many people have German names but are not German. Even some Spaniards."

"I hope that you are right. Robert was wounded by the Germans. I am not giving his poems to a German."

"I am sure that he is English, Mama. Positive. And somewhere along the line, they will want to take a photograph of you."

"I am too old for photographs," Maria Jesus snorted.

"Well, maybe it could be of the whole family. Now I will write every few days as usual, but any problems, any doubts, you can talk to Alexandro and Genoveva, or to Vanessa, when they come up to visit. Or you can telephone me."

Contacting Josefina by telephone meant using Carmen's telephone next door, and as often as not leaving a message for Josefina to telephone her back. During the ensuing conversation Carmen would blatantly listen in to what Maria Jesus was saying. It was a line of communication to be avoided if at all possible.

One last time, Josefina showed Maria Jesus how to recharge the batteries of her electric chair using the plug next to her kitchen range.

"There is still an hour or two before you have to leave, Josefina," her mother suddenly said. "Drive me to Son Marroig."

It took less than ten minutes for Josefina to navigate the hairpin bends up to the rotunda built in the gardens of the medieval mansion sitting high above the village: a place she knew her grandparents used to take Maria Jesus for Sunday picnics when she was a child. She parked the car at a viewing point and found a bench overlooking the gorge below, and the sea beyond.

"I had almost forgotten," Maria Jesus said, looking out at the sea.

"Forgotten what, Mama?"

"The grandeur. And memory plays tricks. I have seen the rotunda a thousand times but it is smaller than I had remembered, and I thought that it was closer to the mansion, but it is not. But it isn't the reality that counts, but the memory. What remains in the mind – that becomes the new reality."

She was telling Josefina not to expect too much from the meeting with Justine Goodenough.

They sat on for almost an hour, talking about Maria Jesus' parents and her childhood walks with them into the mountains and woods surrounding Deià.

When it was time to go, Josefina, helping her mother to her feet, said, "Your recollections of Graves are only the half of it, Mama. People want to see a piece of surviving humanity, who was known, touched, loved maybe, by a man whose memory they revere. Do not worry – you have much to give the English. They will not feel that they will go away empty handed."

"And they will have the poems as well? Must I give them up?"

"What would happen to them if you don't? At least, whilst you are still with us, you will have the chance to see them go to a safe place where they will be valued."

She realised too late that she had spoken of her mother's death, albeit obliquely. "And you will have the rest of the money," she said quickly. The wheelchair had proved surprisingly successful, although she was aware that the novelty might soon wear off.

"I've been thinking," Maria Jesus said, pausing before climbing into the car. "I might have a makeover."

"A makeover?" Josefina could hardly believe what her mother had said.

"Yes. Get a new hairdo; have a massage; have my nails clipped in one of those new beauty salons in Palma, and maybe buy some new clothes."

"But Mama, I would have arranged all of that for you at any time. I just didn't think it was what you wanted."

"But don't you see? This is Robert's money, not yours. Money he would be spending on me. Treating me, just as he did in the old days."

It all might work out alright after all, Josefina said to herself as she was driving to the airport. At least as far as her mother was concerned. Whether or not it will be alright for the English would be an entirely different matter.

TWENTY-TWO

Christian Tennenbaum's long friendship with the Bursar was paying dividends.

There would need to be a carefully managed press conference to whet academic appetites, followed by decisions as to the displaying or archiving of the papers, depending on the quality of the work and, of course, the reaction of the public. Justine Goodenough no doubt would expect to be paid for her services, but sensitively handled, she would be an important component at the press conference. They might even need an event manager to ensure a successful, if not triumphant, presentation. It would all cost money. Not a great deal, but there should be no corner cutting. And that was where the Bursar came in.

Further down the line, he had it in mind to collaborate with a Graves expert, possibly a junior fellow at St John's College Oxford, to dovetail the papers into Graves' mainstream oeuvres. As long as he was in charge, of course. The English Department of the College of Katherine the Queen was going through a particularly lean patch, lecturers coming and going, so he would have to rely on a little outsourcing. But he would be generous to his Oxford competitors – as generous as Graves himself had been to his alma mater.

Three weeks before the deadline agreed with the Spanish, he was sounding out the Bursar for the funding required for the trip and the subsequent marketing campaign. Anthony Grace was being his usual, careful, Bursar-like self.

They were sitting in a pub in Grantchester, the Spread

Eagle, away from what Christian Tennenbaum called the college bubble.

"You've driven a coach and four through the college slush fund already. Six thousand euros gone, and twenty-seven thousand euros to go." The precise figures were etched onto the Bursar's memory. "For what?" He then answered his own question. "Not much so far. That Spanish kid not only beat you right up to the limit, but gave us a very peculiar exchange rate figure."

"I know, Anthony, but we had to go along with it or they would have taken the poems elsewhere."

"They had us over a barrel, you're saying."

"Pretty well, but we won't be sorry, I can assure you, Anthony." He leant forward confidentially. "Think of it. That poem we were allowed to see was written the year Graves died, when we thought he had lost the plot."

The Bursar looked at him vacantly.

"So what came before must be of even higher quality!"

Christian Tennenbaum took a swig of beer to give himself a little courage.

"Now Justine and I may have to do some entertaining in Mallorca, so we'll need to keep the pump primed."

"Justine? What's this to do with her?"

"Ridiculous as it may sound, she created quite an impression on the Spanish and they want her to conduct the interview with the old lady, not Tristram."

"So three of you are going to Mallorca?"

"Relax, Anthony. Tristram is going, but I've told him that it has to be at his own expense."

"I suppose I'm meant to be thankful for small mercies."

"And there may have to be a few more outlays when we return with the merchandise – publicity, marketing, tapping into the American market. I may even want Justine to co-edit a paper with me, and she'll have to be paid."

Anthony Grace looked across the table in despair. "Just try and keep these outlays, as you call them, to a minimum,

Christian. Please. And for God sake, make sure that the money is well spent."

The term crawled by. Usually Christian Tennenbaum was sorry when the academic year came to an end, never having very much to do in the long summer recess. Not that he hadn't tried to do something about it. When his parents had died he had used some of his inheritance to buy a cottage in a small Norfolk village. His retreat, he had called it, just an hour's drive from Cambridge.

At first he had enjoyed modernising the cottage, discussing his plans with builders, giving them instructions, meeting his new neighbours. But as time went by it had lost something of its appeal. The locals were a little in awe of him, a Cambridge professor, and the friends and colleagues who he thought would jump at spending a few days with him in the country were not as enthusiastic as he had expected. And then there were the women. He was disappointed to discover that the prospect of a long weekend alone with him in a remote corner of the Brecklands did not hold much attraction for the opposite sex.

But now, he knew, the cottage would come into its own. It was the ideal place to take the Gonzalez papers on his return to England. There, in its seclusion, his preliminary examination could take place away from the eyes and ears of Cambridge. Although, to his credit, Tristram Jones had honoured his request not to speak to others about the papers, and Justine Goodenough was completely unaware of their existence at all, the news would soon be out and it would be good to have a few days alone with them, away from the throng.

All was set in his mind. He just had to be patient for a few days more; mark the year-end papers, chat up the external examiners, see his third-year students through their vivas, present them for graduation, eat cream teas with their parents on the college lawns, and be off.

He had come round to Tristram Jones accompanying him to Mallorca. There was now an uneasy truce between the two of them. It was perhaps only fair that he should witness the denouement after all that he had done, not least preserving him from a moment of idiocy. An understandable lapse, Christian Tennenbaum now decided, as a result of becoming too closely associated in his mind with the object of his study. Role playing. That's what it was. But still, Tristram Jones had averted what could have been a highly embarrassing incident and he was, in retrospect, grateful to him for that.

*   *   *   *

When Justine Goodenough first took up her post at the college, she had made it clear that her priority would be her work on Lorca. She gave a specified number of lectures and tutorials on Spanish literature and diligently assisted with the year-end marking process, but then removed herself from Cambridge to Granada for the rest of the summer, ducking the round of graduation ceremonies and celebrations.

The renting of an apartment in the Realejo, the old Jewish quarter of Granada, had been a long standing arrangement with an elderly Spaniard, who was glad to leave the heat and noise of the city for a few weeks in the summer to join his son and wife working as caretakers of a block of flats in St John's Wood.

Justine Goodenough found it hard to forgive herself for capitulating under Christian Tennenbaum's pressure. The view from her Granada apartment window did not confer its usual enchantment with the trip to Mallorca hanging over her. The slow, luxurious adjustment to her selfish desires and whims – studying and researching to her order and no one else's, sleeping and taking her meals when and as she wanted, and picking up on friends of the same sexual orientation as herself – were all to be disrupted because in a moment of weakness she had agreed that ten days into her time in Granada she would fly to Mallorca. And for what? She wasn't even sure. Why was this particular old lady friend of Robert Graves so important? After all, he had only died thirty or so years ago, and there must be many old people still alive who knew him in Mallorca.

The one compensation would be to see Vanessa Gonzalez again. She was a little flattered that the beautiful girl at the fatuous fellows' dinner had remembered her, and been grateful for her friendship amongst all those drunken men.

As the sun set behind the Alhambra, she opened her luggage and started to fill the bedroom drawers and wardrobe with her clothes. Before she was overcome with tiredness there might just be time to visit her favourite tapas bar, where she knew she would receive a tumultuous welcome from the proprietor, Pepe.

And then her mobile rang. Before thinking what she was doing, she answered it.

Christian Tennenbaum's voice boomed loud and clear. "You've arrived, Justine."

Her heart sank. "Yes Christian, I've arrived."

"What's the weather like?"

"What do you think it's like, you oaf? This is the oven of Spain. It's bloody hot."

"Sorry. And you're all set for your sortie in ten days' time?"

"I'm not a child, Christian. I don't need reminding."

"And Josefina Gonzalez will meet you at Palma airport and take you to your hotel," he said assuringly.

"I know that, Christian. Please leave me alone now."

"And Tristram and I will be along to Mallorca on Wednesday."

"Tristram? He's coming as well?" she said in astonishment. "Why, for God's sake?"

"Well I suppose he's coming along for the ride, Justine, but it's your special skills we need. And then there are one or two jottings of Graves', some bits and pieces in the old lady's possession, which we shall have to pick up. I'll let you go now. Please don't hesitate to contact me if there are any problems."

"I won't, Christian. Goodnight." She pressed the off button, threw her mobile on her bed, and rammed her fists against her temples. "Why didn't I say no?" she cried out-loud. "Why didn't I just say no?"

PART FOUR

TWENTY-THREE

Justine Goodenough strode resolutely into Palma airport's Arrivals Hall, pulling her maroon suitcase behind her. It was just big enough to hold all she needed for a four-night stay in Mallorca, and small enough to travel with her as cabin baggage.

Seething with frustration at having to abandon her carefully crafted critique of Lorca's duende to fulfil her promise to Christian Tennenbaum, she was feeling nether sociable nor friendly. Scanning the faces of the noisy melee before her awaiting the arrival of friends and relations, her attention was attracted by a little wave from a fine-looking lady a year or two older than her.

"*Hola, bastante buena*," the woman said, a wide smile on her face. Justine Goodenough was taken aback. It was how she had described herself to Vanessa in Cambridge. Much of her anger and irritation drained from her.

"How did you know it was me?"

"An English lady professor on a Spanish internal flight would always be very obvious."

"You mean I look conspicuous?"

"No," Josefina added hastily, "you are just different."

"I'm afraid I'm not a professor, just a humble university lecturer."

"There is no such thing. At least in Spain."

"And neither in England." Justine Goodenough laughed, holding out her hand.

Josefina shook her hand in an awkward up-and-down

pumping motion. "I like your formality," she said. "In Spain people are getting a little too casual. And impolite. I have great problems in my school teaching the children some old-fashioned manners."

Justine Goodenough followed Josefina to her Seat in the car park. "But we must never fall into the trap of thinking that we and our times were better than young people's," Josefina said over her shoulder. "That's what my mother thinks, as you'll find out tomorrow, and it isn't helpful."

Josefina was easy going. The visit to Mallorca might not be such a burden after all.

"Now, I think it is best," Josefina said, as they turned onto the stretch of motorway leading to the Palma docks, "to tell you little about my mother before tomorrow's meeting so that you approach her with an open mind. What I will say, though, is that she is not an easy-going woman."

"Do you think that she might like me?"

"She will like that you are English and clever, that's for sure. After all, her Robert was English and clever. And you speak quaint Spanish. I think that she will like that too."

"Quaint Spanish?"

"Yes. You speak like an Andaluza. She will, I think, find that amusing. And I must say that I find it interesting. When I heard your voice on the telephone, I thought that I would be meeting a dark-haired girl with a pair of castanets."

"I've spent too much time in Granada, I suppose."

"Andalucía is a very interesting part of Spain. Sometimes I think that up in the north we have too low an opinion of the people down there. Find them too basic. Too primitive."

"There's something to be said for the primitive," Justine Goodenough said almost wistfully.

"A refreshing change from Cambridge?"

"Exactly. And Barcelona?"

"For people such as me, it has its pros and cons," Josefina replied after a time.

They remained in their own thoughts until Josefina pulled into the forecourt of the Can Cera hotel and helped Justine Goodenough into the foyer with her case.

"This is very grand," Justine Goodenough said, looking around.

"My brother is a big-wig in the local tourist board. He's pulled a few strings with the hotel manager and got a deal. Professor Tennenbaum said that you were to be provided with the very best during your time in Palma."

"Thoughtful of him," Justine Goodenough said guardedly.

Josefina collected the room key from reception and conducted Justine Goodenough to a palatial suite on the first floor, overlooking the Plaça Major.

"My brother took Professor Tennenbaum at his word." Josefina smiled as Justine Goodenough looked admiringly at the paintings and tapestries on the walls.

"I think this is an original Gaudí," Justine Goodenough said, staring at a framed, gaudy daubing.

"It might well be, though I think I could have done better. Now, if you would like, and if it would not be an imposition, I could join you for some dinner downstairs."

"That would be very nice indeed. Please give me twenty minutes to freshen up, and then I'd be delighted if we could have dinner together."

*   *   *   *

Josefina was waiting on a marble bench in the atrium.

"Come," she said as the lift doors opened, ushering Justine Goodenough along a high-ceilinged corridor and into the dining room. "Here. Will this table do?"

They sat opposite each other beneath an ornate crystal chandelier. Justine Goodenough suddenly felt exposed under Josefina's gaze. "I'm afraid I'm a little underdressed," she said. "I like to be casual when I'm in Granada. Go a little native even. I never imagined that Palma could be so sophisticated."

She was wearing a low-cut green polka dot dress, with rows of imitation pearls descending as far as her waist.

"No. You are very clever. The simplicity of your dress suits you perfectly. But look at me. I am wearing my suit for visiting the parents of difficult pupils. Power dressing."

"So you thought I might be a problem?"

"No, but for some reason I thought I needed to impress the lady from England." Josefina placed a hand on Justine Goodenough's bare arm. "But now we know each other a little, we can just be ourselves."

They gave their orders and then sat in silence, as if needing some time to adjust to each other's company.

"Vanessa tells me that you are translating the works of Lorca into English," Josefina said at last.

The dining room was all but deserted. The over attentive waiters had just swept away their soup plates and they were awaiting the main course.

"Yes indeed."

"Tell me of your love for him."

"I find almost everything about him attractive."

"Not just his poetry and plays, then?"

"No."

"What then?"

She was interested, not just making conversation. Justine Goodenough detected a sparkle in her hazel-green eyes.

"His contempt for the wealthy class into which he was born. His bravery. His opposition to the fascists which cost him his life. His fervour for music, for flamenco, for Andalucía, and his youth."

"His youth?"

"Yes. To be executed by barbarians for your ideals at the age of thirty-six should buy you respect and immortality."

"And his homosexuality?"

"That I admire above all else."

"You admire someone for their homosexuality?"

"I admire the fact that Lorca was not ashamed of his homosexuality. He didn't hide it at a time when it was dangerous to be a practising homosexual, and it was almost certainly the principal reason why he was executed."

They ate their main course of Mallorcan fish stew, Josefina's recommendation, Justine Goodenough from time to time complimenting the local cuisine. When they had finished, Josefina fixed her eyes on Justine Goodenough and said in an urgent voice, "How much do you think has changed in Spain?"

"How do you mean?"

"What prospect is there for a young homosexual in Spain?"

"The laws have changed. Times have changed."

"You cannot change people's hearts with laws. Spain is a big country – a conservative country. It is fine to be homosexual in Madrid or Barcelona, but maybe not in the Extremadura, or in rural Andalucía. We still have a long way to go."

"We?" Justine Goodenough said, her head tilted to one side.

"We, they, it is all the same," Josefina said. "But I think you know what I mean."

The conversation had become too intense, too personal for people who had only known one other for an hour or two. They smiled at each other a little awkwardly.

The waiters were lounging just within earshot. "I think they want to go home," Justine Goodenough said. "Shall we just have some coffee?"

Josefina signalled that they were finished and ordered a pot of filter coffee.

"And then there was Lorca's duende, his inspiration," Justine Goodenough said reflectively, pouring coffee into Josefina's cup and then into her own. "Not an easy word to translate into English. Not a muse – that was a female entity, entirely impossible in Lorca's case for obvious reasons – not even a person, more a spirit. He took the idea from the gypsies, whose duendes forced them to dance and play flamenco until they dropped."

"A little different to my mother. She was more flesh and blood than spirit."

"How do you mean?"

"Was she not a muse for Robert Graves? His last muse?"

"I hadn't realised. I thought they were just friends."

"I think they were more than just friends, Justine, despite their differences in age. She was his last inspiration."

"I haven't read much Graves, but if that is the case then presumably there are literary works written in her honour."

"Well there are, in a manner of speaking."

"That sounds very enigmatic. Can you explain?"

"He was very old at the time, Justine. But, nevertheless, he dedicated some pieces to my mother. No one else has ever seen them. It is why Professor Tennenbaum is so interested in having them. I thought you would know all of this."

So that was what all the excitement was about. Why Christian Tennenbaum could not have told her right from the start, she could not imagine. The first hint she had been given was when he had referred to some 'jottings' during the telephone conversation a few days before. She could only presume that it was all to do with professional jealousy. He had stumbled upon something special, unique, and he wanted to keep it all to himself until he decided the time was right to break the news with himself the centre of attention. But it was important that Josefina should not see that she had been given only part of the picture. The English must be seen as working as one at all costs. She owed that much to the college, and to the integrity of research. She shook her head vigorously from side to side, as if to clear it of cobwebs.

"Academic overload, I suppose," she said. A suitably innocuous remark which could be taken as meaning either that she had been told and forgotten, or that Christian Tennenbaum had forgotten to tell her.

"Did you meet Robert Graves when you were a child?" she

said, opening up a new avenue of conversation to conceal her anger at being kept in the dark by Christian Tennenbaum.

"Yes. Quite a few times."

"What was he like?"

"Special. Very special. Not just for his personality, his aura, but for what he did for my mother."

"In what way?"

"My mother was a hard-working widow who could see no further than the end of the week, when she would receive her pay from the hotel where she was no more than a chambermaid. Graves lifted her out of all that. Gave her a self-respect, a freedom beyond imagining. I can never thank him enough for that. But maybe it has all gone to her head a little. But you will make your own judgment tomorrow."

They pushed their chairs back from the table. "The waiters will put the dinner on the bill. All will be taken care of by my brother," Josefina said.

"Where are you staying?" Justine Goodenough asked.

"When I'm in Mallorca I usually stay with my mother, but with all the comings and goings of you English I'm staying in Palma. My brother's fixed me up with a nice room in a three star hotel round the corner."

Josefina accompanied Justine Goodenough to the lifts. "My mother is an early riser, and at her best in the mornings. Can I pick you up at, say, eight o'clock?"

"That would be perfect."

When the lift doors opened they gave each other a peck on the cheek, and a small wave as the doors closed.

TWENTY-FOUR

Josefina was enchanted by Justine Goodenough's gentle, patient handling of her mother. She entered her cottage with courteous deference, shook Maria Jesus' hand with a small curtsy, and stood until she was asked to sit down. An expression of delight on her face, she looked around the cluttered room, admiring the ornaments on the shelves and pictures on the walls.

"She smiles a lot. I think she is a happy woman," Maria Jesus said to her daughter, flipping a hand towards Justine Goodenough.

It was true. From the moment she had been met by Josefina at Palma airport, a happiness had descended upon her and increased by the hour. Even her annoyance with Christian Tennenbaum had soon evaporated, despite the discovery of his duplicity over dinner the night before. She had slept soundly in the coolness of her air-conditioned room in the Can Cera – a stark contrast to the noise and heat of the Granada Jewish quarter which, although exhilarating, could also be enervating. But here in the hills above Palma, the rudiments of the cottage, a combination of utility and beauty, seemed designed to provide contentment: a contentment which came from simplicity, hard work, and modest expectations. That, she was sure, was part of the attraction for Graves.

"Is this a photograph of Josefina?" she asked, pointing to a framed picture of a young woman in a gown, placed beside the television.

"Yes. She had just passed her teachers' exams. She is the clever one."

"Justine is clever as well," Josefina said. "She is translating the poems of Lorca into English."

"'At five in the afternoon,'" Maria Jesus quoted.

"So you know his poetry?" Justine Goodenough said, a little surprised.

"We all knew his poetry," Maria Jesus said, throwing back her head with pride. "Because, you see, it was banned."

"Banned, Mama?" Josefina cried.

"Yes. When I was a child, no one could speak of Lorca, the anti-fascist. Five in the afternoon. Nothing to do with the death of bullfighters, but all to do with the death of Spain at the hands of the fascists. Justine will know that."

Justine Goodenough nodded in confirmation.

Josefina hoped that the mention of Lorca and his poetry would seamlessly take the conversation on to Graves, but instead it wandered off, as if it had a mind of its own.

"I like your dress," Maria Jesus said. "Josefina, do you like Justine's dress?"

"Very much, Mama."

It was a floral-patterned, bright green shift, which Justine Goodenough would never have worn in England but which could be absorbed into the more colourful Spanish scene.

"You're not married?" Maria Jesus asked, scrutinising Justine Goodenough's fingers for a wedding ring.

"No, I am not."

"How old are you?"

"Forty-four."

"A year younger than my daughter. Time is passing you by. Maybe has passed you by."

Josefina shifted uneasily in her chair. "My mother's own marriage was sadly cut short."

"I'm sorry to hear that," Justine Goodenough said softly.

"I loved my husband after a fashion, but if our marriage had

170

not been cut short, as Josefina says, I would never have met my great love. Robert."

At last, Josefina thought, we have got round to him.

"And you see, he was never a marriage breaker. He would never have courted me if I was a married woman. He was a gentleman, and she was a lady."

"She?" Justine Goodenough asked softly.

"Señora Graves. Nothing would have been possible without her consent."

"So she knew?"

"She knew everything. Above all, she knew that without me, there would have been no last poetry."

"You must be very proud."

"I don't know what I am. It is difficult to be proud of something only you know about. But now the secret is out, thanks to my granddaughter, yes I suppose I am a little proud. Proud that something about me enticed, enraptured, the great man. I have been thinking much about it lately. My body, yes, it was still firm and beautiful at your age, as is Josefina's – as is yours for that matter – but I must have had something else. After all, there are any number of comely women of your age who would be only too pleased to be the muse, if not the mistress of a great and famous man: to share, to claim a little of his charisma, but I must have had something extra."

"Your simplicity, perhaps." It was not the most complimentary remark to make, but Justine Goodenough felt it to be the most accurate.

Maria Jesus thought hard. "You are very clever, Justine. Maybe you are right. I was a haven from all those intellectual people who came and went from his house all the time. I could give him silence at a time he was falling silent. And now, everyone is clamouring for my poems, the poems which Robert dedicated to me, just to me, and which a little time ago no one had seen."

Josefina could hardly believe that her mother had produced so much eloquence for a stranger. In the space of less than an hour this English lady had won Maria Jesus' confidence and respect, and broken the barriers she erected against those who would delve into matters she did not deem to be their business.

"The poems which you will now share with my colleagues in England," Justine Goodenough said, with an engaging smile. The jottings, as that secretive idiot Christian Tennenbaum called them, she thought, and which Josefina presumed she knew all about.

"Share? Sell, more like," Josefina said, with quiet significance.

The whole tawdry business of selling for a ridiculous sum a few scraps of paper to the men of Cambridge was weighing heavily on Josefina. It was going to go wrong. She had taken an instant liking to Justine Goodenough, which was growing apace. She did not want her to be deceived. It would relieve her mind if Justine Goodenough could look at the papers and give her professional opinion as to their worth. If necessary, the whole deal could be called off. Alexandro would throw a fit, but he would just have to accept the reality of the farrago into which he had led his mother and the family.

"Mama, show Justine your chocolate box. I know she is here just for an interview with you, but I'm sure she would also like to see the subject of all the excitement."

"Gladly," Maria Jesus said. "Why not? Justine, you are a lover of poetry, I can tell."

Josefina watched Justine Goodenough deferentially examine each piece of paper. It was clear at once that she was the professional, able to assess the true value of what her mother had hoarded for so long. It almost seemed to Josefina as if Justine Goodenough was wearing an invisible pair of the white gloves which are donned when ancient papers of great worth are examined. Even the pages with just a few strokes of a pen were carefully scrutinised. When her examination was complete, she replaced the sheets in the same order as she had found them and cleared her throat.

"What I see here are two poems, with accompanying

photocopies, which are complete, albeit short, works of artistic integrity."

"Those are the two which Alexandro copied and took to England, to show the men of Cambridge," Maria Jesus interrupted.

Justine Goodenough glanced at the faces of her audience – Maria Jesus' showing satisfaction, Josefina's anxiety – before continuing. She needed to be as tactful, yet honest, as it was possible to be. Searching carefully for her words, after a slight pause she said reflectively, "Otherwise the remainder is of value not so much to the fraternity of pure literature, but more to a wider circle of cognitive and medical researchers and scientists."

Maria Jesus was a little blinded by the technical nature of Justine Goodenough's assessment. "So they are important?" she exclaimed. "All of them important?"

"Most certainly they are. Most certainly."

"I cannot thank you enough," Josefina murmured. Justine Goodenough knew what she meant: I cannot thank you enough for not crushing my mother's fantasies.

"And these are to be delivered to Christian Tennenbaum in two days' time, I understand?" Justine Goodenough asked.

"Yes. This is all that he will receive," Josefina said emphatically, as if to forestall any assumption that there might be something else. "But he will also be supplied with a little personal detail of my mother, and something about the origins of the poetry, which you will provide – not forgetting a photograph, which can be taken on the day of the hand over when my mother will be in her Sunday best."

"Of course." Justine Goodenough smiled and nodded at Maria Jesus and Josefina as if everything was running totally according to plan.

Josefina jumped to her feet. "I will prepare a light lunch for us all."

She unhooked a pinafore from behind the door leading to the stairs and tied it behind her waist in a large bow. Gliding dexterously around the kitchen she had known all her life, she removed plates from cupboards and took down dishes from shelves, her hands moving with a knowledge and familiarity of their own.

Surreptitiously, Justine Goodenough watched her from the corner of her eyes as Maria Jesus told her how the village had changed since the Graves' house had been open to the public, with daily coach loads of tourists seeping into the back streets and peering into peoples' houses.

Josefina was wearing a sleeveless cotton blouse and as she reached to the top shelves, stretching the material across her breasts, Justine Goodenough noticed a shadow of hair downing her armpits. She probably hasn't shaved her armpits since she left Barcelona, Justine Goodenough decided. Josefina was home amongst people who would not concern themselves with the details of her grooming. For a reason she could not fathom, the thought pleased her.

At one point, Josefina opened the door to cut some chives growing in Maria Jesus' pots. A shaft of light flooded the room, silhouetting Josefina in the doorway when she returned with the chives in one hand, scissors in the other. It was a moment that gave a meaning and justification to Justine Goodenough's expedition to Mallorca which otherwise, she was beginning to believe, was a fruitless escapade.

"It is very simple," Josefina said, placing plates of cold meat and a tomato and cheese salad on the table.

"Wine!" Maria Jesus cried. "We must have wine!"

"You really have made an impression on Mama," Josefina said, opening a cupboard door and removing a bottle and three glasses. "But do not worry. This is our local wine. A glass or two should not have too great an effect, even at this time of day."

"To Robert," Justine Goodenough said, holding her glass aloft, when the wine had been poured.

"And to Lorca!" Maria Jesus replied. "I think," she continued, after sipping at her glass, "that I will give my poetry to this

174

professor at Son Marroig. I do not want him here, and I'm not going to Palma."

"That is a very good idea, Mama." Josefina turned to Justine Goodenough. "Son Marroig is a rotunda a kilometre or so out of the village. It is where my mother used to be taken for picnics by my grandparents many years ago. There is a beautiful view across the island. You can see for miles."

"I don't want a German in my home," Maria Jesus said, pursuing her own line of thinking.

"How do you mean?" Justine Goodenough asked.

"Tennenbaum. He must be German. They were cruel to Robert. Shot him. Broke his mother's heart. And they helped that upstart Franco to take our country from us."

"All in the long distant past, Mama. And anyway, he's not German, is he, Justine?"

"Absolutely not."

"We could take that photograph up at the rotunda," Josefina said.

"Maybe," Maria Jesus said, off-handedly.

It was time to go. Her mother was becoming a little difficult. It might be just the wine, but Josefina was anxious not to let things deteriorate, to descend from the friendly atmosphere created so skilfully by Justine Goodenough.

Josefina and Justine Goodenough cleared the table and washed up the plates in the sink.

"Alexandro is meeting Professor Tennenbaum at the airport tomorrow," Josefina said, as they prepared to leave, "and the whole business will be settled the following day, or the day after. Alexandro will keep you informed. Nothing for you to worry about, Mama."

Josefina kissed her mother, and Justine Goodenough shook her hand.

"Tell them," Maria Jesus said, as her parting shot, "that whatever the day, I will hand over the box at five in the afternoon precisely. At the rotunda."

TWENTY-FIVE

"You didn't make any notes," Josefina said to Justine Goodenough, as they drove out of Deià.

"It's not necessary. I can remember exactly what was said; I'll concoct a report which will make Tennenbaum happy, as and when. Seasoned with a little poetic license."

Josefina smiled connivingly. "Mustn't let the facts get in the way of a good story."

As they turned towards Palma, Josefina pointed up the mountain. "That is where my mother has decided the box will be handed over to Professor Tennenbaum. You can just see the rotunda."

"I like your mother, Josefina," Justine Goodenough said, craning her neck. "She's got style."

"Yes. But it takes someone such as you to bring it to the surface."

"Josefina," Justine Goodenough said, as they began the descent towards Palma, "how much is Tennenbaum paying for what he calls Robert Graves' jottings?"

"Thirty-three thousand euros."

"What did you say?"

"Thirty-three thousand euros. To include the interview you have just conducted, and a photograph."

"Thirty-three thousand euros?" Justine Goodenough repeated, staring blankly through the wind screen. "Doesn't he know then? What little there is?"

"No. It seems that Alexandro produced those two photocopies, and that was that."

"So on the strength of those two poems, Tennenbaum convinced himself that he had to have everything else supposedly written by Graves and given to your mother?" Justine Goodenough asked incredulously.

"Or else Alexandro persuaded him there was more of substance, in which case the money paid so far will have to be returned and not a penny more will be forthcoming."

"Unless your brother says that it's a done deal, and he wants the money anyway."

"In which case, I can see a lawsuit looming."

"It's disgusting, isn't it?" Josefina said after a few kilometres, breaking the ensuing silence. "We must do something about it. Stop the deal going ahead."

Justine Goodenough began to laugh.

"I don't think it's very funny, Justine."

"Oh, but it is. Tennenbaum is greedy for fame, and your brother is greedy for money. Let the best man win!"

"So we let matters take their course?"

"Why not? It's not our problem. They've brought it upon themselves."

Josefina smirked, and then she chuckled, a little at first, but by the time she drove her Seat into the Can Cera car park they both were rocking with laughter. "How stupid and venal men can be," she said, following Justine Goodenough into the hotel.

"Shall we have a cup of coffee in the lounge?" Justine Goodenough asked.

Josefina took Justine Goodenough's hand in hers, stroked it, and then raised it to her lips. "Coffee is a time waster, Justine. Please, let's not waste any more time, Justine. We should go straight to your room."

Slowly and luxuriously they undressed each other, caressing and kissing each part of their bodies as they were revealed before sinking into the great soft bed of the Can Cera honeymoon suite. Gently at first, and then more violently, they orgasmed over and over again until they had no energy left.

"At last," Josefina murmured, when they were spent. "At last I have found you."

"If it had not been me, who then would it have been?"

"It was always to be you."

"There are many women in the world."

"That is irrelevant. I have waited, Justine, just for you."

"So never before?"

"Nothing that mattered. Nothing that could be permanent. I have always feared my mother's disapproval. But today you broke the spell."

"Very Spanish. You took me home for your mother's approval."

"And you passed muster. I tried with men, to please her, but it could not work. I was going to wait for my mother to die."

"And now, you don't have to wait."

"No. I have waited too long," Josefina said, nuzzling Justine Goodenough's breasts, "and the wait is over, my primitive Andaluza."

Hours later, they woke as twilight descended and the street lights were lit.

"You smell of Spain," Justine Goodenough said dreamily, as they tightened their arms around each other.

"And what is the smell of Spain?"

"Garlic and heat."

"And you smell of England."

"And what is the smell of England?"

"Carbolic soap."

"*Viva la diferencia!*"

"What would that be in English?"

"It doesn't work in English. Only in Spanish or French – *vive la différence*. 'Long live differences' doesn't have the right ring about it."

"Graves would have approved," Justine Goodenough said after a moment or two.

Josefina sat up. "Graves would have approved? How do you know?"

"He liked women as women: not just for what they could do for men, or for how men saw them. It's there in his poetry, time and time again."

"So you know his poetry?"

"Every student of literature, at least of my generation, knows something of his poetry."

The telephone rang, loud and brash, shattering their universe.

Justine Goodenough picked up the receiver beside the bed. She turned to Josefina. "A Señor Gonzalez and his family are in reception," she said.

"Damn, damn, damn. I forgot. My brother said he would come round this evening with Genoveva and Vanessa to meet you. Check that everything went OK with our mother. I was meant to tell you. Say we'll be down in five minutes."

As they were dressing, Justine Goodenough sidled up behind Josefina, and slid her arms around her neck. "We must get rid of them. Tell them everything's fine. Just get rid of them."

"They'll want to have dinner with us."

Justine Goodenough pressed her forehead against the nape of Josefina's neck, and thought hard. "Tell them you are helping me with my report for Tennenbaum. We have to write it up while it is still fresh in our minds."

Josefina rubbed her cheeks against Justine Goodenough's inner arms. "My mother's right. You are clever."

They were standing close together under the hotel's atrium: Alexandro, his face full of anticipation, wearing his best suit; Genoveva overdressed in the clothes she wore for her rare visits to church, attempting to look sophisticated in honour of the English academic. Only Vanessa, in a simple skirt and T-shirt with 'Stop the bloody bullfighting' emblazoned across the front, looked relaxed. Her mother had gently tried to persuade her to dress up a little, but had been told in no uncertain terms that

Justine Goodenough had last seen her in all her finery and now she was to see the real Vanessa.

Vanessa introduced Justine Goodenough to her parents; she was her trophy, brought to Mallorca on her advice, and it was immediately evident that it had been a good decision.

"We did not have the pleasure of getting to know each other when you were in Cambridge," Justine Goodenough said when she took Alexandro's hand.

"I am afraid not. But now you have met all of us, including my mother."

"And what an enchanting lady she is."

"You got on well?" Alexandro could hardly conceal his surprise.

"They got on beautifully," Josefina said, her eyes shining. "Justine has worked wonders. But please, Alexandro, I know it will be disappointing but we want to persevere with our report for Professor Tennenbaum. Do you mind very much if we skip dinner? We can have some sandwiches sent up later and keep writing until we are satisfied."

"The work must come first, I suppose," Alexandro said, crestfallen. "I will see you tomorrow then. I am picking up the professor from the airport at eleven, together with the young Englishman, Tristram Jones."

"Yes, I understand that he is to join the party," Justine Goodenough said without enthusiasm.

"Apparently so. The professor told me as much when he emailed with his flight times. I have arranged rooms for them here in the Can Cera."

"We must get back to work while everything is still fresh," Josefina said, blowing a kiss at the trio standing before her. "Bye for now."

Genoveva was crushed. She had decked herself out for an evening in her favourite hotel restaurant, and now it was being taken away from her. And what was more, her sister-in-law was treating the lady from England almost as her private property, when it was Vanessa who had been clever enough to find her in the first place.

But there was something else. Josefina looked young. Radiant. Too much enjoying life. And smug; not intellectually smug, but smug as if she had just made an astounding discovery about life itself.

"There's something going on," Genoveva declared on the steps of the Can Cera.

"How do you mean?" Alexandro asked.

"There's something going on."

"Nothing's going on. They're concentrating on my mother's statement."

"Your mother's statement? Don't be ridiculous, Alexandro, she's got nothing to say that would need two bluestocking women to pore over half the night. And did you see Josefina's eyes? I've always been suspicious of her."

"Suspicious of what, Mama?" Vanessa asked.

"Suspicious that she likes women more than is decent, and now this English woman in particular."

"If my aunt has found love that is all to the good, isn't it?"

"So you think they're in love, do you, Vanessa?"

"I hope they are. She could never have chosen better than Justine Goodenough; she's lovely."

"It's unnatural."

"No, it's not. Love can never be unnatural. I do hope that you're right. What do you think, Papa?"

"Please leave me out of this," Alexandro pleaded. "I've got enough on my plate without having to worry whether or not my sister's a lesbian. And now it's beginning to rain. We better get a taxi home."

TWENTY-SIX

Josefina ushered Justine Goodenough into the bedroom, slammed the door behind them and burst into tears.

"What is it, darling?" Justine Goodenough asked, holding Josefina in her arms.

"She knows. That bloody sister-in-law of mine, she knows. She's like a bitch on permanent heat, always on the lookout. She's got sexual antennae."

"That doesn't make much biological sense, but I know what you mean. But does it matter?"

"I don't want us to be the subject of her gossip."

"But she would have known sooner or later."

"Yes, but I wanted to break the news to my family and my friends here in Mallorca, not her. I want people to know from me, from you, not from her warped mind."

"And your friends in Barcelona?"

"Barcelona is a liberal city, but I will have to decide how to deal with the teachers and parents at my school."

Josefina searched for a handkerchief in her bag and blew her nose. "This is for real, isn't it, Justine?" she asked tremulously.

Justine Goodenough took her in her arms again. "It is not just for real; it is the only reality."

"I can't go back to how it was before."

"You don't have to."

Josefina wrenched the Gaudi daubing off the wall, opened a window, checked there was no one below, and threw it as far as she could across the square.

"What did you do that for?" a shocked Justine Goodenough asked.

"I don't know, but it's made me feel better. Anyway, I hate his stuff. He's not only mucked up half of Barcelona, but he even had a go at our cathedral here in Mallorca. I don't know how he got away with it. And it's not just him, but the coachloads of people cruising around Barcelona staring at his rubbish in awe, people who wouldn't know a Gaudi from a Dali. People like Genoveva. It's raining by the way."

"Close the window and come here" Justine Goodenough said.

Obediently Josefina stood before Justine Goodenough. "And now take off your clothes, and get into bed," Justine Goodenough ordered.

It was after midnight when they rolled apart and stared at the ceiling, with the rain pummelling the window.

"How long will it last?" Justine Goodenough asked. "The rain, I mean."

"It will pass by morning," Josefina said. "It is one of our Mallorcan specials, soon blowing itself out."

"But now," Justine Goodenough said, "it is as if it is cocooning us. Protecting us."

"Yes. Protecting us from those who would condemn, or mock, or abuse."

"Or try to persuade us to be other than we are."

"The rain has come to keep us safe from the wagging tongues."

"Preserve us, God, from the proselyte's wordy hell," Justine Goodenough said in English.

"Say that again, but without the word 'God'. I am not fond of that word."

"Preserve us from the proselyte's wordy hell."

"That could be poetry, Justine. 'Preserve us from the proselyte's wordy hell,'" Josefina repeated, in heavily accentuated English. "In fact, it is poetry. Make of it a poem."

"Give me a moment or two."

Justine Goodenough wrapped a sheet around herself and made for the dressing table.

"Justine!" Josefina cried. "Do not hide yourself from me. You've been hidden from me for too long."

Justine Goodenough allowed the sheet to fall from her shoulders, sat at the dressing table and started to write with a hotel biro on a pad of crested hotel notepaper.

"I cannot bear to be apart from you," Josefina said, stealing across the room, and kneeling by the dressing table.

"You are a distraction." Justine Goodenough laughed. "How can I concentrate with you so close?"

"I will stay quiet as a mouse, querida, so you can write my poem."

At this, Josefina lay across Justine Goodenough's knees, her dark hair cascading to the floor, and hummed quietly to herself.

"That is not very mouse-like, darling," Justine Goodenough said. "What is it that you are singing?"

"It is a Catalan folk song my mother used to soothe me with, when I was a child."

"You're not a headmistress now, just a little girl," Justine Goodenough said, stroking Josefina's broad back with her left hand and writing with her right.

"You have been my inspiration, my muse," Justine Goodenough said a few minutes later. "It is finished."

"Read it to me," Josefina commanded, sitting up, and pressing herself against Justine Goodenough.

"Very well. I hope that it makes some sense for you, because it comes with all my love."

There was just enough light from the street for the writing and the reciting. Justine Goodenough tore the page off the pad, and after a final caress of Josefina's back, began to read.

"Your spinal column runs proud and pale
Like the mountains of the moon
Down to my hand, resting on your roundness.

And through your breast on my knee,
Your heart beats beats beats noiselessly.
Preserve us from the proselyte's wordy hell
(Feed on her too in silence with thanksgiving).
Let's pray the mists will clear for them as well,
To show the sculptured landscapes of the living."

Josefina took the page from Justine Goodenough's hands, and stared at the words. "It is so beautiful. Read it to me again."

Justine Goodenough did as she was asked.

"So beautiful, so beautiful," Josefina murmured.

"It is very short."

"That does not matter, querida. Better short and beautiful than long and intellectual. It is mine?"

"Of course it is," Justine Goodenough said, handing the page to Josefina.

"It is a love song," Josefina proclaimed, tears once more running down her cheeks, "for all those which have not been written, and for all those which could not have been written, but which you have now written."

"You are talking in riddles, Josefina."

"My mother's box. The empty pages. The page just headed 'Madonna'. Perhaps you have written what was in Graves' head, but which he could not express. These lines of yours would fit on any of those blank pages but, I hope you would agree, best on the page headed 'Madonna'. And after all, you and Graves are English, my mother and I are Spanish. It is more than just coincidence."

"Of course, Josefina, you are now my Madonna. But how do you mean, for those which could not be written?"

"Lorca, of course. Think of all the poetry, including love songs, which were killed with him when he was only thirty-six. This beautiful poem of yours, which you have dedicated to me, and of which I am not worthy, I want to fill a little of those gaps."

"Gaps?"

185

"The gaps in my mother's chocolate box, and the gaps in Lorca's love poetry. I can do nothing for Lorca, but I can do something for Graves and my mother."

"I'm lost," Justine Goodenough said, a little uneasily.

"My poem, which it now is, I will present to the world as Graves' last poem to my mother: the last poem he ever wrote. Indeed, it is a poem that transcends people and personality, a mighty paean to love. I know that I should not do this without your consent, so please say that you agree."

"But that would be dishonest."

"You are so English, querida. You and I, we have been compelled to live dishonestly for so long. This will be the last little dishonesty, which we will impose on a society which forced dishonesty upon us. Made us ashamed of ourselves. It will be a little revenge. The last dishonesty before we appear to people as we are."

"But how could it be done? Your brother has seen the contents of the box; your mother would never agree, and anyway, the box never leaves her cottage."

"I must find a way." Josefina paced between the bed and dressing table. "I will find a way. I want revenge. I want people to be duped one more time, just as I have had to dupe them about myself."

"It is not very Graves like," Justine Goodenough said, picking up the sheet and re-reading her poem.

"People will believe what they want to believe. Tell them it's from Graves, and they'll want to believe it's from Graves. You will be immortalised, and I will be immortalised as well."

"Fraudulently. Anonymously. Secretly."

"So what? It'll be fun. A joke which maybe only we can share, but which will bind us together. And what is more, it will make everyone happy."

"I just don't see how you can do it."

"I will find a way, querida. I must." She took Justine Goodenough's hands, and stared pleadingly into her eyes.

"And now," she said, "write a little more for me. A little more fraudulent Graves."

"Darling, tempestuous, mischievous Josefina, my Spanish muse, there is nothing which I can refuse you."

TWENTY-SEVEN

Josefina opened her eyes and stared blankly at Justine Goodenough coming out of the bathroom, a towel wrapped around her hair.

"Are you alright, darling?" Justine Goodenough asked, perching on the edge of the bed.

"For a moment I had forgotten where I was. I have been dreaming."

"What of?"

"I was young – about sixteen – and had just met you, and somehow all that had happened since had not happened. How long have you been up?"

"About an hour."

"You have been writing?"

"Yes. A little."

"Good." Josefina looked at her watch. "Seven o'clock. I must get back to my hotel. I'll wash and change there and be back at ten. Would that suit you?"

"Of course."

"And I must phone my brother. Tell him my mother's demands before he leaves for the airport to pick up your colleagues."

"What demands?"

"Don't you remember? The box to be handed over at the rotunda at five in the afternoon. I should have told him last night, but I just wanted to get rid of him."

"Which day at five in the afternoon?"

"Tomorrow, I suppose."

"Please, Josefina, arrange it for the day after. So that we can have one more day like this. Together."

"I will try. But anyway, I think that we will have to do a little ducking and diving, to keep clear of my family and their guests for the next day or so. For a start, my brother's bound to want to see us today. Gather us all together," Josefina said, pulling on her clothes.

"Bonding. That's what it's called. We're all engaged on the same project, united in one common endeavour. As long as Tennenbaum doesn't want a group hug. Make it this evening please, Josefina. Anyway, I have to write my report for Tennenbaum before we see him, and I will need your help."

Josefina circled her arms around Justine Goodenough. "I want to take you where I used to bathe in the sea as a child. Maybe you could write your report on the beach."

"I don't have a bathing costume."

"Then we shall have to go shopping. Until ten, querida," Josefina said as she kissed Justine Goodenough, and then for a moment rested her head on her shoulder. Gathering up her bag, she slipped out of the suite and strode out of the Can Cera to her hotel.

*   *   *   *

"As I thought, my brother wants a party," Josefina announced on her return to the Can Cera. "He's arranging something at his apartment for seven this evening. There will be the professor, and the other Cambridge teacher from the Spanish Department."

"Tristram Jones."

"Yes, that's right. Tristram Jones."

"I've no idea why Tristram is coming to Mallorca as well," Justine Goodenough said. It could have been worse though, she thought. He might have brought that pompous ass Gilbert Pym. She shuddered as she recalled him ogling Vanessa over his raised wine glass and shouting '*Arriba España*!'

"This Tristram Jones met Vanessa in Cambridge. Apparently they got on well," Josefina said.

"Yes. They were both at that infamous Cambridge dinner. They were the youngest in the room, by far. And did you tell your brother of your mother's requirements? For the handover at five in the afternoon?"

"Yes, but I think that the irony was lost on him. But some good news. My brother has agreed that the box will be handed over the day after tomorrow, so we will have a free day together."

Justine Goodenough waved her arms in the air in triumph, and then embraced Josefina. "Thank you, my darling."

"Now, let us forget these people for a few hours, and concentrate on ourselves," Josefina said. "First, how do you say? We must shop until we drop."

After a lengthy choosing of bikinis and towels in El Corte Inglés, Josefina drove them away from Palma eastwards along the coast.

"Where are we going?" Justine Goodenough asked.

"I told you. Where I learnt to swim as a child."

Seated at a bar on a small beach hemmed in by granite cliffs, Josefina ordered a plate of shellfish and rice, and two forks. She looked admiringly at Justine Goodenough.

"It's years since I have worn a bikini," Justine Goodenough said coyly, colouring a little, as she looked down at her body.

"Why querida? You are still young, and see how it suits you."

Why Justine Goodenough had allowed herself to drift into premature middle age, she could not fathom. Josefina had come along just in time.

"Why me?" Justine Goodenough asked, prodding at a crayfish.

It was a question waiting to be asked, a question Josefina had been thinking of asking for herself.

"When you spoke of Lorca that first evening," Josefina said, slowly, "I realised I had stumbled upon someone with such a great heart, such a compassion and love for things that mean so much to me, that I was no longer on my own. And you are strong. You have intellectual strength as well as moral strength. I don't believe that you have ever gone out of your way to hide what you are in the same way as I have. Unlike me, you are not a coward. And from companionship and admiration has come love."

Josefina sipped at her glass of white wine, allowing Justine Goodenough time to think through what she had just said before leaning forward. "And why me? Am I just a holiday romance?" she asked, a little timidly.

"No. You're not. It is hard to explain, but when I saw you preparing lunch in your mother's cottage yesterday, you seemed to be everything that is so fine and good about women which is so ignored, so taken for granted – at times by me, as well as by men. I envied what you are and wanted, if not to be a part of it, at least to be close to it. Not just for a day or two but for however long you can tolerate me."

Josefina laughed. "Domesticity! I had never thought of that as my main attraction."

They sat in silence, looking at the sea, considering what each had said.

"And now to work," Justine Goodenough announced at last, pushing the half-eaten plate of shellfish to one side. She removed a blue notebook from the briefcase at her feet, together with a range of pens which she spread on the table before them. "We must provide something to gladden Tennenbaum's heart."

Her long flowing script covered page after page until the notebook was all but filled. At first the barman had looked curiously at her, but Josefina had assured her in English that he would soon get bored and turn his attentions elsewhere.

"Querida," Josefina said, when Justine Goodenough had finished, flicking through the pages, "you are a novelist as well as a poet. My mother hardly merits more than a page or two, but you have written a small book."

"It will make Tennenbaum happy. But do not underestimate

191

your mother. Some small inventions, perhaps. Some elaborations. But all grounded in the person I think her to be."

"We must swim now, before it gets too late."

Josefina ran into the sea, and then cut through the water with a strong front crawl. "Come," she shouted. "Come and join me."

Justine Goodenough hesitantly stepped across the shingle and then, on reaching the sea, with a splash threw herself onto her back. Turning in the water, she slowly swam towards Josefina using her breast stroke. It seemed feeble compared to Josefina's scything crawl.

"You swim like a fish," Justine Goodenough panted, when she drew up to Josefina.

"At last. There is something I can do better than you. But then, my father taught me to swim almost as soon as I could walk."

She placed her arms around Justine Goodenough. "I like to think of you as a little frail sometimes. Someone who might need my strength, just occasionally."

They dried themselves on the beach and wriggled into their clothes.

"Josefina," Justine Goodenough said tentatively, as they walked towards the car, "in the cold light of day maybe those poems of mine, of yours, cannot magically get into your mother's possession and become love poems written for her by Graves."

"I hate the cold light of day, but however hard I think I cannot see how that is going to be possible. But the next best thing is that they are just for me. And I want to see the others you wrote last night while I was asleep."

"Of course, darling," Justine Goodenough said with relief, wrapping an arm around Josefina.

* * * *

Christian Tennenbaum was ill at ease. He had to rely on his smattering of Spanish and the few English words the Gonzalez were able to offer to make himself understood. It was Tristram Jones who was looking relaxed and in his element. That was inevitable, Christian Tennenbaum supposed, given his command of the language. But nonetheless, he felt well and truly shut out from what was being said.

Genoveva was being the perfect hostess, offering plates of tapas to the pair of them and from time to time topping up their glasses with rioja.

"How was your flight?" she had asked him twice now, in broken English, and twice he had assured her that it had gone well.

Genoveva relished these evenings: showing off her flat, buying in readymade refreshments, hostessing in her own expansive way. She had convinced herself that much of Alexandro's success in his career was down to her contribution as his wife, entertaining the people who counted in the Ministry of Tourism. And then, of course, if her guests were men a little flirting would not be out of order. She might be old enough to have a teenage daughter who turned a few heads in the Plaça Major, but she still retained a pulling power of her own, particularly with men of a certain age. This English professor, though, seemed impervious to her charms.

Try as he might to feel otherwise, it piqued Christian Tennenbaum to see Tristram Jones leaning against the wall by the window, glass in hand, engaged in heavy conversation with Vanessa about God knows what, whilst Alexandro was bobbing up and down, impatient for the arrival of his sister and Justine Goodenough to complete the party. "That idiot wants to seduce your daughter," he longed to tell him. But as he had learnt to his cost, there is much that is best left in your head.

But he could hardly complain. In addition to paying their fares, the Bursar had provided some pocket money, as he called it, for himself and Justine Goodenough. But true to his word, Tristram Jones was self-funding, footing his own bills, even refusing to allow Alexandro to put his room charge at the Can Cera on his Tourist Ministry account.

From time to time Alexandro peered out of the window to

see if his sister could be spotted entering the square with Justine Goodenough.

"Alexandro, my dear," an exasperated Genoveva finally said to her husband, "do please relax. Your sister will be here soon enough with Professor Goodenough, I am sure."

By the time the bell on the street had been rung by Josefina, and Alexandro had pressed the entrance button on the box in the hall to open the front door, the party was running out of steam. Genoveva's reserves of charm were all but exhausted, and conversation between Vanessa and Tristram Jones was drying up.

Josefina and Justine Goodenough bounced into the room. Justine Goodenough was only too conscious that they resembled naughty school girls, guilty of some prank. "I'm sorry if we're late," she said in Spanish.

"In Spain," Tristram Jones said, pecking her on the cheek, "everyone is late. Don't worry. Lovely to see that you've been able to drag yourself away from Lorca. And this must be Miss Gonzalez."

To Christian Tennenbaum's irritation, Tristram Jones, having introduced himself to Josefina, then took it upon himself to introduce Josefina to him, Christian Tennenbaum. And there was a distinct element of bathos in his being presented to her as the 'august and learned professor.'

"Your brother has told me that you and Justine have, by all accounts, had a successful interview with your mother," Christian Tennenbaum said.

Josefina nodded. "Yes. I think you will be pleased. Very pleased. Justine, show the professor what you have written."

Justine Goodenough produced her notebook from her briefcase and presented it to Christian Tennenbaum with a flourish. "It's the best I could do, in the circumstances."

"What circumstances?"

"The circumstances of you not telling me the full story,"

Justine Goodenough said rapidly, in the hope that the Spanish would not pick up on what she was saying.

"What full story?"

"The college buying the poems."

"You didn't tell her?" Tristram Jones cried in amazement.

"Please let us not have any differences here," Christian Tennenbaum said urgently. "We must not be seen to be divided. I apologise, Justine. It was stupid of me, but the Bursar has certain sensibilities about expenditure which I had to respect."

"But nonetheless, Professor, Justine has done a very good job," Josefina said, making it clear that she, at least, understood what had just passed between the squabbling English academics.

Christian Tennenbaum opened the notebook at random and began to read. "This is good, Justine. So good. More than I could ever have hoped for."

"It still needs some tweaking," Justine Goodenough said, taking the notebook from him. "Josefina has some input as well, which I want to include."

"Understood. But otherwise, I think that we are all set. Your report is all but complete, and Tristram has brought his camera." Turning to Alexandro, he repeated slowly and deliberately, "We are all set."

Alexandro nodded nervously.

"Five in the afternoon, day after tomorrow," Tristram Jones proclaimed. "That's when, according to Señor Gonzalez, we are all to gather together on a hill top for the last scene of the drama. So tomorrow is a free day. Vanessa has very kindly offered to take me on a railway excursion into the mountains, so my day's sorted."

"What was that, Vanessa?" Genoveva asked her daughter.

"Tristram was kind to me in England. Took me on a trip to a place whose name I have forgotten."

"Ely," Tristram Jones said.

"Yes. So I am returning the compliment. I am taking him to Sóller on the electric train."

"Oh, that's a wonderful trip," Alexandro exclaimed. "Our heritage railway line is one of our great tourist attractions. Perhaps we could all go," he suggested.

"No!" Vanessa snapped. "Just Tristram and myself."

"I will be putting tomorrow to good use. I need to revise parts of my report, with Josefina's help," Justine Goodenough said.

"Perhaps you could do that at our hotel," Christian Tennenbaum suggested. "Maybe the three of us could have lunch together. After all, you and I are staying under the same roof, and I understand that Miss Gonzalez is staying close by."

"No. Too much coming and going. Josefina is going to find a quiet spot where the two of us can work in peace."

Genoveva smiled graciously at Christian Tennenbaum. "Professor," she said, "please allow my husband and I to accompany you tomorrow."

He looked so forlorn, so alone, he not only needed but deserved some of her special attention. The young would be together, though God knows what her daughter saw in that Englishman, and the two lesbians were now joined at the hip.

"Thank you," Christian Tennenbaum said lamely. "That would be very kind."

TWENTY-EIGHT

Vanessa's motive for taking Tristram Jones for a ride on the vintage Sóller railway was, in reality, a far cry from that of reciprocal hospitality. She needed to put some sense into the only person who, in her judgment, would listen to her and do something to halt the unfolding crisis.

When she had haggled over her grandmother's chocolate box at the College of Katherine the Queen, it had all been a game. She and her friends were proud of their bargaining skills, honed in the boutiques and markets of Palma, and it had been fun to take on the clever men of Cambridge, beating them up to a ridiculous figure for a few scraps of paper. But she hadn't thought through the consequences. On the flight to England, her father had told her of his doubts about the value of the remaining pages in the box, but she had said they would cross that bridge if and when they came to it. And they had come to it now. In a few hours, the paucity of the merchandise would be revealed and the English would see themselves as cheated. There would be repercussions for certain, but she wasn't sure what or how. The only option was for the whole sordid business to be stopped before it was too late.

The problem was, who would be willing to take the bull by the horns? Time and again, she had run down the list to identify someone who would listen to her. To talk to her father was out of the question. Sensing an impending disaster, he would be quite incapable of doing anything about it. He would either go into denial or become mentally paralysed. He might even decide that matters would have to take their course, expecting a miracle to occur – the English would be delighted with the few snatches of writing, and everyone would be happy. But Vanessa knew that was not going to happen.

And then there was her mother. She was hardly worth considering. Cruising along in a world of her own, showing off her apartment, testing her charms on the professor; she would tell Vanessa that she was talking nonsense, and should not interfere anyway in what were her father's affairs.

Her aunt knew, and by now Justine Goodenough would know, but they were so wrapped up in themselves Vanessa doubted they cared. Besides, it would be a shame to distract them from their obsession with each other by regaling them with her anxieties. If there was anything good that had come out of the whole sorry mess, it was to see her aunt so happy, and with a woman of such kindness and decency.

To speak to the professor was out of the question. He was remote and introverted; she couldn't even think of approaching him.

The only person left was Tristram Jones.

*   *   *   *

Standing beside her on the narrow platform of Palma railway terminus, Vanessa examined Tristram Jones critically.

He was wearing a Panama hat with a broad blue band, a red and blue striped blazer, a paisley patterned cravat, and a pair of cavalry twill trousers. He brought to mind a character out of one of P.G. Wodehouse's novels, which had recently enjoyed a phase of popularity in Spain. How she had allowed him to snog her in Cambridge she could not now imagine.

When the train reversed to a halt, he was all but knocked over by the surge of tourists. It was all she could do to grasp him by the elbow and propel him into a double seat, facing the engine.

They sat opposite a young couple who Vanessa assumed were Russians. She was blond and willowy, whilst he wore a vest displaying his formidable biceps. It seemed that they sulked for Russia, speaking nothing to each other, just staring surlily out of the window. It suited Vanessa's book, not having to shout the words she needed to say to Tristram Jones over the cries of thrilled tourists.

"We have to stop them," Vanessa said almost as soon as the train had lurched and clanked out of the station. "Stop them before it's too late."

Tristram Jones looked at her uncomprehendingly.

"I'm partly to blame," Vanessa continued, fidgeting in her seat, and twisting her rail ticket in her hands. "I just didn't think."

"Think about what?"

"That you and the professor were being duped. There's nothing worth having in that box. Nothing worth having. It will be humiliating for my grandmother, and humiliating for my father. I cannot bear it any longer."

The train continued on its way, winding through the suburbs of Palma and into open countryside.

Quietly, she began to cry. Tristram Jones handed her a handkerchief from the top pocket of his blazer, and put an arm around her, as the Russians redirected their silent gaze from the window to the pair opposite them.

"It's not your problem, Vanessa, and it's certainly not mine."

"Why is it not your problem?" Vanessa asked, unwinding his arm from around her shoulders.

"Because when Justine was nominated the go-between in my place, I was told that I was surplus to requirements."

"Then why are you here?"

"As a self-funding observer."

"You mean you are paying for your room at the Can Cera out of your own pocket?"

"Sure. Once I was given the sack the college certainly was not going to pay, and I wouldn't allow your father to pay. So you see, Vanessa, it really isn't my problem."

"Then why is it not my problem? What has happened is

dishonest, and I did the bargaining. For what? For nothing. It's immoral."

"Who decides what is immoral? Not even two theologians could agree on that."

"Don't be pedantic, Tristram."

"It was a fair negotiation. If the college got a little carried away that really is down to our stupidity, and no one else is to blame."

"So you will not help me to stop the whole affair going ahead?"

"Of course not. I'm going to have some fun."

"What do you mean, 'fun?'" Vanessa said in outrage.

"Vanessa, you've forgotten. When we were at that pub in Ely you told me to have fun. Warned me against becoming stuffy. Well, I came here for some fun, and from what you've just said I think I will be having more fun than I could ever have expected. And you should too."

"What about my family's honour?" Vanessa cried indignantly. "We could be dragged through the courts."

"You are sounding very Spanish, Vanessa, talking about honour. We are not living in the sixteenth century. And as far as litigation is concerned, I can assure you that Christian would not want his own stupidity to be the subject of forensic examination or mockery. It's all rather comic, you must admit."

Tristram Jones patted Vanessa's hand patronisingly.

It all sounded so simple. The professor would be a little disappointed, but acknowledge his stupidity; her grandmother would be seen as a senile old woman, hoarding papers of no worth, and her father as a small time crook out to make a fast euro, aided and abetted by his streetwise daughter. But they would all see the funny side of things, come to some sort of compromise, and that would be the end of it.

The train was drawing into the first stop on the line, Bunyola. There was a stationary train on the other platform, going back to Palma. Nimbly, Vanessa jumped out of the carriage and ran across the platform to join the Palma train just before it pulled out of the station, leaving Tristram Jones to continue to Sóller with the Russians.

Vanessa stared bleakly out of the window as the train rocked through the vineyards. He was right. They could well be a public laughing stock, but she didn't like being laughed at. Yes, she had told Tristram Jones to have fun that lunchtime at that English pub, but not at her expense. If they were not seen as petty thieves, then the alternative was ridicule. People trying to sell something for nothing. She was not sure which alternative was more disagreeable.

As a final resort, there remained her grandmother. She was no fool. And she had a morality. A strange, old-fashioned morality, but still a morality of sorts. If she could overcome her delusions, be persuaded to see the futility and danger, if not dishonesty, of going ahead with tomorrow's handover, then she could simply say nothing doing and it would all grind to a halt. There would be some details to untangle, but with goodwill on all sides it was not impossible for it all to be done quickly and amicably.

She stood outside the railway terminus to allow herself to settle down. She looked at her watch. It was twelve forty-five. At one, Rafael would be leaving his morning lecture at Palma technical college when she would phone him. She needed him to chauffeur her up to Deià. At times it annoyed her how much he would do at her behest, like an obedient puppy, but today it was going to be put to good use. And most important of all, he knew nothing of what was going on.

"Park up here. By the cemetery. And wait, please, to take me home when I've finished speaking to my grandmother."

She had said little from the time he had dutifully picked her up at the railway station. Asking no questions, he just wanted to please the girl with whom he was besotted.

Maria Jesus was sitting in her usual place beside the fireplace when Vanessa lifted the latch. Looking up as she entered she showed no surprise, almost as if Vanessa's visit was expected.

"First your father, and then you, Vanessa. Two visits from my family in one day. I am truly honoured."

Vanessa was not sure whether she was being sarcastic or not.

"I thought my father was looking after Professor Tennenbaum today."

"No. Apparently this morning that was your mother's chore. Taking him around the cathedral. Your father is meeting them for lunch, and then they're taking the German to Valldemossa."

"That will be very..." Vanessa shrugged her shoulders, "nice, I suppose."

"Your father wanted to know if I would like to join them, but why would I want to go to Valldemossa? Even more tourists there than here, prodding at the memory of Chopin. What for? They want a bit of the greatness of great men, but that you can't have unless you have been part of great men's lives. Like me."

She pulled and stroked the hair at the back of her head before continuing. "I asked him to leave me alone now, until he picks me up tomorrow afternoon for the meeting at the rotunda. Leave me alone. Give me my last few hours with my poems. Just the two of us. Before they are surrendered to the German."

Twice now, she had called Christian Tennenbaum a German. It irked Vanessa. She was sure that nothing could be further from the truth. Nothing could be more English than the College of Katherine the Queen, and no one more English than its head of the English Department.

"He's not German, Grandma. I'm sure of it."

"With a name like Tennenbaum, he's German. You can be sure of it."

"I'll check."

Vanessa removed her iPhone from her bag. It was all a distraction from the purpose of her visit, but she needed to be right. Sure, it was a German sounding name, but maybe part of the family or tribe came to England so long ago it made no difference. Just as some Spanish names down south had

Moorish origins, but no one thought of the people as anything but Spanish.

She pressed the buttons on her keypad and stared at the information which appeared on the screen. Her face fell.

"Read it, Vanessa," Maria Jesus ordered.

"The name is a variant of Tannenbaum."

"And?"

"Old German."

Maria Jesus leant back in her chair with satisfaction.

"It doesn't matter, Grandma, what he is. What does matter is that we call this whole business off."

Whether or not Maria Jesus heard Vanessa's request to abort the proceedings, she was not going to let her assertion that Christian Tennenbaum's supposed nationality was of no importance pass unchallenged.

"Doesn't matter?" she cried. "Doesn't matter? That clever telephone of yours, dial in 'Guernica.'"

Vanessa did as she was told, and then began to read. "Guernica is a town in the mountainous Basque region of Vizcaya..."

"No!" Maria Jesus interrupted. "Dial in 'destruction of Guernica.'"

"We all know how it suffered, Grandma. Picasso has made sure of that."

"Picasso?" she blazed. "A raging bull and a light bulb? I want to know what it," she flicked a hand at Vanessa's iPhone, "says."

Vanessa could not refuse. She was always fascinated to discover what information her iPhone could provide. Her fingers seemed to have a will of their own as they tapped on the screen. "Here it is," she declared after a moment or two.

"Read," Maria Jesus snarled.

"At four forty in the afternoon of the twenty-sixth April 1937, Heinkel bombers of the German Condor Legion appeared over the mountains and started bombing the town of Guernica. By five in the afternoon it was ablaze. The Heinkels were followed by Junker 52s. Civilians who fled to the countryside were machine gunned from the air. Until a quarter to eight, wave after wave of aircraft dropped high explosives onto the defenceless town...." Vanessa looked up, tears streaming down her face. "I don't want to go on, Grandma. It's horrible."

"It is, isn't it! Read it again, right to the end."

"But why?" Vanessa screamed. "You hate the Germans, and this just feeds your hate. But it's history. It no longer counts. And anyway, you don't even like the Basque people, so why should you care? Why? Just to hate the Germans a little more? And you hate Picasso. He saw Guernica as a raging bull and a light bulb, so maybe that was how it was – certainly how it was for him. And if it wasn't for him and his picture, no one in the world would hardly know what happened. No one! For God's sake, Grandma, stop hating. We have become what you don't like, but it doesn't mean that you are better. Just try and love us, all of us, just a little bit. You were loved once by Graves, but you treat love as private property and keep it in a box. Love people in the here and now, not in the past."

Sobbing, Vanessa sank into the chair on the other side of the hearth and dropped her head on to her knees. "Even my aunt Josefina has found love," she said in a scarcely audible voice through her sobs.

A deathly silence fell between the two.

"What did you say?" Maria Jesus asked finally.

"Even my aunt has found love," Vanessa repeated boldly. "With the English professor, Justine Goodenough."

Maria Jesus narrowed her eyes. "That woman comes here to talk to me about Robert, but instead seduces my own daughter?"

"It doesn't matter about Graves, Granny," Vanessa said quietly. "All that matters is love, and Graves would be the first to see that. And he would be happy for them, to think that in a strange way it is he who has brought them together."

She had said too much, but she didn't care. And now there was no point in prolonging her visit, least of all in attempting to persuade her grandmother to call a halt to the fiasco which

Vanessa knew was going to end in disaster. Her grandmother's mind would now be on Josefina, Guernica, and God knows what else. She wiped her eyes, gathered up her bag, kissed Maria Jesus on her forehead and left the cottage.

"Where to?" Rafael asked, as she slammed the passenger door of his car. "Home?"

"Anywhere except home." She thought for a moment. "I want to go to the cinema first – they're showing a re-run of *Apocalypse Now*, and then this evening I want to go dancing."

"Not that old Spanish stuff you did on your eighteenth?" he said with a grin.

"No, Rafael. You're going to take me clubbing. Clubbing until late."

TWENTY-NINE

"I feel I'm being watched. Monitored. Tennenbaum wanted to know over breakfast where we were going to finish the report. He just can't seem to leave me alone."

"Don't worry, querida, my sister-in-law will keep him occupied today. And she certainly will keep clear of us, you can be sure."

Justine Goodenough and Josefina were standing in the lobby of Josefina's hotel, a short walk from the Can Cera. They had spent the night apart, anxious not to be caught out by the English. *In flagrante delicto* is what Christian Tennenbaum would have called any discovery of intimacy, Justine Goodenough had decided. The tag carried a veneer of learning, concealing a multitude of undiagnosed impropriety.

"But this evening he'll expect me to be available. For dinner. On-tap to translate, or relieve his boredom," Justine Goodenough said in despair.

Josefina thought for a moment.

"I too feel that I am being stalked. By my brother. There is nothing for it but to leave the island. Let us go to Menorca. Just for twenty-four hours."

"Is that possible?"

"Of course. If we hurry, we can catch the eleven o'clock ferry."

"Will we be back in time for the rendezvous at the rotunda tomorrow at five?"

"For sure, but we need to hurry."

With each mile that the ferry ploughed its way to Menorca,

Justine Goodenough felt an increasing sense of liberation. They leant over the stern of the vessel, watching Mallorca recede into the distance.

"It is strange to think that small rock in the ocean, getting smaller by the minute, holds all the people you love. It seems so tiny, and soon, it will slip beneath the horizon," Justine Goodenough said wistfully.

"And those people I love are going to have to love you as well."

"Will that be a problem for them?"

"No. I don't think so, except perhaps for my mother. Genoveva for a time will be a little judgemental, but Vanessa will sort that out. My brother won't care; we have a love – well, a love of sorts – for each other that can overcome most things. But my mother..." Josefina tilted her head. "She likes you: but will she still like you, love me, when she knows? I am not sure."

"It is difficult for the old to adapt."

"Particularly my mother. But what of your parents? Do they know, how shall I put it, the way you are?"

"Yes, they do. But since I've said, my mother hasn't spoken to me. Not for years."

"And your father?"

"He speaks to me regularly on the telephone, when my mother is out of the house, and sees me when he can."

"That is hard for you, querida."

"Harder for my father."

On the quay at Ciutadella, Josefina conducted a brisk conversation with a taxi driver in Mallorquín before she gestured to Justine Goodenough to throw her bag in the boot and get in the back of the car.

"Where are we going?"

"Wait and see. And this is all down to me. I am paying for this little excursion."

The taxi drove south from the town, weaving through vineyards until the road ran parallel with the coast. Passing through a fishing village, it took a sharp right onto a promontory

207

surrounded by the sea and drew up outside a *finca*, an old aristocratic house converted into a hotel.

"Surely we are not staying here?" Justine Goodenough asked. "It's far too grand. It reminds me of the Can Cera."

"No, but look," Josefina said, tapping on the window of the taxi and pointing. In the grounds of the house, close to the sea, stood an old cottage converted for tourists. "That cottage was once used by the lord of the manor to meet his mistresses. Our driver thinks it's free. I will check in the finca."

"It is stunning, Josefina. So beautiful. But how did you know about it?"

"The islands are small and there is little that the locals don't know. I've always wanted to come here, but never until now have I found the right person to accompany me."

Josefina ran into the finca and returned a few minutes later with the key to the cottage, holding it aloft. "Twenty-four hours of freedom," she said in English, and then, turning to the taxi driver, she paid what he asked and arranged for him to pick them up at ten the following morning.

"We must swim," Josefina said, as soon as they had unpacked their overnight bags. "You have brought your bikini, haven't you?"

"I wouldn't have dared to leave it behind."

"I have always lived by the sea, either in Mallorca or Barcelona. I could not bear for it to be otherwise."

"Neither Cambridge nor Granada are close to the sea, Josefina. You are going to have to compromise."

"For you, I am prepared to make some sacrifices."

After they had swum they lay silently on their towels, side by side, until Josefina said, "You are muttering, querida."

"Yes I am. A poem is coming. Wait."

Justine Goodenough hurried into the cottage and returned with her notebook and a pen. After writing, crossing out, and re-writing, she held the notebook at arm's length. "It's finished, I think," she said, examining her work critically.

"Read it to me, querida."

"It is short and simple."

"Like me. So it must be my poem."

"They are all your poems, Josefina," Justine Goodenough said earnestly. "As I said, you are my muse. Here goes:

'If you should ever wish to hear
An echo of my love,
Go down to the sea and standing there,
Listen to the waters as they move
Against the shore eternally,
The mirror and pledge of my love's constancy.'"

"It is lovely. So uncomplicated, but saying so much. Could Graves have written it?"

"Graves?" Justine Goodenough burst into laughter. "Graves? Not in a month of Sundays. It's far too commonplace. Graves could never write anything commonplace."

"It is not commonplace. You do not do yourself justice. And it is my poem, so I should know."

They booked an early dinner in the finca and returned to the cottage as the sun sank beneath the sea.

"How many poems have you written since you met me?" Josefina asked, as they were preparing for bed.

"Four or five, I suppose."

"Keep writing them, please. I want a book of poems all to myself. I am greedy for your poems."

   *   *   *   *

Dinner in the Can Cera was not the enjoyable experience which Genoveva had been anticipating two evenings previously. It had been a long dreary day entertaining the professor, and now she and Alexandro had to shoulder the burden of his company with only Tristram Jones as an addition to the party.

Vanessa had phoned her to say that she would not be home until late. It was a brief conversation, Vanessa assuring her mother that Tristram Jones had been thrilled with the trip on the old railway, but that she was now going to spend the evening with Rafael. And then there had come the bombshell. Josefina had left a brief message with the desk at the Can Cera to the effect that she and Justine Goodenough had decided to go to Menorca. There, the short note declared, they would be able to complete their report well away from the clamour of Palma. Distance would put what they had to say into some perspective, as the end result would demonstrate. They would be back in good time for the rendezvous at the rotunda.

"Menorca?" Christian Tennenbaum had said in astonishment when he was told why the dinner party was so depleted. "Menorca? But that's miles away!"

"Not really," Alexandro had said assuringly. "They probably took the mid-morning boat, and if they catch the same boat on its return tomorrow they should be up at the rotunda in good time."

It was totally out of character for his sister to act on impulse. Reluctantly, he had come to the same conclusion as his wife; Josefina had fallen in love, and was now making up for lost time, kicking over the traces, tearing away the prim, starchy, school ma'am persona and behaving a little more like the girl he had known as a child. But he could not afford to dwell on his sister's affairs. It was important to make sure that as far as he was able to dictate events, the financial aspects of the following day's transaction would run smoothly.

He waited until the meal was all but over, ignoring the urgent glances from his wife, drinking glass after glass of local Binissalem wine to pluck up courage.

"Forgive me for asking, Professor, but I take it that all necessary arrangements for the transfer of funds are in place?" he said at last.

"One telephone call to our Bursar. That is all that will be needed."

"As soon as the papers are in your hands, you will make the call?"

"Yes."

"Unequivocally?"

"Of course."

Tristram Jones, faithfully translating the exchange, could hardly suppress his glee. If what Vanessa had said was correct, Christian Tennenbaum had made himself a hostage to fortune. It would serve him right discarding his, Tristram Jones' services, and letting his, Christian Tennenbaum's, ambitions run riot. He exculpated himself from any guilt with the thought that the money was coming out of the college's slush fund. It could well afford to lose a few quid, and maybe it would learn not to be soft headed in future, particularly when dealing with real people in the real world such as Vanessa Gonzalez.

On the other hand, of course, despite what he had said to Vanessa on that ill-fated train trip, it could all turn out nasty – Alexandro wanting the money and Christian Tennenbaum refusing to pay up. In that case he would quietly melt away, leaving the debacle to be sorted out with the assistance of the other participants in the drama. And that included the two ladies of an indeterminate age now spending so much of their time together, Justine Goodenough and Josefina, or the bosom pals as he was beginning to think of them. They were a decent couple, and quite capable of knocking some sense into Christian Tennenbaum and Alexandro. Either way, his conscience was clear.

"Twenty-seven thousand euros," Genoveva said, between mouthfuls of torta della nonna. "And remember, it's not just the chocolate box that you will be getting, Professor, but also that all important interview which Justine is writing up now as we speak."

"Not forgetting the photograph," Tristram Jones added. "I've brought my father's old Zeiss camera, and I've plenty of film. I've been thinking; maybe a black and white shot of Señora

Gonzalez would be better than colour. A reminder of the good old days. And one or two shots with the background slightly out of focus, like something from the 1960s French cinema."

To be on the safe side, he would make sure that he got his photos in before the box was opened.

Alexandro and Genoveva nodded enthusiastically. Tristram Jones then translated what he had just said for the benefit of Christian Tennenbaum.

God, Christian Tennenbaum said to himself when Tristram Jones had finished, why I let him tag along, I just can't fathom.

THIRTY

Once again it had been Vanessa, little more than a child, who had dared to speak her mind to her grandmother, just as she had when Maria Jesus had been foolish enough to show her the box of Robert's poems.

Hours after Vanessa had left her to her solitude, when the dusk was enveloping her cottage, Maria Jesus needed something to bring her comfort. It would be the memory of the girl's eighteenth birthday, when she had danced the fandango as passionately as an Andaluza duende. Afterwards she had said to her son that maybe there was still hope: hope that all had not been lost of the old Spain. And maybe in the hands of the new generation of Vanessas there would be hope for the new Spain as well.

It was the generation of liars and concealers which she hated. When the nightmare had finally come to an end, there was a national conspiracy of pretence. "These things are painful," whined those who had benefitted from the system for all those years. "Put the past behind you, because otherwise it will only damage the unity which our country so desperately needs to prove that we are now a fit and proper democracy, ready to be accepted as an equal by all the civilized nations of Europe. Look! We are as civilized as Britain, as France, as Germany!"

But the past cannot be discarded that easily. Vanessa did not like what she read on her iPhone, but at least she could remonstrate and argue with her grandmother. Maria Jesus was intrigued by what she had said – if one man had seen Guernica as a light bulb and a raging bull, maybe that was what it was. At least talk about it, get it out of your system, even if your argument was patent nonsense.

And it was good that it was Vanessa who had told her about Josefina and the English woman. It was so more palatable, coming from Vanessa's lips, than being fudged and excused by Alexandro or Genoveva. Thinking about it afterwards, it was she, Maria Jesus, who had been complicit in ignoring all the indications of Josefina's sexual orientation. The truth had almost come as a relief, and if that was the way she was, Josefina could do no better than find happiness with such a gracious lady as Justine Goodenough.

All she asked for was honesty. Where there was hate and destruction, be honest about it. She hated the people, the regimes, which had brought the fascists to power. Spain had suffered from their evil for thirty years after Germany and Italy had been brought to justice for what they had done to their own countries as well as to swathes of Europe. But they had never been brought to book for using Spain as their plaything.

Her husband Manuel had been a buffoon, but he did not deserve what they had done to him, and no one had been held to account for what was done to him. There was much to be avenged.

She could not be a Robert, placidly telling her how he had been left for dead in the carnage of the trenches, his mother brutally notified of his death. And now she was expected to surrender the last poetic outpourings of that great man to a member of the nation which had brought down such misery upon Robert, his family, her family, and Spain.

*   *   *   *

After a disturbed and restless night, Alexandro awoke in a state of nervous tension. There was nothing that Genoveva could do but send him to the office in the hope that a few hours at his desk might get his mind temporarily off the clinching of the deal with the English that afternoon. She then decided to take it upon herself to conduct Christian Tennenbaum and Tristram Jones to the world-renowned Palma Museum. They were after all, academics, and therefore could never be exposed to enough culture.

Vanessa had come home late, emerging bleary eyed from her bedroom just as Genoveva was leaving to collect the English from the Can Cera. Normally she would have given her daughter a piece of her mind, but today of all days it was vital for the family to remain calm and harmonious.

"You had a good evening?"

Vanessa made a hint of a nod.

"It was a very long one."

Vanessa turned her eyes to the ceiling.

"Your father wants us all to be at the rotunda at five. To give your grandmother our support. He is picking us up at four, and then with the English he is driving us up to the rotunda. He will leave us there for a few minutes while he collects Granny."

"Will my aunt be there?"

"Yes. With Goodenough. They will be getting back from Menorca just in time."

Vanessa raised an eyebrow. "Menorca?"

"Yes. Menorca," Genoveva said in a crisp, emphatic tone of voice that made it clear there was to be no discussion as to why Josefina and Justine Goodenough had made their way with no warning across eighty kilometres of sea to Menorca.

"So there will be seven of us to witness the catastrophe."

"Try not to be so negative, Vanessa, if only for your father's sake."

Vanessa stared at the door of the apartment long after her mother had slammed it on making her exit. Her mind was blank. Totally blank. There was nothing more to be done, nothing more to say but to wait for the hours to tick by until five in the afternoon.

The mansion of Son Marroig, set high in the mountains above Deià, was rescued from ruin by Archduke Ludwig Salvator, an Austrian aristocrat who came to Mallorca in the nineteenth century, fell in love with the island, married a local girl, and remained for the rest of his life. It was now open to the public, last admission tickets being sold at three-thirty. Within the gardens and overlooking the sea, Salvator built a white marble rotunda: a focus point for walkers, picnickers, and lovers.

By late afternoon, the last buses of foreign tourists were juddering away from the house and grounds, and down to the coastal hotels for their human cargo to prepare themselves for evening dips in the sea, sundowners, and dinner.

In the opposite direction Alexandro was at the wheel of his car, driving up the winding road to Son Marroig, his wife beside him, and in the back, Christian Tennenbaum and Vanessa, with Tristram Jones, his camera on his knee, wedged between them.

It seemed that it was only Tristram Jones who had any appetite for conversation.

"This reminds me," he said, looking through the windscreen, "of a scene from the film of Graves' masterpiece, *I Claudius*. Do you remember how that Roman emperor built his villa high on a mountain top in Capri, overlooking the sea?"

His remark was met with silence.

Unperturbed, he pressed on. "What was the name of that actor with the brilliant stammer?"

"I remember now," he said, two hairpin bends later, "Derek Jacobi. That's who it was." He only fell silent when the car navigated the final gradient towards the summit, when he felt a little travel sick.

Alexandro brought the car to a standstill behind Josefina's white Seat, parked opposite the rotunda. They all spilled out to join Josefina and Justine Goodenough staring over the edge of the mountain, talking animatedly as Josefina pointed out villages along the coast from Sóller.

"How long have you been here?" Tristram Jones asked Justine Goodenough.

"About five minutes. The boat bringing us back from Menorca docked bang on time."

There was no need to ask if the excursion to Menorca had been a success. The two women exuded joy and suntanned health. Vanessa felt a surge of pride. I'm responsible for that, she said to herself. Me. I brought them together.

"Stay here please, all of you" Alexandro ordered, in a state of agitation, "whilst I collect my mother."

To his relief, when he hesitantly opened the door of his mother's cottage, he found Maria Jesus sitting beside her hearth dressed in the twin set she had last worn for Vanessa's eighteenth birthday party, and holding on her knees the all-important chocolate box.

"I shall need my chair, Alexandro," she said, nodding towards her electric wheelchair, its batteries recharging on the plug by the range. "Disconnect it and put it in the car, please."

Alexandro disconnected the charge lead and dismantled the chair. He carefully stowed the pieces in the boot of his car, and then helped his mother into the passenger seat. On the short journey to the rotunda she stared fixedly through the windscreen, the chocolate box held firmly in her grasp.

"Stop here!" she demanded, as soon as they drew within a few yards of the group of people waiting for her with welcoming smiles and, in Genoveva's case, a little wave and a blown kiss.

"Tell them to stay where they are, and put my chair together again."

Alexandro did as he was told. When the chair was re-assembled, he helped Maria Jesus onto the seat with the chocolate box firmly in her hands. Tristram Jones looked through his camera lens and adjusted the focus.

"Tennenbaum, I suppose," she said to Alexandro, as they moved towards the welcoming group standing in a line, "is that large man in the middle."

"Yes, indeed, Mama. That is indeed the professor."

With a blood curdling cry of "*No Pasarán!*", Maria Jesus accelerated her chair at full throttle straight at Christian Tennenbaum, knocking him off his feet. The impact spun her chair around before it began to move away from the rotunda and down the gradient, slowly at first, but then picking up speed as it went.

It was a moment or two before anyone could absorb what had happened. Genoveva stood rooted to the spot, while Justine Goodenough and Josefina helped Christian Tennenbaum to his feet.

"Are you all right, Professor?" Josefina asked solicitously, brushing dust and gravel off the back of Christian Tennenbaum's suit.

"Never mind him, we must catch her," Alexandro cried, as his mother bumped down the road, the chocolate box still in her grasp.

They all gave chase to the receding figure of Maria Jesus, sitting upright in her chair, Tristram Jones and Vanessa in the lead followed by Alexandro; some way behind came Josefina and Justine Goodenough, with the rear taken up by Christian Tennenbaum, limping slightly, and Genoveva doing her best in her high heels.

"I think she must have taken it out of gear," Tristram Jones shouted, his camera bouncing against his chest.

"Just catch her, Tristram," Vanessa panted, sprinting beside him.

At the first hairpin bend the chair struck the parapet, went through a one-hundred and eighty degree turn, and then careered on.

Tristram Jones glanced over his shoulder: the remaining pursuers were falling behind. Alexandro was holding his side, reduced to little more than a walking pace, whilst the others had still not made it to the first bend. Somehow, Maria Jesus just managed to negotiate the next bend.

As Maria Jesus approached the third bend, Tristram Jones made a supreme spurt, drew level, and made a grab at her arm, just before she hit the parapet. The force of the impact against the curved steel propelled her out of the chair, over the edge and into the abyss, leaving him holding the box.

"Give it to me!" Vanessa screamed, as she caught up with him a moment later.

Tristram Jones held onto the box. "It's safe," was all he could manage to say.

"You stupid, stupid man!" Vanessa shrieked, tearing the box from his hands and flinging it into the gorge below. Immediately, she threw herself onto the tarmac, beat her hands on the ground and howled, "My grandmother is dead! My grandmother is dead!"

There was no need for any explanations. As each of Alexandro, Josefina, Justine Goodenough, Christian Tennenbaum and finally Genoveva arrived on the scene, the empty chair and Vanessa's hysterics told the full story. In turn, they looked over the parapet in a state of shock at the prone figure of Maria Jesus spread-eagled on a rock thirty yards below them.

Josefina and Genoveva tenderly lifted up Vanessa and enveloped her in their arms, tears falling down their cheeks. Alexandro continued to stare blankly over the side of the road at his mother's body until Justine Goodenough gently led him away from the edge.

Christian Tennenbaum limped up to Tristram Jones. "And the poems gone as well, I suppose."

It was not an appropriate remark, which he immediately regretted, but he felt the need to say something.

Tristram Jones nodded. "Afraid so. There's one now, if I'm not mistaken." He pointed at a piece of paper being taken by the wind towards the sea.

PART FIVE

THIRTY-ONE

In the immediate aftermath of the disaster Alexandro had taken the initiative, instructing his sister to ferry the English and his wife and daughter back to Palma, telephoning the fire brigade, and then waiting on the mountain until later that evening two men scaled down the face of the precipice on ropes to put Maria Jesus in a body bag and raise her up to the road.

But after he had identified his mother in the morgue, he could do no more. He was overcome with guilt, he confided in Genoveva that evening. Guilty for starting up the whole business of the marketing of the poems in the first place. She rose to the occasion, taking him under her wifely wing, providing the support and the words he needed to hear. She assured him that he should feel no self-recriminations, acting in the interests of the family and the wider interests of art. She forbad him to take any further part in the formalities, informing Josefina that from then on she should take responsibility for all necessary arrangements.

Josefina was relieved to be in control. Her brother was quite capable of making a hash of things, as she put it to Justine Goodenough.

"At times like this, one must be bold. Confront destiny, death, even your own mistakes. Look them all in the face unflinchingly. I love my brother, he has many qualities, but he is not bold. Not as my mother was.

They were walking along the front at Sóller, arm in arm. It was three days after the disaster. Three tumultuous days of

222

police enquiry, statements made to the coroner, the newspapers, and explanations to friends and neighbours. There seemed no reason to say precisely why the Gonzalez and some English friends had been at the rotunda in the first place. It had all been a simple outing to a local beauty spot which had ended in tragedy, when the matriarch of the family had lost control of her electric wheelchair and, despite everyone's best efforts to save her, had catapulted over the side.

"My mother was bold," Josefina continued. "Did I tell you how she used to go into the police stations to bring my father home when he was in trouble with the Guardia Civil? In the days when no one wanted to go into those places? And then, the whole Graves affair. It was bold, in a small village, to allow him to visit. He was a foreigner, an artist. Conventions meant nothing to him, he would always be excused: but it was not so for my mother. She could have been ostracised, or worse. But she took the risk, and it paid off."

"How did it pay off?"

"She had a rich life."

"But a horrible death, Josefina."

"A horrible death, yes, but a defiant death. She never wanted to hand over those poems."

"Particularly to someone she had decided was German," Justine Goodenough said tentatively.

By unspoken mutual agreement, so far they had kept clear of raising between them the matter of Maria Jesus' deliberate act of violence against Christian Tennenbaum.

"Who knows what goes through the minds of people who have seen and lived through terrible times?" Josefina said resignedly. Her mother was to be forgiven – must be forgiven. It was too late for rebuke or accusation.

Justine Goodenough paused to watch the sun sinking into the sea. "Her death was too early. She was too young. There were more sunsets she should have seen."

"Yes, I agree. She wasn't even eighty. But in a way, she had completed her life's work."

"How do you mean?"

"Inspiring great art from a great creative genius."

"Josefina, I think that you are losing touch with reality. There was little left in Robert Graves to inspire, as you know."

Josefina had been waiting for the right moment to say what was burning in her mind, and time was ticking by. It would have to be now. She could wait no longer. Christian Tennenbaum and Tristram Jones had, out of respect for Maria Jesus, elected to stay on until the funeral, but then they would be going home.

"But we can do something about that," Josefina said softly, but urgently. "But, like my mother, we must be bold. And also I want to salvage good from something bad. Maybe even fulfil that contract for the men of Cambridge."

It was crystal clear where Josefina was leading. It was important to nip her plotting in the bud right away.

"Nothing need or should be done, Josefina. To all intents and purposes, the contract is null and void. What do they call it? 'Act of God.' Tennenbaum, Tristram, and the college will never know that the box was all but empty. The lawyers will have to do some unravelling, but the whole escapade is over. And above all, the family's honour, your mother's honour, even Graves' honour, are all intact. If there's anything good, as you say, to be salvaged from something so horrible, it's that."

"A little deception could make everyone happy, querida, especially myself." She gave Justine Goodenough's arm a squeeze.

"Josefina, you have given your professional life to teaching: imparting to the children in your care standards and values to make them honest and decent citizens. What I believe you are suggesting is intellectually dishonest. The disaster which has afflicted your mother has relieved us all, especially your family, of an impending embarrassment, to say the least. We should not now be planning to put ourselves in further difficulties."

"What you say is right, but the values I have instilled in my children have always been at my expense."

"How do you mean?"

"I have had to praise and support all those standards which by implication condemn me. I have had to pose as a dedicated teacher serving a narrow and prejudiced society. But you have changed all that. I have found someone who sees and loves me for myself. To put in the public domain your love poems to me, for everyone to see and marvel, will be my revenge. A gentle, harmless revenge, which will give me so much happiness."

"But if you remember, we made our final decision on that beach where your father taught you to swim. In the cold light of day."

Josefina ignored the remark and snuggled closer to Justine Goodenough. "And only we will know, querida. Just us two, and no one else."

"No one will know?" Justine Goodenough cried. "I have told you before, these are not the outpourings of a towering genius but simple expressions of my love for you."

"But that towering genius was losing his mind. You just said that."

"That is hardly a compliment to my own poetic endeavours."

"In Spain, we say that everyone who is in love is a little mad."

"You are being devious and disingenuous, Josefina."

They lowered themselves onto a bench facing the sea. Justine Goodenough looked across the bay at a yacht spangled with garish white lights as the evening drew in. Had they, the people on board, lived the life of probity and restraint which she had followed? Probity and restraint, which so easily could lead to a desiccated self-denial and an empty old age. She had met Josefina just in time and for once, at her urging, was going to do something wild and out of character.

"Just one, Josefina. Just one," she relented.

"To whet their appetites!" Josefina said excitedly.

"To whet their appetites for more, which they will not get."

"It is a compromise," Josefina sighed. "Just one. But how to choose?" She opened her handbag and withdrew a sheaf of papers. "Mine, all mine," she said, rifling through them. "But which?"

"That is for you to decide, Josefina."

"No, we must decide together. I very much like this one, the one you wrote as I awoke in Menorca." She pulled a page out from the others. "Read it to me, querida."

Balancing the poem on her knees, and bending low, the last glimmering of the setting sun provided just enough light for Justine Goodenough to read the words.

"*She softly wakes and spreads her arms*
Outside the sunlit counterpane,
And all her sweet and mystic charms
Now re-possess her glad domain.
Duty and truth I now reject –
I'm freed at last from Adam's curse;
She devastates my intellect
And circumscribes my universe!"

"That is so beautiful. Let it be that one."

"I don't think so. It's a far cry from Graves, and besides, I'm not sure that he ever saw your mother in bed."

"We shall never know," Josefina giggled. "But to be on the safe side, let's have the first. The very first you wrote for me."

Justine Goodenough nodded. "Yes. I think that would be the best. Now, how are you going to accomplish the impossible? Are you going to say that the poem was discovered at the bottom of the chasm, stuck to a holly bush?" Justine Goodenough clamped her hand against her mouth. "Oh, Josefina, that was so insensitive. Please forgive me. I got a little carried away."

"Do not worry. But I have a better idea than your holly bush. Just wait."

"Tell me your idea."

"No, querida. You must be patient. And now, I think, it is time to take you back to Palma."

They had not spent a night together since Maria Jesus had died. Josefina was now staying in her mother's cottage, tidying and clearing the remnants of almost eighty years of life, sifting through old photographs and papers whilst Justine Goodenough spent much of her day with Christian Tennenbaum and Tristram Jones. It seemed that one meal ran into another; after a long breakfast, either Christian Tennenbaum or Tristram Jones would suggest a mid-morning drink in a tapas bar, and then it was time for lunch. Justine Goodenough had to wait until the afternoon before Josefina's Seat appeared at the front door of the Can Cera to take her off to the mountains or to the beach.

"What time will you pick me up tomorrow?" Justine Goodenough asked, as they dawdled their way to the car.

"Two-thirty. I have to see the priest at twelve, to put the finishing touches to the funeral arrangements, but then I shall be free."

They drove in silence over the mountain, close to the rotunda and past Deià, the memory of the calamity of three days before bearing down upon them.

"You think maybe, that I am not sad, or that I should be more sad," Josefina said, negotiating the bends below the village. "But my mother was not sentimental. She hated anything like that. So you see, mourning my mother is not so difficult, at least for me. And believe it or not, curiously I am finding enjoyment in clearing away her life, organising her funeral. It is like a release.

"I cannot wait for Sitges," Josefina concluded, as they moved through the traffic lights on the outskirts of Palma.

They had planned to spend a week together in the resort a few miles south of Barcelona after the funeral. Josefina had made the arrangements. "Sitges is a place," she had said, "where anything goes. A place where no one will stare at us for holding hands or kissing in broad daylight. For a long time it has been an oasis in Spain. Like your Brighton, I think."

Justine Goodenough put her hand on Josefina's, working the gear stick. "We just have to be patient for a little longer, and then we both shall be free."

As they drew up outside the Can Cera, Justine Goodenough saw Christian Tennenbaum and Tristram Jones behind the hotel's plate glass window drinking coffee in the lounge, bulbous glasses of brandy before them.

"I know it is hard for you, querida, to spend the rest of your evening with them, but please remember that it is polite of them to stay for my mother's funeral. I know that my brother appreciates the gesture, and anyway, I want them to witness my little surprise with that poem."

Justine Goodenough felt a pang of regret that she had capitulated over the matter of the poem. She wanted to ask Josefina not to do anything crazy with it, but it was too late for that now. There was a wild, unpredictable, Latin streak in Josefina which made her so alluring, demonstrated when she had thrown the picture out of the bedroom window or suggested on impulse that they go to Menorca. She wasn't sure if Josefina had always been such, or whether their love had released it.

She leant over and kissed Josefina openly and brazenly. "Until tomorrow," she said. "Two-thirty."

She stood and watched as the car tore heedlessly into the traffic before making her way to the hotel lounge to join Christian Tennenbaum and Tristram Jones.

THIRTY-TWO

Christian Tennenbaum soon regretted staying on in Mallorca for the funeral. It had been a magnanimous offer made to Alexandro the day after Maria Jesus' death which, to his consternation, had been accepted with enthusiasm.

"It would be an honour for the whole family if you were to be present," Alexandro had said, Genoveva nodding next to him, black rings around her sleepless eyes.

Tristram Jones had cancelled their return flights and rebooked for both of them on his iPhone. He had assumed that Christian Tennenbaum's offer to stay on included himself.

But it was less of a sacrifice for him. He spoke Spanish and was in his element, joking with waiters and waitresses when they bought their drinks or meals, and planning afternoon excursions for the two of them to places of interest to him, Tristram Jones.

The day after the calamity at the rotunda, Christian Tennenbaum had had a brief telephone conversation with Anthony Grace. He didn't feel bound to say exactly what had happened, except that the contract had been frustrated.

"Frustrated?" the Bursar had boomed. "What the hell does that mean?"

"*Force majeure*, Anthony. I'll explain when I get back."

"What of the funds already paid?"

Christian Tennenbaum terminated the call. He needed to think about that. It was not something which could be decently raised with Alexandro in his bereaved state. If the worst came to the worst and Anthony Grace made a song and dance about it, he would restore the college's slush fund from his own resources.

But it was Justine Goodenough's behaviour which had first baffled, and then dismayed him.

He had long held a soft spot for her, moving fragrantly around the college, always unruffled, always serene. And when the old lady had lost control of her chair and pranged into him, she had been caring and attentive, helping him to his feet and checking that he was unscathed. It had been no mean feat to persuade her to come to Mallorca, but when she had arrived she rose to the occasion with a vengeance. He admired that. But then she had become inseparable from the old lady's daughter. It was Tristram Jones who had opened his eyes.

They had been sitting in a café off the Cathedral Square two evenings after the tragedy at the rotunda, when he said, as casually as he could, "You know, Tristram, I think I might just ask Justine out. Take her to dinner at a nice restaurant one evening. Give her a break from the Gonzalez family. You wouldn't mind, would you, fending for yourself for an hour or two?"

"Not at all, Christian, feel free," Tristram Jones had said.

"Thank you, Tristram. I'll do that."

Tristram Jones swirled his Spanish brandy around the bottom of his glass, looking at Christian Tennenbaum suspiciously. "But if, Christian," he said, "you have any romantic inclinations towards Justine, I think you'll find that you're barking up the wrong tree."

It became clear in a flash. Christian Tennenbaum felt himself crumple. "Barking up the wrong tree again," he said quietly.

Tristram Jones silently nodded.

This kid's like a bloody nanny to me, Christian Tennenbaum said to himself. That flight home can't come soon enough.

*   *   *   *

The day before the funeral at eight in the morning, when Alexandro was preparing to leave for the office, there was a prolonged ring on the bell.

Genoveva, still wearing her candlewick dressing gown, pressed the answerphone. It was Josefina.

"Let me in, please," she said.

Josefina was not her usual calm self, launching immediately into the purpose of her visit.

"Alexandro, I am having a problem with the priest."

"What priest?"

"The priest at Deià of course. The man who will be burying Mama tomorrow."

Genoveva took a cup and saucer out of the kitchen cupboard, poured it to the brim from the pot on the stove, and pushed it into Josefina's hands. "Sit down," she said. It was an entirely fresh experience to see her sister-in-law in a state, needing a little attention from herself or Alexandro. It made her feel a trifle superior.

Vanessa, woken by the bell, emerged from her bedroom in her night dress, mechanically poured herself a cup of coffee, and sat opposite her aunt at the kitchen table.

"What has the priest done?" Alexandro asked.

"Nothing. It's what he will not do which is the problem. He is beginning to annoy me, to put it mildly."

"What will this man not do?" Vanessa demanded. It was unusual for Josefina not to get her own way. It seemed unbelievable that a simple parish priest could have the temerity, the gall, to thwart or obstruct her.

Josefina took a deep breath. "I have been clearing Mama's cottage, as you know: going through her things, getting rid of rubbish, but throwing nothing away that is in any way important to us."

She sipped at her coffee before continuing. "And it was then that I made this discovery."

"What discovery?"

"A poem by Graves. Written for Mama. Dedicated just to her."

"But they are all lost," Vanessa said quickly. "Gone. With Grandma."

231

"This one must have been very special to her. Very very special. She kept it separate from the others. I found it folded at the bottom of her jewel box."

"Just one?" Alexandro asked hopefully.

"Yes. Just one. So I took it to Justine to look at. She said that it was very fine, very beautiful. One of the most beautiful poems by Graves that she had ever seen."

"So where does the priest come in?" Genoveva opened her hands in exaggerated ignorance.

"Because it must be read at Mama's service tomorrow. I have been going over all the procedures with him, what hymns we sing, at what point you, Alexandro, make your tribute to Mama, and so on. So I suggested that just before the coffin is removed from the church and taken into the graveyard, one of the English, maybe Professor Tennenbaum, reads the poem to the congregation in final tribute to Mama's powers of inspiration."

"A brilliant idea, Aunty," Vanessa cried. "But why did the priest object?"

"He wanted to see the poem."

"And?"

"He said that he knew enough English to see that it was pornographic, and he wouldn't allow it into his church let alone be read." Josefina's scheme for the reading of the poem had, with some misgivings, been approved by Justine Goodenough, but was now being blocked by the sanctimonious numskull of a villlage priest.

"Do you have the poem with you?"

Josefina opened her hand bag and handed a folded piece of paper to Vanessa. She then sat back and drained her cup whilst Vanessa slowly read, line by line.

"What do you think?" Genoveva asked, when Vanessa looked up from the page.

"It is beautiful," Vanessa declared, handing the poem back to Josefina. "My English may not be up to much, but I can see that it is beautiful. And it is all about my grandmother. I hope that one day a man will write such words for me."

That was all Genoveva needed to hear. "Right. Leave this to me. Alexandro, don't be late for work. Vanessa, we must get dressed at once. You're coming with me."

"Try and stop me!" Vanessa threw over her shoulder as she made for her bedroom.

Thank God, Josefina said to herself. They are so incensed with the priest that they don't even pause to doubt or question my little jewel box fabrication.

"Shall I come too?"

"No!" Genoveva said imperiously. To break the priest's intransigence demanded more earthy skills than her cerebral sister-in-law could offer.

As Genoveva parked Alexandro's car outside the small manse attached to the Church of Sant Joan Baptista in Deià, they saw Father Ramon locking his front door.

"Quick! Get him!" Genoveva cried.

Vanessa sprang from the car and raced over to the priest. "Father," she said, placing a restraining hand on his arm, "my mother and I need to speak to you urgently."

"I have a meeting with the bishop in Palma," he replied briskly. "It will have to be this afternoon."

"It will only take a minute or two," Vanessa pleaded. "We are in desperate need."

Genoveva joined them. "Please help us, Father," she said piously, fixing him with large cow-like eyes and plucking at his sleeve.

"Very well, but we must be quick."

As soon as he had led them into his small, book lined study, their demeanour changed.

"Allow me to introduce myself, Father. I am Genoveva Gonzalez, the daughter-in-law of the long-time resident of this village you are burying in your churchyard tomorrow, and this is my daughter Vanessa. How long have you been the priest here?"

"Two years."

"Then you will know little or nothing of my mother-in-law."

"As far as I know, she never came to mass."

"No, she didn't, and I'm not surprised."

As the priest looked towards the door, Vanessa crossed the room and leant against it.

"Why are you not surprised?" the priest asked witheringly.

"You adhere to a hate-filled, bigoted Christianity. You belong to the days when Spain was a dreary, miserable country from which people wanted to flee. What example do you set for young people? My daughter is a faithful Catholic, but how can she hold fast her faith when people such as yourself try to close people's minds to the generous, inclusive country which Spain has become?"

Father Ramon decided to go for a quick knock-out blow to bring the interview to a speedy end, making his position, harsh as it might seem, clear and unnegotiable.

"I presume that you are speaking of my refusal to allow the reading of a vulgar poem by a promiscuous Protestant, or maybe even an atheist, in my church, at your mother-in-law's funeral tomorrow," he said with contempt.

Vanessa felt her heart beat faster and a red flush move up her neck. "He was a man who lived," she said hoarsely, struggling to control her voice. "And my grandmother knew how to live."

She moved closer to the priest, standing directly in front of him. She had not had time to think what she should wear when she left the apartment, and the top she had thrown on was slipping down one shoulder.

"But you?" she continued. "You? What do you know of life? Nothing. You can't even tell the difference between art and pornography. You preach love but know nothing about it. But nonetheless, you seem to know all about sex. In fact, I think that you're a little bit obsessed with sex. It seems to take up too much of your thinking. And you would condemn the multitude of people who love, but not in the way you think they should.

People like my aunt Josefina who came to you for help with the burial of my grandmother."

"I don't understand."

"She's a lesbian," Vanessa sneered. "A lesbian," she repeated, as if to taunt the priest. "A practising, unapologetic lesbian. And what's more she's a Catholic, and a better Catholic than you."

Motioning her daughter to calm down, Genoveva moved towards the door. "My husband," she said cold-bloodedly, "is head of the Mallorcan Spanish tourist board. If you prevent or obstruct the reading of this poem at his mother's funeral, he will ensure that the busloads of tourists who come to this village every day to visit the house of that great man are informed that here resides the bigot priest, who hates Graves and what he stands for. A man who pitted himself against all that is of worth, all that makes our lives endurable. At best you will be a laughing stock, but more likely hated and reviled."

Genoveva opened the study door. "You are a busy man, Father. We must go. But make no mistake, the poem will be read. Thwart us at your peril."

Genoveva paused to look down at Maria Jesus' cottage before unlocking Alexandro's car.

"Grandma would have been proud of you today," Vanessa said.

Genoveva nodded. "Your grandmother always saw me as a bit of a bimbo. A waste of space. I hope that today she might have changed her mind."

THIRTY-THREE

At lunchtime Alexandro telephoned Josefina on her mobile to say that Genoveva and Vanessa had had a confrontation with the priest over the poem. After a struggle, they had forced him to concede that it could after all be read at their mother's funeral.

"How did they manage it?" Josefina had asked

"They make a formidable pair," was all Alexandro could reply. "Quite a team. Something I've learnt from experience."

Josefina pressed her mobile to her chest so Alexandro could not hear, and punched the air with her free hand. "Barcelona one, Vatican City nil," she shouted out loud in her mother's cottage.

"I hope you agree that the professor should read the poem," she said, resuming the conversation.

"Agreed. Maybe it would be something of a consolation prize for him."

That evening, Josefina parked her car behind the Can Cera and walked through the back entrance into the lounge with Justine Goodenough in tow.

Christian Tennenbaum and Tristram Jones were seated in their usual corner offering a long view of the promenaders in the street. They sprang to their feet as soon as Josefina appeared with Justine Goodenough, weaving between the tables.

"What a pleasure!" Christian Tennenbaum cried. "Justine graces us with her company most evenings, but this is a double treat."

Tristram Jones gestured to the waiter for attention.

"I cannot stay long. Tomorrow, as you know, is the funeral,

and there are still one or two loose ends to tie," Josefina said, sitting down. She turned an expression of solicitude onto Christian Tennenbaum and Tristram Jones. "It is so kind of you to stay on for Mama's send off, but by now you must be heartily sick of our little island. When will you be going home?"

"Tomorrow. On the six p.m. plane to Stansted," Tristram Jones said. "We have organised a taxi to pick us up from Deià at three, drop in here to collect our suitcases, and then carry on to the airport."

When the waiter arrived, Josefina resisted all Tristram Jones' urgings to stay for a drink.

"No, I must go back," she said. "But there is something very important I want of you, Professor. A big favour."

"Anything, Josefina."

"Believe it or not, Professor, but when clearing out my mother's most intimate possessions I discovered a poem by Robert Graves."

"You what?" Christian Tennenbaum exclaimed in disbelief, springing to life.

"Yes. A poem kept separate from all the others. A very special poem." She treated Justine Goodenough to a broad smile. "Justine has corroborated that."

"Short, but special," Justine Goodenough said nervously.

"This poem will not have seen the light of day for many years," Josefina continued. "I want it to have its debut tomorrow, at Mama's funeral."

"Very appropriate," Christian Tennenbaum affirmed, his eyes bright with anticipation. "But where do I come in?"

"The poem, Professor, is of course in English."

"Of course. Goes without saying."

"And all my family feel that nothing could be more fitting than you, a Cambridge professor of English literature, reading it to us in church."

"It would be an abiding honour," Christian Tennenbaum

proclaimed, collapsing into the back of his chair. "This is so exciting. Please let me see the poem."

"No!" Josefina cried senatorially. "This poem will have its debut tomorrow, not just before my mother and her family, but also before the whole English-speaking world, represented by you, Professor. My mother's funeral will be a double ceremony, of death and of birth."

Justine Goodenough had made the reading conditional on the poem not being released to Christian Tennenbaum before the funeral. It might not stand up to scrutiny, and he should be spared the temptation of copying it. Somehow, after the service, it would also be necessary to relieve him of it. Again, it would hardly withstand examination by the Graves' experts back in England.

"Doesn't the poem belong to the college anyway?" Tristram Jones said to Justine Goodenough in a clearly audible whisper.

"That, Tristram, is a pretty cheap remark to make, in all the circumstances," Justine Goodenough snapped indignantly. "All that side of things will have to be sorted out when Christian gets home. And anyway, it was never in that wretched box."

Josefina stood to go. "I, or my brother, will direct you to the lectern when the moment comes for the poem to be read, Professor. And that is where it will be. Waiting for its first exposure for many unknown years."

She's overdoing it, Justine Goodenough said to herself. But nonetheless, she's magnificent.

"I am collecting Justine at twelve midday tomorrow," Josefina continued. "Would you like a lift in my car? There'd be room for all of us."

"Thank you, thank you," Christian Tennenbaum and Tristram Jones chorused.

"Your English has improved," Justine Goodenough said to Josefina as she accompanied her to her car.

"It was never so bad, querida, and being with you it has excelled. What do they call it? Symbiosis I think is the word."

238

Maria Jesus had lived the life of a semi-recluse for as long as anyone cared to remember, and as a result, her funeral was not particularly well attended.

Her long-time neighbour, Carmen, was there, displaying a measure of public bereavement. A few other villagers attended as much out of curiosity as respect or love for the neighbour they had lost. Three or four employees of Alexandro's had considered it diplomatic to attend, and Genoveva had persuaded a family of her cousins to support her in her grief. In addition, the local mayor and his wife deemed their attendance obligatory – one more item in their busy calendar.

Josefina had cleaned and polished her mother's cottage in preparation for the reception after the funeral, buying in bottles of rioja and sweet white wine and setting out cakes and tapas supplied by the local village shop.

By the time she drew up outside the church at one forty-five with her carload of English academics, the coffin had been delivered by the undertakers and was set on a stand in front of the altar. The priest, tight lipped, was lighting an array of candles arranged on long candlesticks around the catafalque, to the strains of Handel's Largo solemnly sounding from the organ.

In the front pew sat Alexandro and Genoveva, beside them Vanessa and Rafael. Genoveva and Vanessa clutched white lace handkerchiefs contrasting with the long black shawls draped around their shoulders. Each had covered their head with a black mantilla, elevated in Vanessa's case by a large tortoiseshell comb.

Josefina, in the formal suit she had worn to welcome Justine Goodenough at the airport a few days earlier, took her place with her family while the English shuffled into the pew behind, left vacant by a sign marked '*reservado*' which Josefina had prepared and installed that morning.

The funeral liturgy was beyond Christian Tennenbaum. Even Tristram Jones cautiously remained silent during the responses. The only familiarity was the hymn sung to the tune of 'Abide With Me.'

Before Alexandro moved to the lectern to deliver his tribute, Josefina handed him the poem copied out by Justine Goodenough in large script.

Alexandro spoke warmly of his mother's old-fashioned qualities: her wisdom, her tenacity, her stability, anchoring the family through turbulent times of change. An example for them all to follow in whatever difficulties might lie ahead. Finally, he said that his mother had had an extraordinary, if not unique, brush with greatness, as an inspiration for one of the most significant creative geniuses of her time. They were now to hear a recently discovered panegyric to his mother's beauty and charms, written by that genius, to be read by no less than a celebrated professor of English poetry.

When he was ended he collected up his notes, leaving the poem on the lectern. On his return to his seat he indicated with a nod to Christian Tennenbaum that the time had come for the reading of the poem.

Walking with a slow and dignified step to the lectern, Christian Tennenbaum removed a pair of spectacles from the inside pocket of a navy-blue blazer he had purchased in Palma that morning, together with as dark and sombre a tie as he could find.

He spent a moment scanning the first line or two before beginning his reading in a loud, authoritative voice.

"Your spinal column runs proud and pale
Like the mountains of the moon
Down to my hand, resting on your roundness."

A little disconcerted, he glanced at the next line. This was not the stuff fit for funerals, but there could be no going back now.

"And through your breast on my knee,
Your heart beats beats beats noiselessly."

He looked up, straight into the face of Tristram Jones smirking broadly at him. He needed to get on with the reading and return to his seat as quickly as possible.

"*Preserve us from the proselyte's wordy hell*
(Feed on her too in silence with thanksgiving)"

There was a sudden involuntary movement from the priest, an outraged spasm, at the allusion to the distribution of the host. Christian Tennenbaum did his level best not to rush the last two lines.

"*Let's pray the mists will clear for them as well,*
To show the sculptured landscapes of the living."

He had planned to say a word or two to the effect that they had all been privileged to hear lines of great moment befitting a great lady, but thinking better of it he collected up the poem and made for his seat.

With great solemnity, the funeral undertakers slowly marched down the aisle, surrounded Maria Jesus' coffin, and hoisted it onto their shoulders. The priest, leading the procession, spoke the words of committal in a booming, sonorous voice, as if to cleanse and purge his church of the filth to which it had just been subjected. The family and friends followed the coffin into the graveyard where, after some forty years, Manuel Gonzalez' grave had been opened for his wife's coffin to be lowered upon his.

Josefina had indicated to Justine Goodenough that she should accompany the funeral party as she was all but family now, leaving Christian Tennenbaum and Tristram Jones sitting alone in the empty church.

"Appropriate or not for a funeral, Tristram, this," Christian Tennenbaum said, shaking the sheet of paper in his hand, "is great poetry."

Tristram Jones said nothing, the eerie silence of the church acting as a condemnation.

"My God, Tristram," Christian Tennenbaum said after they had sat on for a while. "What has been lost?"

"How do you mean?"

"What was in that box?" He shook his head in despair. "What has been lost to art? To humanity?"

They looked round to the sound of footsteps in the aisle. It was Josefina and Justine Goodenough.

"Your taxi has arrived, gentlemen," Josefina said. "And please, Professor," she held out her hand. "The poem."

Without demur, Christian Tennenbaum handed the sheet to her.

"Thank you, Professor. And beautifully read."

Vanessa appeared at the church door, Rafael hovering behind her. "My parents have particularly asked that you say goodbye to them before you leave."

She walked up to Tristram Jones and offered him her hand. "*Recuerdos felices*," she said.

"That sounds lovelier in Spanish than in English," Justine Goodenough murmured.

"Why, what does it mean?" Christian Tennenbaum asked.

"Happy memories. Recuerdos felices. I believe they're amongst the most complimentary words you can say to anyone."

Lightning Source UK Ltd.
Milton Keynes UK
UKHW020641301220
376134UK00013B/1276